THE BABY FARM
Paul Kestell

First published by Black Cormorant Books
©2019 Paul Kestell.

It hides in the undergrowth, knives sharpened. This is the throat-slitter, the wandering minstrel, the kind of animal you pray to on Sundays, the goat glutton, existing with sheer willpower. Its will is to slide the knife across your throat till rich blood flows, but not satisfied with that, it wants to see that deep black blood, the stuff that bleeds the life out of you, the squealer, pudding dripper, the moment when your blood boils, explosions when your dreams burst. It awaits as you innocently pass by.

From the novel Deep in the Woods by T. Fleming

When Mary Ryan came here there wasn't any snow, but I'm told that it snows here most years. I guess she came at the wrong time. There isn't much to this place, but maybe the interesting things lie all around it. I think it is a little like standing in a dark wood but through the gaps in the trees you can see the sparkling stars. This place is pretty, though you can't see Upper Lough Lyn from the main road, but you know it is there because the mountain moulds into a saucer so it must contain water. The lower lake is bland, stretching a mile across, eating into the base of the hills, and there are wild islands too small to be of use, and they are covered with trees and the white horses riding the waves gravitate towards them. The village is one long main street with a few criss-cross lanes hiding secret homes. I see folk appear erratically; they gravitate to the square that is the centre of business where the main street ends. The Lough Lyn Hotel is big and bold beside the neon Spar shop that lights the square, and the benches nearby are caked with snow that melts like ice-cream onto the planted patches of dead flower beds below; even the evergreens are struggling for breath.

Marcia Mellon greets me gruffly. Methinks she is dull and pissed with the world for she is obese, very mature; she looks hairy, complete with a lazy moustache. Marcia looks at me like I am mad, like she is trying desperately to figure me out. Putting her head down she flicks through the pages of her register and I guess she is trying to find some excuse to refuse me or at least to delay me in some way.

'I booked online!' I say.

'Yeah, I know. The broadband is down again, so I have to use this thing.'

She keeps flicking through the pages that are thick and heavy. They are sticking to her fat fingers. She flutters and licks her fingers to rid herself of the invasive register.

'Swan … Avril Swan.' She keeps turning the pages. 'We're very busy with the snow. It came early this year. Usually it doesn't fall till February, but not this year. People are booking in. They don't want to travel.' She finds my name and stops for a second. She can't believe her eyes. 'You're staying a few weeks?'

'That's the plan.'

'You won't be able to go anywhere with the snow. I hope you brought lots of reading material.'

'I'll manage.'

'Room 12, top of the stairs to the right. We serve breakfast till ten and you can have other meals. Just let us know and we'll look after you.'

Mary Ryan stayed in Room 10. I should ask her to change just to have the same view, but I don't bother as Marcia has her head stuck in her register once more. I can see the flakes of dandruff nestled in her hair.

They resemble the flakes of snow outside as they descend gloriously from her head onto the counter. I feel queasy.

Room 12 is just two doors up, but both rooms look out over the square. There is nobody about and away from the Spar the world recedes into dark shadows with the snow obliterating the view. I tidy my things into the chest of drawers beside the bed. I fold my smalls and I hang my one dress and my hand-knitted cardigan in the wardrobe. I brought two winter jackets, two woollen sweaters, two brand new pairs of jeans, an old pair for luck, and two pairs of leather boots. I also squeezed in a pair of wellingtons. I guess I was used to snow. How could you hail from Maine and not know about snow? Maine is entirely different from here. Bangor, Maine, is more grandiose and when it snows, the folk crawl out of their shells to greet it, not like in Ireland where one gets the impression that people are fearful of it, even though it snows most years for a few days at least.

Marcia Mellon serves me whiskey and I am not at all worried about it, as it is 7 p.m., just the right time for a tipple. She offers me ice and I wanna tell her that where I'm from ice and whiskey don't mix but I don't bother. I end up watching her heave her way to the end of the bar to pull a pint of stout for this dishevelled fella.

He is bearded he looks like Ben Gunn out of *Treasure Island*, and I think he is like the 'Wild Man from Borneo' my grandmother yelled about when me or my sister came in late from a date – yeah, and her other one, 'Yer like a cat who's been dragged through a hedge backwards.' She is some mean oul witch, but I love her, mean and all as she is, but how can you love someone that is so mean. Do I love her because she is mean, or is it that she isn't so mean, that she is in fact kind and the meanness is all a front? Was that the stuff that Mary spoke about in her research? She said that she couldn't unravel evil, like she couldn't isolate it. What causes it in all its manifestations? Is that what happened to Mary? Was it this place or was it what she found out here doing her research that caused her to go missing? The 'Wild Man from Borneo' has intelligent eyes. He watches a soap on the television, straining his neck. When he looks along the bar his eyes glow through his animal hair, and those eyes aren't unkind either, but I don't care much about him as Professor Black never mentioned him. So, Mary didn't mention him in her notes. Who knows, maybe Mary never met this guy?

Marcia Mellon takes his money and goes slovenly to the till, and he watches her deposit the cash and return his few cents change. Together they lift their heads to watch the soap once again.

Someone turns down the heat at night, so I grab the blankets, pulling them up over my head, expelling air and feeling the fog cling to my lips. Back home the heat is constant; nobody in Maine turns off the switches; this is our way to deal with the cold. I dream of woollen hats and hot water bottles, but my sleep is disturbed. I imagine Mary's voice; it is shaking and pleading.

I follow her path.

* * *

He is overweight. Maybe it is the local diet. His head is big, pushing out his shoulders, and I'd say that he used to be fair, but time has paled him. Sergeant Boyle, at fifty-four, retains his deep blue eyes and looks at me lazily as he wipes the pile of files out of the way with his left hand. I see rings. His wedding ring looks expensive, but it probably isn't, and he sizes me up, but then he chooses to lie back lazily in his chair. This chair is made with cheap imitation leather and I hope his weight doesn't capsize it. That will be a mess.

'She was very quiet and studious, not like you. Maybe you have more about you?'

'Me, being ten years older and all, Sergeant – is that what you're implying?'

'No.'

'Perhaps, having done ten years in the Bangor police department?'

'Maybe. Are you a mature student too?'

'No, I'm a private detective. Mary's people are trying to find her.'

'A private detective around here?'

'You seem uninterested in her disappearance.'

He sits forward now, putting the weight of his elbows onto the desk. 'Lots of people go missin', many by their own free will. We can't be responsible for everyone who takes off on a whim. I have the file open. It's current but it's not suspicious. A student comes to Lough Lyn to do some research, then she goes missin'. Maybe she just ups and leaves? Nearly a year goes by, Ms Swan. There was nothin' suspicious. We never found any trace of her. Where is her car and the rest of her belongings? Yeah, she left a few things at the hotel but what does that tell me? That she left in a hurry. You say she was in contact with this Professor Black. Did she sound scared? You know I met her many times. She was fine. To be honest it was like she was enjoyin' her time here, so maybe she just suddenly decided to move on.'

'It's a year ago, Sergeant, and no sight of her. She left without a word. Nobody, not even her mother, has heard from her since, and yes, I do believe that her research was revealing things, stuff that frightened her. According to Professor Black she felt very scared by the facts she was unravelling, but as you say it all just stopped very suddenly.'

'We had teams from Dublin lookin' at it. They spent a week here and still nobody knows what happened to her. She just vanished without a trace. If someone can give me a shred of evidence to go on there is no better man to chase it up, but we are poor out here. We don't have the resources. I have lots on my plate and I don't have time to chase shadows, if you get me. Look, if you're here to continue the search so be it. Personally, I don't have a clue as to what she was lookin' at and I don't care either – and neither does anyone else around here, if the truth be known – but I tell you straight up, there isn't any point in hasslin' old Ms Bauer. She was giving out about your friend. She made several complaints, her and the security firm over at St Michael's. Mary was very persistent. Don't get me wrong – these people came and made their complaints, but they weren't about to take the law into their own hands.'

* * *

I'm glad I brought the jeep. The walk is no more than a couple of hundred yards, but the snow is falling heavily again; besides, there is hunger. I see no place to eat except at the hotel, or I could get a takeout from the Spar. A small pub on the corner advertises food but it serves it at the weekend only. I try the hotel. Marcia Mellon is on duty again. Is she the only person that works here? I order a sandwich and a pot of coffee and she shuffles away, scraping her feet along the tiles. The fire is good; she has stacked it up with decent-sized logs on top of coal and the wet logs sizzle. In time she brings the food on a silver tray, placing it on the table beside me. She allows me time to sort out my stuff and make room for it all, and I notice she puffs and pants. The place is empty. What would she be like if it were full?

'I'll bring you mustard for the ham,' she says, belting off like something is chasing her, but she slows to a crawl as she reaches the kitchen door.

I wanna shout after her, 'I don't like fuckin' mustard,' but I don't and Marcia returns with a yellow bottle of Colman's.

'You remember Mary?' I ask, holding up the only photograph I possess.

Marcia leans over like she is pleading for more light. 'She stayed here last year. Is she your friend?'

'Not exactly. I'm just wondering did you know her?'

'Know her?'

Marcia straightens up and dusts the front of her apron. 'I didn't know her well enough. She left us without settlin' her bill!'

'Oh.'

I never thought of that – how much could she have owed. I am thinking of my fee. Do the Ryan family want me to settle Mary's bill?

'She owes us a thousand euros. The police were here lookin' at her things and askin' us all sorts. She went missin' and they thought it very suspicious, but the boss sort of wrote it off, you know. Mrs Breslin, she put it down to experience.'

'That's kind.'

'You don't know where she is do ya? Can you fix Mrs Breslin up? She hasn't much since Charlie passed. He left her with nuthin' she says – not a cent.'

Marcia is tidying again, picking up the silver tray. It seems heavier now that it is empty.

'Ah no, I'm here to try and find her,' I say. 'We weren't friends at all.'

'Pity. She was a very nice girl otherwise, very respectable.'

Marcia leaves and I watch as she disappears behind the bar.

* * *

Old Ms Bauer lives several miles out of the village, sharing the big house bordering the lower lake with her son Arnold and his wife Julia. The old lady is in her late seventies now and I wanna drive out to see her. I am screwed though, as the snow is still falling and the country lanes are impassable. So I am stuck. I go to the bar for a whiskey and end up sitting by the fire where I ate my lunch. All this time I am wondering if I can afford to settle Mary's bill. But I would need to reconcile my accounts, especially when I don't know how long I will need to stay in this place myself. I'll contact the Ryan family for permission. Of course the human spirit has a terrific way of exonerating the conscience. I'm here to find Mary, but I don't feel indelibly tied to her, and her only link to me is through my job as an investigator, so I'm hardly responsible for where she slept or what she ate, even if I am a sort of representative of her family. I drink three whiskies and on the third my rationale changes. The cheek of Marcia Mellon to speak about unpaid hotel bills. She and the sergeant are just typical of the prevailing attitude in these parts. Where is the concern that a perfectly healthy twenty-seven-year-old woman could just vanish from their midst and disappear into thin air? Where is the empathy or any notion of responsibility? Do they really think she just upped and left, leaving some of her belongings behind, and are they only concerned about unpaid bills? Perhaps their worries are deeper. Is there a shared secret they don't want the world to know about?

'I hear you're looking for Mary?'

The woman with a closed left eye stares at me and I immediately think of pirates and other one-eyed baddies as she sits opposite me. She is uninvited, but she warms herself just the same. She looks over her right shoulder to catch the eye of the young girl behind the bar and nods. The girl responds, and in a minute, two whiskies arrive. I'm impressed.

'Moya Breslin. Cheers.'

Moya puts her whiskey down. This time she doesn't turn around. The girl brings over the bottle and tops Moya up; she refills my glass too, even though I've barely touched mine.

'Make some room, woman,' Moya snarls, but she is just amusing herself.

I do, and the whiskey is good. The girl stays a few seconds more, but then she gives up and leaves the bottle on the table.

'It was a great shock about Mary. You know I really liked her. The wee lass used to sit there, right where you're sittin', but she drank coffee not whiskey. I think she did take a drink. Where did you learn to drink? You swallow like you've drunk lots of whiskey in yer time!'

'My mother taught me. Believe me, she is the best of teachers.'

'Where did she learn it?'

'As a girl in Portland, New England. My gran taught her and she wasn't short of a drink when we moved to Bangor, Maine, either!' I drink a half glass in salute. 'Gran is ninety-two!'

'She's a good age, so. I'll be eighty-nine in March. I'm catching her up.'

Moya tops up both glasses.

'She left you a bill, Mrs Breslin?' I say.

'She did. I tell you, this thing about Mary going missin' is a sore point around here. You needn't be concerned about me, dear. This old place is fallin' down and it isn't goin' to go any faster because of her unpaid bill. Me and Charlie made a right go of it when we started out and we managed to spirit away a wee few bob, so we'll say nuthin'. I don't tell the staff my personal business, you know, but the folk around here aren't happy about Mary. It casts a long shadow over the village. We're the talk of the country – the place where the mature student disappeared – so we're all suspects in a crime that nobody's sure was committed. But as the sergeant said to me off the record, she hardly just got fed up and left. There's no evidence. They found nothin' – not her car or her clothes or anythin' belongin' to her. She just vanished.'

* * *

Someone plays a car radio loudly in the street. I look out. The snow has stopped falling at last. The square is dark and the neon sign from the Spar is quashed. The loud radio is from an SUV parked at the hotel front door. Somebody is waiting for a person. The engine ticks over loudly and the radio DJ is over-cheerful for the hour of the day. For a moment I think I'm home in Bangor; the accent is so familiar. Then just as quick the music reverts to boom boom, and I feel the cold against the window pane. My work brings me here to this small place, the village that I imagined is so different. What I envisaged is so much more like home. Where are the fast-food joints and the cafés? Here the cars come by slowly and infrequently. This place is the true back of beyond. I am thinking of what the professor said. Mary was doing some research on St Michael's – now defunct; it is only a ruin – and she rang Professor Black in a panicked state. The academic thought her hysterical. She was going on about discovering the truth. She was so excited, and the professor told me that she was crying. She kept repeating that she had found the source of evil! What happened to Mary Ryan? Wherever did she go and why did she disappear?

Moya Breslin sets me right, telling me that the convent closed in 1979 and it suffered a fire back in 1950, destroying the chapel. This old woman has a good memory. Telling me she used to play in the convent grounds as a child, she says the land was full of trees and most of the children from the village used to play in the woods. Moya tells me that Mary went to the old ruins regularly. It is guarded by a security firm, but the driver might not visit for days at a time. I wonder did Mary find what she wanted there, as the professor back in Maine was unsure. She said that Mary was researching a paper on young Irish women who were incarcerated in these institutions. Some reports said their babies were confiscated after birth and many were sold off for adoption; indeed, many went to childless couples in the United States. Mary was particularly interested in those that ended up in New England wanted to know if any ended up in Bangor, Maine.

The convent ruins are on my list, but I also need to visit the retired schoolteacher Jane Watts. She is the local historian and she gives free talks and advice on all matters of local history, but I decide to drive out by the lower lake to browse and think. The snow has eased but the dark roads are full of slush. Happily the jeep keeps traction and I arrive at a small jetty. It has crumbled from lack of use, so part of it is detached, looking lonely all on its own. The lake is full of white horses and the water slurps to the edge. All is wide and populated by nameless islands choked with trees. It's a wonderful place to lower a car with a body in it. Perhaps one dark night someone rowed across the water with a precious cargo. Those islands could hide a multitude, and I imagine the sound of shovels digging into the hard, frosted earth, the sharp blades sparking off the solid ground. I am fighting with myself whether to go over to the ruins of the convent or to start interviewing the few people that Mary mentioned in her correspondence with Professor Black. I have a torch in the trunk, so maybe the convent first, but it starts to snow again, so I go back to the village and slip the jeep into a perfect space at the rear of the hotel.

Marcia Mellon is on. She takes delight in giving me a glass of whiskey.

'Where did ya get to today? Did I see ya down by the lake? It's freezin' out der. De wind's bitter.'

'Back home we would call that a cold one – nothin' more dramatic. You have it so warm in here. It makes a body glad to come back.'

'D'ya want a menu?'

'Yeah. I wanna see what else you have besides sandwiches?'

She hands me a hard-backed book with 'Menu' embossed in gold on the cover.

It is mostly sandwiches but some are toasted; the only alternative is an all-day breakfast, so I order that and Marcia Mellon goes away.

I look up more of Professor Black's notes and she mentions three interviewees: Mr Tobin, the undertaker's father, is ninety-three years old, Jane Watts who lives at No. 33 Rathlin Lane, and Kevin Witherspoon, who makes ceramics and sells them from a little window at the front of his house. Professor Black has added a note – 'Mary thinks he is mad' – that interests me, so I decide to call on Kevin Witherspoon as soon as I finish eating.

I order another whiskey as I will be walking in the snow for the afternoon. The food warms me and the sausages and rashers are good. By now I think that Marcia likes my face, for she smiles at me constantly.

* * *

Kevin Witherspoon looks at me like he is lost and I am the first human being he has seen in years. Susan, his wife, is unkempt and ugly. She has prominent teeth that are black and green in places and I realise that he must never kiss her cause if he did, it would make him a pervert or some sort of conspirator in the dark arts.

'Susan will look after things here.'

He walks through a stringed paper curtain and I am expected to follow. Susan looks at the ceramic jewels with disdain. She is to stay and sell these tiny objects to non-existent customers. Kevin sits at a bare table below a window that looks out on a dark yard which is surrounded by an old, high wall. I see two scrawny cats lying idle at its base. They suddenly attack each other, biting at the throat, but just as easily they are distracted by movement in a bush on the far side of the yard and their dispute ends. Kevin plays with his beard. I notice that his teeth are in poor shape too. He tells me he has been living in Lough Lyn for over seventy years, but he has never lost the North of England accent he was born with.

'I knew a bit about the convent. Me father came here originally to fit the staircase. They wanted granite and he was the stonemason they needed. Our dad was as good as you'd get – a right genius, they said.'

'So it says here, Mr Witherspoon. Mary Ryan's notes are very thorough.'

'She was very foolish. There's no good in openin' old wounds, bringin' folk back to a time they wanna forget. You know people leave stuff behind them, things they want to bury and leave in the past. I tell you, girl, she was doin' no good remindin' them. I told her that straight to her face.'

One of the scrawny cats jumps up to the windowsill. She is looking for heat and presses her little body up against the glass.

'Der not oours. They belong to the Grainger's that own the garage. Pity they feed them nought. Susan feeds them or they wud starve.'

'So, Mary Ryan was interested in your father?'

'She had no interest in him, only his work. I was tellin' ya he was the stonemason up at the convent. That's a long time ago. You see, I took her out the back there. We have photos of him and the granite stone in me shed.'

'I'd love to see them!'

'Too damn cold today. We'd freeze to death out there. More things dyin' out there than in me father's slaughterhouse out the road. He went into the killin' business once the war was over. There wasn't much of a demand for stonemasons, not in Lough Lyn anyhow, so he took to killin' pigs mostly. But we killed lots of lambs in season.' He laughs. 'The old place still reeks of death.'

* * *

Jane Watts is not what I expect. I was thinking schoolteacher 'looking over the top of her glasses' type. Jane lives down the dark lane beside the Spar. It gets darker as it narrows near its end, and you can barely get a bicycle down it never mind a car. The house, though small, is neat and she shows me into a small living room with a good sofa and a piano alongside a fine big flat-screen TV. Jane is in her late sixties, but she looks younger. She is pretty and was most likely a stunner in her youth, and I wonder how she avoided men, as Jane never married, nor did she openly have a relationship with either a man or woman. There lies a mystery.

'I'm still in shock,' she says. 'We don't have much to chat about around here – well, not anything strange. If anything's murky about this place it's all in the past and believe me that's where we like to keep it. I liked Mary though. She was a very good researcher, very driven. I tell you there was no way she wasn't going to find something. She left no stone unturned. To be honest with you I'd say she ruffled a lot of feathers, especially some of the big noises around here. You get me?'

I wanna say 'I don't get ya,' but I don't, and she says, 'I don't buy it for a second that she just upped and left out of frustration. The dogs in the street know that's not the case!'

'What do you think happened to her?'

Jane is surprised by my directness. 'I dunno. The guards don't know. Who knows. Maybe she drowned out in the lower lake. She spent a lot of time out there. Maybe she drowned.'

'But they found no trace of her car.'

'No, but the car could be anywhere. The car could be in the lake too.'

I am taken with Jane Watts. She has a funny dimple on her chin that moves when she speaks and her eyes kind of sparkle with genuineness somehow. She is drawing me in, but this makes me a little uncomfortable, so I move in my seat every so often.

'She visited the Bauer's a lot. I think she found them fascinating – you know, with the grandfather and all that.'

'Yeah, I'm reading her professor's notes. But what's your take on all that?'

'On old Hugo?'

'Yes.'

'He came here after the war, and evidently there was a bit of a cloud over him as he worked for some of the eminent academics in Berlin. These were the advisors to Hitler on Aryanism, on natural selection, you know – the foundations of true eugenics. Our Hugo was a disciple, if you get me. Then he came here and they gave him that big house out the road.'

'Hold on, who?'

'Who what?'

'Who gave him the house out the road?'

'The bishop, the diocese. They wanted him to work as a consultant to the convent. He was an expert in eugenics, a disciple of Darwinism. They wanted him to consult on what Bishop Cassidy referred to as the 'unmarried mother problem'. I have the notes in my study. I'll get them. They're the minutes of some meetings held in the diocesan house way back in 1948.'

'Yeah, sure. The professor mentions them in her notes.'

Jane goes from the room and I am left to admire the piano crushed against the far wall. It has to be loved and played often to accept such modest surroundings. I am thinking of Mary. I have been visualising her as I sit up at night browsing over her professor's notes, but there is nothing like hearing folk such as Jane Watts tell you stuff straight from the horse's mouth. She comes back with a thick grey file, which she places on the small coffee table.

'The bishop had a special interest in eugenics and he was also a noted astronomer. Let me see, Bishop Cassidy was sixty in 1948, but Hugo was only in his early thirties.'

* * *

There is a smell of old people. I know that smell as my gran has it and she knows it, which makes it worse for both of us. Mr Tobin sits beside the blazing fire. His son Eoin is grey and friendly but very protective. He places his hands on his father's shoulders as he speaks.

'I must go out the front in a minute – clients, you know.'

I do know, and I wonder why he whispers the last bit, but the old man doesn't look too bad. He has young-looking skin even though it is patched up with plasters covering what I presume to be cancerous skin extractions. He still has a mop of sandy hair, and he is fitted into a decent suit. His eyes wander like he might be having some problem focusing, but then he settles and all is well.

I remind him about Mary Ryan and he keeps repeating 'who?', but then he stops and says, 'I liked her. She was a very nice young woman.' He laughs. 'She wanted to know so much. I told her, sure most of those people are long dead, long dead and in the grave, but she was very keen. She told me to tell her anyhow. She said it didn't matter whether they were dead or not.'

He stops again suddenly taking a deep breath. it takes him an age to exhale and I am worried for him.

'I told her about my sister Martha, so I did. I told her about the wood.'

'What about the wood, Mr Tobin?'

'Martha was the youngest in our family. She's long dead now. Funny how the youngest dies and the oldest still lives – if you call this living!'

He laughs and splutters, clearing phlegm, then takes a dirty handkerchief from his pocket to wipe his mouth.

'Martha used to play in the woods. It's all the one place. The grounds of St Michael's run into the woods and she and her friends played there most days in the summer. "Strange," Martha said to me, "we hear children playing up in the garden of St Michael's. We only ever hear them squealing and screeching. One day we crept closer to the edge of the wood to get a better look, but as we got near, the screeching and the squealing stopped and we saw nuthin'. There wasn't a sinner to be seen." She swore to me that in all that time they played in the woods, they only ever heard the voices of children, they never saw any, not a one?'

* * *

The snow is pelting down on the cars in the square and I go to my room where it is warm. Someone has had the sense to put on the heating and the radiators are piping hot. I lay out Professor Black's notes on the single bed. I think for the umpteenth time that I should read over them again, but I am too tired for anything. This whole experience is exhausting, and I am concerned how I will sustain this pace. I am confused as the live versions of events are full of menace compared to the wandering conjectures of the professor's notes based on Mary's research. I guess that I just want to sleep and sleep for a long time. I want to banish all thought, let it go no matter what the consequences.

My cell rings and I answer it.

'Avril Swan?'

'Yeah, who is this?'

'My name is Mike Fallon. I'm a journalist. You might know me. I did an article on Mary Ryan. I work for the *Irish Review*. You know it?'

'Yeah, kinda. What is it you want?'

'Just a chat.'

'Hey, I'm out west now. I'm stuck here in the goddamn snow trying to figure all this out. You're in Dublin, right?'

'No, I'm downstairs in the bar. I booked in for the weekend. I thought maybe we could help each other – share notes, that sort of thing.'

'You're here in the hotel?'

'Yeah.'

'Wow!'

'Can you come down for a coffee or a drink?'

'Well, I suppose. To tell you the truth I'm running on empty right now, but yeah, I guess I can squeeze you in for half an hour or so.'

He's small, not athletic but he isn't fat either. Mike isn't the type that works out but he smokes too – I can tell by his fingers and his pallor. His tight beard hugs some life into him and I like his bright green eyes; they sparkle like they are made of glitter. He holds out his hand, which is too big for the rest of him, and ushers me into a seat opposite.

'I ordered a beer,' he says. 'What would you like?'

'I'll have an Irish whiskey, please.' I try to sound casual but my heart is beating too fast. I want to bang my chest to change its rhythm.

'I came here in August, a few months after she vanished,' he said. 'I didn't find much but I am willing to tell you all that I know, little and all as it is.'

'Why, that's too kind.'

I was playing softball.

3

1948

Hugo Bauer arrived by car, and the driver did as he requested and left him and his suitcases at the gate. Bauer was a fit man in his early thirties, so two suitcases and the fifty-yard uphill walk were well within his range. He stopped to survey his new house, taking a deep breath. Hugo then lifted the suitcases, one in each hand, and walked. He struggled at first but with twenty yards left he increased his speed. Arriving at the front door breathless, he dropped the cases before running around the back of the house in his excitement to take everything in. Hugo was caught suddenly by a gust of wind and he was overawed by the chilly air that stung his throat. The lake was choppy, with white horses churning the water, making dark mixes of brown. The waves rolled right up to a large boathouse and a small jetty. The water looked deep and he suspected that it all was much friendlier in summer. Hugo had an urge to remove his clothes and just dive in to satisfy his curiosity, but he didn't as he was sure it was far too cold. How things had changed. One day he and his young wife were in grave danger; now this new world lay at his feet, what with this new house and a boat and the lake. A great fortune had bestowed itself on him, and Addie was so excited. She hated the stinking apartment in Berlin, and Hedy, how delighted she will finally be. She will have a place to breathe and play happily in newly found freedom. The house had wonderful lawns both front and rear, with the rear lawn running right down to the jetty, so it was a good job the bishop had offered the services of a gardener, and even a part-time maid and cook. To think that one day he was convinced he was destined for interrogation in Nuremberg, and now he was in this magical place, all safe and sound with his wife and daughter following on.

'I have asked Jennings to bring your suitcases into the hall. I hope that is alright for you. He is shy and didn't want to disturb you. This view is wonderful, but it only comes to life in summer. I'm sure you and your wife will appreciate it hugely. You will probably want to place a few deckchairs and a summer table with those modern parasols down by the water. Hey, you may even have one of these American barbecues. I hear they're all the rage. Herr Bauer – or is it doctor?'

The man Hugo looked at was thin and middle-aged, but he still had dark hair that was stuck to his head with lashings of hair oil. Hugo thought him a mature man trapped in a boy's body. He was dressed in an elegant suit topped off by a radical dickie bow that was arrogant and out of place.

'I'm a doctor and I don't smoke any more, but you can call me Hugo. It's my name, you know.'

'I'm a medical doctor myself, Hugo, but I haven't practised for many years – a case of not needing to, I'm afraid, as my family are filthy rich. I spend my time travelling to Africa and helping the bishop when I'm home, although when you meet him, he might dispute that. He's a pithy sort. He's mad into science and astronomy. Many of his disciples think he is more into those particular subjects than his chosen religion, but we shall leave that for now.'

Dr Hammond held his hand out for Hugo to shake and Hugo took it gently, but the doctor gave it an strong squeeze, which almost forced Hugo to withdraw. Somehow he braved it out to the end.

'Come, I will introduce you to Jennings. He's a fine chap, if very quiet, and an ideal gardener and houseman. Jennings says little to anyone, which, Hugo, you will find a blessing in these parts.'

Hugo was introduced to Jennings who was a little younger than Dr Hammond intimated. The man looked odd. He had untidy blonde hair and his nose was squashed and wretched, like he had been a victim of a beating. He wore an unkempt old suit jacket under a worn and torn gabardine. His teeth were black at the sides and one of his front teeth was missing altogether. But he was prompt and courteous, and he had a penchant for arduous work. On that first day Jennings carried the two suitcases up the spiral stairs on his own. He made the fires in the kitchen and the dining room before fixing one up in the bedroom upstairs, heaving the coal bucket from place to place. Hugo then met Mrs Rooke in the kitchen. She looked well-worn, but Hugo was shocked to hear that she had only just gone forty-five years old. He'd have put another ten years on her. Mrs Rooke was married with three children, but her husband Don died from a rare cancer when he was only forty. She lived in the house next door, which was half a mile away, but the job was still handy for her, and Hugo found her pleasant, if a little suspicious. It was true that some people were still nervous of Germans since the war, so he did his best to placate her, making sure to be polite in all his dealings.

When Addie and Hedy arrived Mrs Rooke became more relaxed. It seemed that she felt much safer with other women in the house, taking to Hedy straight away. She teased her about her next birthday, with Hedy insisting that she would be five but Mrs Rooke telling her that a girl of her beauty and height must have reached eight, and Mrs Rooke was right, of course. It was Hedy's playtime with her dolls and she never told her little troupe the truth about her age. Addie took to Mrs Rooke but in a different fashion. While Addie held her composure always, she didn't want the cook to become confused about her place, and she made sure to pass on a few instructions about how she liked their food to be cooked, and what time of day she wanted dinner served. At first Hugo fretted that his wife may have overstepped the mark, but Mrs Rooke took the instructions dutifully. Her only reply was that she wouldn't be doing breakfast through the winter as she had to get her own youngest off to school in the village.

* * *

On the first night, Dr Hammond treated him to a meal in the Lough Lyn Hotel.

Dr Hammond said, 'You're a studier of human beings no doubt, Herr Bauer.'

'I am doctor, but then aren't we all?'

'Bishop Cassidy has an interest in all of this science, but me, I'm more of an Adam-and-Eve man. I can confide in you, I'm sure. Are you ready to order yet? Here's an idea for you to study. Tell me, why does a man in his fifties want to drink rather than eat? I keep hoping for a delay in the delivery of food as it will prolong my intake of whiskey!'

'I'm ready when you are, Doctor, but feel free to drink.'

'You Germans get a bad press I feel. Yes, I know what they say in those British newspapers, but you people get things done and with a certain amount of panache too. Let's say you folk want to civilise the world and you want us all to adhere to your delectable standards.'

'To answer your question, Doctor, it's quite in order for a man to want to drink, as alcohol suppresses our inhibitions and allows us to relax as we meet new acquaintances, whereas food is just fuel and nothing else really. It can insult or delight the palate, but it is only like crude oil when it comes down to it. I raise my glass of wine to your Irish whiskey, sir, and wish you happy drinking.'

'You are just perfect, Herr Bauer, absolutely perfect.'

The food arrived, much to the disappointment of Dr Hammond, but he made light of it.

'It's not that this delicious food stops me from drinking. It's the fact that it reduces the room I have left to absorb my alcohol I'm afraid.'

'You'll enjoy the whiskey more, now that you have something to wash your food down with. Food should be washed down – it makes it all run very smoothly.'

'You are correct, Hugo. You Germans are a special people. Hush, I shouldn't say that too loudly.'

Dr Hammond started on his grilled trout caught locally in the Eske River, a small tributary that emptied into the lower lake.

'Is the fish good?' Hugo asked.

'The fish is succulent, devoid of bones. The chef is a wonder, but it's the Brussel sprouts that tempt me most. You have no issue with Brussels, Hugo?'

'You surprise me, Doctor – why should I?'

'No reason. I just didn't think you'd care for Belgians. After all, you might tell me that what they did in the Congo involved the worst terrors ever imaginable on African soil, even worse than you Germans.'

'Far from it. My mother is Belgian, my father was German and just because I worked as a research assistant for Viktor Brack doesn't make me a Nazi. Nor did I sympathise with their methods. In fact, I believe their methods were out of touch, indeed alien to the human condition. If a race is to be perfect, then it must use imperfection to establish a barometer of what perfection really is. I doubt you feel that eugenics go hand in hand with murder.'

'Herr Bauer, you force me to consume far more whiskey than is good for me. As you notice, I have great empathy for the boys in the Congo, so you hardly think that I might agree with the Nazi position on eugenics.'

'As you understand, we are the victims of interpretation. Many things happen by accident over design. History is littered with accidents. Believe me, most disasters happen due to poor interpretation of what it is the great men say, and Darwin is one such beleaguered soul.'

The doctor stopped eating and clapped, causing the other patrons to turn around and Hugo to go red with embarrassment. Dr Hammond was clearly enjoying himself.

'What part of social function is directly related to your area of expertise, Hugo? Now bear with me. For example, why is it we are unequal, either racially or economically. Do the animals in the fields show such differences and does it cause them as much grief?'

The doctor banged the table with his fist and the patrons all looked around once more.

'The social element is mainly cultural and hereditary. We are the result of our genetics. I may pass you this spoon just like my great uncle or my grandfather might have done, but I have inherited their genes for malaise as well. One or other may have died of a heart attack aged twenty-eight. If so, I'm screwed. Let's face it, more than likely the Nazis wanted to play God to end the debate, but true eugenics accepts imperfection and our role is to make the world a better place by improving our genetic content, not by killing or euthanasia. We must work alongside medical progress to create a stronger society, one that can survive the dubious gifts bestowed upon us by our ancestors.'

'So what about the bishop's dilemma?'

'What's this?' Hugo was eating again; his chicken was going cold.

'My good friend the bishop gazes at the stars. He has a viewing tower attached to the roof of the diocesan palace. Now that's wealth, Hugo. He sits there looking through his telescope and he wonders why he has twenty young women languishing in his convent giving birth to babies that are, in reality, fatherless. So, he reasons, why give ourselves all this trouble. He examines what it costs to mind them and feed them; then the babies have to be looked after when they come, homes have to found. Right now, we trawl America. Most of these infants end up for sale in the States. The bishop is perturbed, as the constellations start to shake above, and instead of looking on in wonder the poor man trembles, his lips quivering. What does he do? I tell you, Hugo, he does his research and surprise, surprise – eighteen of these women come from poor backgrounds, like really poor. We refer to it over here as lower class.'

Hugo nods.

'But two of them are from wealthy backgrounds. Like, how does that happen? Can the families not deal with it internally. No, whatever shit happened they come rocking up to the church. The pregnant daughters are given over and we must pick up the bill. So the bishop wants you to look at it. He knows the reality of the whole sad business, but he's damned if he can get his head around it. He'd have a better chance of reaching up and grabbing one of his illusive stars.'

'You're a very funny man. Are all Irish people so funny?'

'There's a tradition of it, but I'm humbled by you.'

'There is no need, Doctor, as I am humbled by *you*, and your beautiful country. I look forward to meeting the bishop. He sounds like a very interesting man. But I must admit that I have this nagging fear since I arrived here, my wife and daughter following me tomorrow. Perhaps I'm a fraud, for the dilemma your bishop describes is outside of my remit. No matter what way I churn it over in my head, I can't for the life of me see how I can be of the slightest assistance to him, and with the diocese having provided such a splendid house and gardens, all I can do is tell my wife and child that we must return to Germany.'

'It's out of the question, Hugo. The bishop wants you to consider these wretched women, but in truth it's the seven children they left behind.'

'Seven children were abandoned?' Hugo says.

'Not quite. We want you to mentor them. But we don't need to go through the job description this evening – there's plenty of time for that. You and your family are very welcome here. I know it's going to be a complete success.'

The driver came to bring Hugo home, but the doctor stayed on in the Lough Lyn Hotel as he liked to do when he was visiting the village. The driver and Hugo had to assist him up the stairs as he was unsteady on his feet. He hit both walls of the stairway with his elbows, and he stumbled on the third step.

Hugo was amazed by the country roads. Having lived in Berlin since childhood, in all his days he had never witnessed such darkness. He got this feeling that the landscape didn't exist beyond the black night curtain. The driver dropped him to the front door and Hugo watched as the old Bentley left the drive, the headlights shining for miles in the distance over the fields.

The old house was in darkness except for the flicker of fire that burned in the upstairs bedroom hearth. He was thinking of the doctor. How interesting he was, yet he was washed out and sad also. Were all Irish people like that? The Irish have a reputation for drinking and telling stories and they have famous playwrights and novelists. Hugo reminded himself to look up some of the Irish legends that he had heard about – the stories his grandmother had read aloud to him when he was a boy. Yes, he would certainly do that. There must be a library nearby.

The fire in his bedroom was still alive and he sat close to its heat. The unpacking could wait until the morning and he could explore, especially down by the lake shore, before Addie and Hedy arrived in the late afternoon. He wondered if there was a boat in the boathouse. By all accounts there should be, and maybe after a while he could get a car. They were all the rage now among successful folk. His mind was, for once, open and bright but some of the Doctor's words brought him back.

All the students at Berlin University had been forced to serve the party, no matter what the faculty, and he and his fellow students did the research for Brack. It was nothing much – stuff about disabilities mainly. His job was to analyse the correlation between the severity of disability to the performance of simple tasks, travelling around to various institutions and meeting with many patients. Some were much worse than others, but some patients showed very little sign of abnormalities at all. The Hadamar Clinic was the worst of places; Hugo spent time there and saw everything. He wanted to leave these memories behind and claim ignorance, but the sudden glow of the fire and the warmth of the red wine just stuck it all in his face once again. Yes, he knew where the death chamber was, where they brought the patients for showers. He could still see them – the little boys with deformities and the Down's syndrome men who looked like boys. But the anger in that girl's crushed face and that beaten look, along with the dreadful stench that crawled up his nose and into his senses – he could never be rid of it.

4

Mike Fallon drives; his jeep is better than mine. I think it grabs hold of the slippery road so much better. He peeps at me every now and then from under his woollen hat, and those sparkling eyes and the snow tyres convince me, but we do have a few hairy moments. I discover his jeep is good on hills but not so good on bends, which isn't good at all as the narrow road to the upper lake is all bad bends. Mike is a good driver and I am comfortable with him. He insists on me calling him Mike, and I do with considerable ease. The road is surrounded by thick woods and then it deteriorates to a track where the snow is deeper and slush gushes into the ditch like it's coming from a power hose.

'He's an odd ball, so be ready,' Mike reminds me, but I can barely hear him as the jeep makes more noise than a snow plough.

'Yeah,' I shout, holding on tight to the handle above the door as the jeep skids heading for a deep ravine.

Mike steers it back gently, and after a gasp and a joint stare, we are set again to continue. I note that he slows a little as we climb and then, through the trees below, I see the upper lake and its frozen shore.

I have heard about log cabins in the woods, but this one is for real, sitting protected by at least twenty conifers, and there is a wooden jetty running into the lake where a small row boat is upturned to the side. I can't help it, I think I am in Norway or Sweden. The sky is dark to the east and there is only a single burning light wedged beyond a cloud out west. Terence Fleming walks onto the veranda. He is sixty-seven years old, completely bald, wafer thin, and he moves slowly like he is suffering some demonic pain. I am concerned and wanna ask him about it, but Mike is already climbing the steps with his hand out for a shake. Terence takes it generously, but I still get the feeling that he is hiding this great pain.

'This is Avril Swan,' Mike says casually, his breath making fog.

'Ah, the good PI comes to visit me. You did well to make it up here in these conditions.'

'Yeah, but it's a beautiful spot.'

I notice the shotgun resting against a garden seat. A German shepherd appears from the woods. He is surprised to see us and stops briefly to look at us suspiciously, but then he comes forward, wagging his tail.

'Bruce!' Terence says. 'He was off chasing rabbits. He never catches them, but it keeps him fit. Come on in out of the cold. I have a pot of coffee brewing.'

I am not good at Irish accents, but I guess he is from Dublin. I know the stage Dublin accent, but his is a kinder version, much softer. Inside, the cabin is huge with a wooden staircase leading up to a loft. A crackling fire burns in the widest fireplace I have ever seen, and I can feel the intense heat from where I stand. In the corner by the window is Terence's writing desk. He has a free-range desktop with an isolated keyboard; a mouse lies abandoned to one side with bundles of paper. Beyond that are hard-back books, standing tall like they are making a statement with a rowdy array of paperbacks trying to diminish them. They are strewn lazily on their sides. In front of the fire I notice an expensive rug, but one end is damaged. Bruce, most likely.

'I have to let him in because of the cold.'

Terence goes to open the door and allow the whimpering dog in.

'He's better now, but God when I first got him he ate everything in sight!'

'Yeah, my brother has a Springer,' Mike says, moving nearer the fire.

Bruce gives us another look before smelling my jeans with deliberate sniffs. He seems to take to Mike, continually butting him with his head for a pet; Mike responds kindly. Terence tells us to sit while he pours coffee, but chairs are at a premium. There is one tight armchair near the fire, and the only other chair is at Terence's desk. I don't think it would be appropriate to sit there. Mike ushers me to the armchair and he leans against the mantelpiece in an effort to show he is relaxing.

'Hold on,' Terence says.

He appears from behind the breakfast counter with two stools and places them strategically near the fire, but not too close as the intense heat might burn through our clothes. Terence gives me a mug of coffee and he tells me to just let my wet jacket dry on the floor. Mike does the same with his jacket. Bruce lies in the wrong place, and when he starts to burn he groans and moves away from the chewed rug and onto the hard tiles.

'I hear you're friends with Mary?' I say. I always try to use the present tense. I feel that it's important to speak of her as still living.

'Many a great chat we had here,' Terence says.

'Terence is writing a new book,' Mike announces.

'Yeah, what is it?'

'A book.' Terence looks at me blandly. 'Authors don't like talking about works in progress. Mary was interested in my research. I let her read some of the drafts. She came up here a lot. Who knows what happened her. I feel a bit responsible.'

'Why?' I ask. I notice Mike stiffen.

'I reckon I was the last person to see her. She stayed here the night before she disappeared.'

'Oh.'

Then Mike follows up with, 'Were you lovers?'

'Lovers?' Terence looks at Mike like he is demented. 'I don't do lovers. We were good friends, if you can call it that, but I hardly knew her, outside of her research and her quest to find out things about Lough Lyn. I had already done a ton of research on this place. I think that might have made me attractive company.'

'You write fiction?' I ask. I am genuinely interested.

'Fiction indeed. I write about this place because I live here – for now anyhow. Where do you live?' He looks at me.

'I live in Bangor, Maine.'

'If I lived there I'd write about Bangor. It's what I do. I'd play God and dig up all its dirty secrets.'

'Sounds fun.'

Terence doesn't see the joke, so Mike says, 'Tell us what you found out about Lough Lyn.'

'Nothing much. It's just the usual shithole.'

Mike laughs. 'Besides that … Hey, you don't think Mary is still alive, do you?' Mike adds suddenly.

Terence glances at me with a frozen look of alarm. 'Why, do you think she's dead?'

'I dunno but I think she could be. It's been so long.'

'Yeah, but that doesn't mean she's dead.'

They both look at me. Going red, Terence reaches for his coffee and drinks most of it down.

'She has to be dead. The body is out there someplace at the bottom of this lake or the lower one. We don't know for sure, I suppose,' Mike offers as a kind of peace deal.

'No, but she's gone too long,' Terence says. 'It's like everything else in this goddamn country. Everyone wants to skim over the truth. If we don't like it, then it didn't happen, and if it did happen, it was back in different times and folk back then didn't know any better. Excuses all the time. It's sick. How can a society survive like that, airbrushing the truth just to make everyone feel good!'

'We're not sayin' she isn't dead,' I say.

'What are you saying then?' Terence eyes me head on and I feel like a young bullock playing with his brother in a field. Wow, my head is going to hurt.

'I'm sayin' we have no proof she's dead. We can only hope, Terence. Yeah, you're right – she is most likely dead. It's the most probable explanation. We were just hopin' you could throw some more light on her disappearance. Maybe your opinion might help.'

He calms himself and offers to make more coffee, but Mike and I say no.

'We became close,' Terence confesses, moving some logs around in the grate.

He is using this giant set of tongs big enough to lift concrete blocks. He is good at it though. He reminds me of a clinician threading a wire into a patient's groin, such is his precision.

'You have to understand where I come from. I used to live in Dublin, out in the leafy south suburbs. People pay millions to buy back their own land from some smart-assed developer, while the folk in the classes below them spend hundreds of thousands doing the same thing. They all end up living in these glorified pigeon lofts. This is where everything is the same. They have the same needs – two cars, send the kids to private schools. All of them share this yearning to become more middle-class so that the generations can reproduce themselves. I wanted away from that, that's why I came here.

'I write these books that nobody reads, and I end up living alone here by the lake. This is Ireland, folks – me living in splendid isolation by this little lake that only the locals know about. Yeah, and I write about the folk that live in the pigeon lofts and then I discover that suburbia spreads right across the island. So when I talk to people here in the rural heartland, they are just the same. They tell me the same things I heard in Dublin. They are all pining for the same stuff as the people in the city. Mary didn't understand that. She wanted to find out what happened here all those years ago, but people here want to wipe out that history, so she was onto a loser. No matter which way she turned, the ghosts kept slamming the door shut. Don't you see? The truth will always be buried even if you manage to drag it out, which is rare. They will bury it by forming a commission of inquiry packed with their own appointees. The powers that be in the law, the judiciary and the media are compliant, don't you see? Most of all, the people don't give a fuck. Why do people allow the church to abuse yet forgive them and act like it didn't happen and still go to mass. People do the same for politicians, even proven liars. The people still come back for more and Mary found this out. No matter what way she turned, the doors were slammed shut in her face.'

* * *

It gets dark early and I am hoping we make it most of the way back down in daylight. By now the tiny sun flicker is covered in a grey mesh and Mike has the headlights tuned onto the dark ditches. The slush is only a sound now as I can no longer see it. I can only hear it gush from under the tyres.

'Did you ever read his stuff?'

'No,' Mike shouts back at me.

'I read about him once. Our arts people did a thing on him. Terence is an oddity. Even within their strange circles I'm afraid he's never going to be popular.'

'Yeah, I guess.'

'He was closer to Mary than he is saying.'

'What makes you say that?' I feel this need to shout over the drone of the engine.

'Because he told me he was very close to her – the first time I met him, men's stuff. I think she stayed up there with him a good bit. I don't know how serious it was. Let's say I think Mary kept his bed warm.'

* * *

Back in the hotel Mike orders a beer and a whiskey and we book a table in the dining room. He wants to go change and shower and so do I, so we agree to meet again in the bar in an hour. That's plenty of time for me. They have changed the bed linen and, as is my habit, I make sure that my briefcase containing the professor's file hasn't been disturbed. It is untouched. I shower and I sing, surprising myself as I only sing when I am happy. Right now I am both exhausted and worried, as my spirits are confused. I am in a strange place, possibly considering the last days of Mary Ryan. What joy can a body derive from that?

I shall move along smartly. Perhaps Mike may cheer me up with his honest face and easy chat. Mike, I am thinking of Mike, and he is cheering me up. Why? Maybe he is good company – just that, a friendly face among these strangers. I know nothing about him, only that he works for the *Irish Review*. What sort of rag is the *Review* anyway? I hear that Irish newspapers are conservative tools. A bit like our own back home, they are all owned by billionaires.

I dry my hair with hotel issue towels as I forgot my plug adaptor and go to admire my face in the bathroom mirror. I am glad it is steamed up as the bits that I wipe aren't kind to me. I inexplicably put on my only dress, the one my sister gave me last birthday. It only got one wear and that was to an award ceremony at the PI convention, but why am I wearing it now – to impress Mike? No, I'm wearing it for me. As a new woman in this new age, I can do things for me. But no, I am really wearing it for Mike. I wonder will he notice, and then I suddenly fret that he might notice. Maybe he will shun me as a woman coming on too strong, too forward, isn't that what men usually say?

Mike is wearing a neat sports jacket. He is showered; he looks dapper in a brand-new white shirt. I like his smells, and it takes me some time to figure out that it's a mix of deodorant and men's perfume spray. He is eager and he savours his beer; he admires my dress, but he doesn't say anything. I decide to go the standard whiskey, then my cell beeps and I receive a text. It's from Jane Watts.

'I need to see you, Avril. I want to show you something. Can you come tonight?'

I reply: 'Yes, but is it really so urgent?'

I am comfortable, and the thought of braving the cold throws me. She doesn't reply, so I tell Mike and he just smiles, taking the interruption on the chin.

'Come on,' he says. 'I'll walk down with you. She's a dramatic sort if I remember correctly?'

Outside some kids have gathered at the bench in the square and the neon light of the Spar captures them firing snowballs. The icy balls break on contact with their victims. The lane is so narrow that I am claustrophobic near its end. Mike rings her bell and then bangs on her door with his fist. There is no sound, yet there is a light on in her hall. We wait for her shadow, but no shadow appears.

He sighs. 'She must have popped out.'

'Yeah, it's probably nothin'.'

'We can call by in the morning,' Mike says.

* * *

He orders a sizzling steak. I want fish but there isn't any available, so I settle for pork belly with some weird seasoning. We love pork back in Maine, but I am raging about the fish. The waitress is tall and thin, and her hair is greasy. I figure that she is probably the daughter of someone important getting a favour. But she is lazy: she doesn't top up the Bordeaux that Mike has ordered so we must do it ourselves. I get the impression that she is on the make, but maybe she is a student and subliminally telling us that someday she will be as good, if not better, than the both of us, so less of this waitressing shit. I am watching her closely when I see the familiar frame of Sergeant Boyle appear behind her, his burly figure catching the tablecloths on either side of him. I am delighted because for once Mike is quiet. Now what has this big man got to tell me?

'We have an incident,' he says, looking at Mike as if he should know who he is but doesn't. He turns back to me. 'It's Jane Watts. We found her dead. Someone said you were knocking on her door earlier. I need to know if you can tell us anything.'

'How did she die?' I ask stupidly as if it makes a difference how she died – but it does!

'She was murdered. You went to see her the other day. Now the place is a mess, with her papers scattered everywhere. Jane kept herself to herself, but maybe you were the last person to see her alive – or you were the last person to visit her.'

'Gee!' The pork belly was going off right in front of my eyes.

'Do you want us to go down to the house with you, Sergeant?' Mike says but he is looking at me. 'We were there just over an hour ago but there was no answer!'

'Here.' I show the sergeant my phone. 'She sent me that message at six fifty-five.'

'I won't disturb your meal, but I will want to talk to both of you later. The crime scene is sealed. The forensic boys are on their way and we can't contaminate the house. Jaysus, we were lucky the neighbour smelled gas and knew where to turn it off, otherwise the whole house coulda blown, with us in it!'

'How was she killed?' I ask and am immediately sorry I did.

'She was stabbed, then strangled we think. Whoever did it really wanted her dead. Her body was carried into the kitchen and her head stuffed into the gas oven. It was brutal.'

'Wow,' Mike says.

'Good luck to you,' the sergeant grunts.

I watch him leave, this time managing to avoid the tablecloths. The folk who are eating have become oblivious to him.

I'm thinking of the lovely Jane Watts. I see her beautiful face in my mind's eye and I'm trying to remember what she said to me. Did I detect any fear in her that day I visited? No, she was calm. If she was in trouble, then she didn't show it. She didn't know she was going to be killed.

5

1948

Hugo thought that Bishop Cassidy's head was like a pencil. It was like someone had put his head into a pencil sharpener, while grabbing his legs and turning him clockwise for a few minutes. When the shavings were wiped away the bishop's head would appear and he was then moulded into shape, his narrow cheekbones the victims of a carpenter's plane. Along with this, his eyes were black, sunken in deep sockets, and he had silver hair pasted to his crown. When the bishop spoke, his eyebrows moved up and down in unison with his gaping mouth. At first Hugo thought it might be some sort of trick, but the others waited eagerly, and Dr Hammond winked at him twice to relay his undoubted friendship. Noel Wade, the Fianna Fáil TD, was clapping his political opponent, John Meaney, on the back at every opportunity. The Fine Gael man took the backslapping gleefully, but he seemed more interested in the cuffs of his new blue suit. Noel Wade was anxious to speak and Hugo thought his big red lips were like that of some ferocious animal, appearing between his giant grey moustache and his full fuzzy beard. Wade also sported a full head of hair, which made him look like a sheep in need of shearing.

'Dr Hammond says yer a hell of a man. I for one was dying to meet you.' Wade looked at the bishop to check that his tone was correct.

The bishop smiled.

'Hugo is very welcome,' he said, his eyebrows following his mouth.

'Yes, we are all delighted,' Meaney added.

'The good doctor loves a good chatterbox. I hear you're an interesting chatter, Herr Bauer.'

'The inspector is late again,' the bishop moaned. 'That man will be late for his own funeral.'

'If only such a thing were possible,' Wade offered, but then he felt foolish. 'Forgive my manners, Herr Bauer. Here I have been charged with pouring the brandy, so push over your glass.'

Hugo watched him fill his glass generously to just over half full.

'We will drink to Germany,' Meaney said. 'That you might rediscover your strength, and very soon find prosperity.'

'Hear, hear,' Wade shouted.

Inspector Whyte arrived. He was very thin, which made him look exceptionally tall. George Whyte had a big red burning face, which informed the world that he was very fond of whiskey and, most likely, drink in general. Hugo looked on as the policeman totally ignored him. The lanky inspector shook hands vigorously with all the others before stooping to say something inaudible to the bishop, who just nodded and smiled sardonically.

'I don't like Krauts!' said the inspector, reaching for a brandy glass. Wade filled it. The inspector swallowed it in one go, so Wade filled it again. 'Now Germans, they're all right.' He downed his second glass of brandy and it was then that Hugo realised the man was drunk.

'Here's to anyone that, eh, didn't think Hitler was all bad.'

The ensemble laughed while the inspector walked clumsily around the table with his huge right hand outstretched. Hugo took it in shock, as he had never seen such behaviour.

'You are a good German?'

'He comes recommended by no less than the good doctor here,' John Meaney said.

'I'm sure he's a top fella, as Doctor Hammond is rarely wrong about these matters. Let's have more brandy, so.'

Wade obliged.

'Now here, gentlemen, let's not confuse our guest.' The bishop stood up, pushing his chair backwards to allow room. 'We shouldn't forget our guest is new here and isn't used to the inspector's idiosyncrasies. We must allow him time to adapt, to learn about our ways and, indeed, our ideas. Inspector Whyte you are too much!'

'I'm meself, am I not. Here's to me!' The inspector drank his brandy down.

'It's all right bishop,' Hugo intervened. 'Back in Germany we have many nights in the beer halls. We should seek such gaiety. Life is so solemn without it.'

Wade clapped at such wisdom, and Meaney shouted, 'Bravo!'

The inspector grunted. Walking away from the table, he sat by the blazing fire. Bishop Cassidy looked at him but he didn't pass comment.

Dr Hammond laughed. 'I think old Whytie has had a liquid lunch, so we may spare him the brandy or Herr Bauer will think we are a bunch of degenerates – and he would be right!'

Hugo was about to protest when 'Whytie' returned to the table.

'We got this fella some years ago. What was 'is name now? – Ernie Timmons. Fuckin' IRA scumbag. We picked him up jus south of here. He was drivin' one of those new vans. Ya know them, Wade? All those fuckin' tradesmen that vote for ya have them. Anyway, after we gave him a hidin', he told us where the stash was, look at this?' Whytie took out a Luger from inside his uniform jacket. 'This they got from the Germans, jus before the war. Fuckin' treason. That's why I don't like Krauts. They'd have toppled this country too!' The inspector stared accusingly at Hugo.

'Hey, that thing isn't loaded, is it?' the doctor asked, trying to stand up but his chair was too close to the table.

'Put that thing down!' the bishop roared. 'Herr Bauer has nothing to do with Lugers or guns. He is a scientist. What's got into you, man?'

Old Whytie moaned and put the Luger flat on the table for all to inspect.

'I don't have bullets far it. I was jus showin' ya what the Krauts gave to the fuckin' IRA. That's what fuckers like that Ernie Timmons were carryin' round. I was hopin' fuckin' De Valera would hang him, but he hadn't the balls, the cunt.'

'Language in front of our esteemed bishop,' the doctor protested, but the inspector ignored him and returned to the fire.

Everyone around the table picked up the Luger in turn, Hugo last of all, each examining it carefully like it was something sacred. Wade pointed it towards the ceiling and went, 'pap pap,' like he was firing shots.

'Lovely gun,' Meaney said. 'My father had a pistol he held onto from the civil war. He used to say he might need it again someday.'

The bishop yawned, glancing at old Whytie who was starting to doze off by the heat of the fire. 'Come, Herr Bauer, let me show you the gardens. We can chat on our way around. Doctor Hammond will organise some food for us. I am sure he will entertain everyone while we are gone. Do come, Herr Bauer, we need to chat properly and without interruption.'

He gave the inspector a caustic glance, and Hugo followed the bishop into the large hallway, taking his coat from the coat stand as it was chilly outside.

'The inspector is a fine man and a great Catholic, but the drink eats away at him I'm afraid,' said the bishop. 'He can go sober for months and then something clicks and he turns up like that. I think it's his nerves. Maybe he imagined you were leading an invasion, as when he drinks he isn't in his right mind. He's had to be incarcerated a few times, but there you go, Herr Bauer, the world is as it is!'

* * *

Addie poured the wine but Hugo was tired, so tired that he could barely keep his eyes open during the meal. Hedy was over-excited earlier and Mrs Rooke had the day off, so the little girl was thrilled to see her mother cooking for once. She stood on a chair to watch as Addie prepared the vegetables. It was a hard slog to get her to bed, and once in bed she failed to settle. She reappeared twice before Hugo carried her up the stairs on his back. He read her two-fairy tales and sang an old German folk song softly before his daughter closed her eyes and was gone. Hugo kissed her gently on the forehead before turning off the bedside lamp. He retreated from the room as quietly as possible, taking care not to trip over some discarded toy, as had happened a week earlier, waking the child and causing general consternation. Addie drank her wine as women do, gentle sips followed by deliberate pauses.

'It's good, Hugo. We should get more of it.'

'I dunno,' Hugo replied. 'It was a present from the good doctor. I didn't ask him where he got it, but if you like it so much, I'll ask him the next time I see him.'

'Thanks, Hugo.'

Addie smiled at him before glancing over to the fire to see if it needed more fuel. Hugo, tired as he was, placed more logs on the fire and waited to see the bright yellow flames spark into life once more.

'How did things go today, my love. Is the bishop as fearsome as they say?' Addie asked.

'The bishop is a lamb compared to the inspector. The man is a drunk – he turned up mad drunk!'

'Did he now.'

'Yes, he was very insulting, calling me a Kraut.'

'My goodness! And what did the others say?'

'They're used to him, Addie. It didn't bother them so much, although I do think they feared the old bugger.'

'You'd think the bishop would have some control over him.'

'He did, but he chose not to be hard on him. Maybe there is something historical between them, I dunno. The bishop brought me for a walk in the garden. That was after the inspector took out a Luger.'

'A Luger?'

'I couldn't believe my eyes.'

'Was it loaded?'

'No, he had taken it from some IRA man a few years back. I think he brought it to show me.'

'Wow!'

'Then the bishop asked me twice did I want him to hear my confession.'

'You poor thing! No wonder you're tired.'

'I hadn't the heart to tell him that my faith has lapsed.'

'No, I bet you hadn't!'

'He presumes me to be still a practising Catholic, so I just made excuses. He was all right about it. I think he was trying to exert some control over me, but when I didn't concede he gave up.'

'You did right. It was never a condition of moving here, you having to be a Catholic, I mean. Nobody ever said that.'

'No, you're right, but I'll just play along to save complications, so be aware of that.'

'Yes, Hugo, of course I will.'

Addie poured herself more wine; Hugo's glass was still full.

Hugo woke in the early hours. Addie was asleep; he could feel her heat and hear the soft sounds of her breathing. Suddenly he got this urge to cry out to her, but he didn't. He just lay there thinking, wishing for the morning to come so he could see around the room.

* * *

The bishop was an enigma, and the whole experience was uncomfortable, not just the drunken policeman with the Luger. That really didn't bother him at all as it was obvious that the man was mad. No, it was the walk in the garden, with its grandiose hedgerows, and the fruit and vegetable areas at the rear of the house. There were no flowers yet but the whole place was surrounded by evergreens. They were tall and pointed, reminding him of a graveyard, so much so that he started to search for gravestones, but there were none. They had walked to the perimeter and he gazed up at the viewing tower. It came through the roof as if it somehow grew there. It was solid with bright clean windows in a circle, and the bishop was mighty proud of it.

'You must come up and see my den. Do you have an interest in the stars?'

'I do – well, a passing interest you might say.'

'Passing is better than none, Herr Bauer. A bit of an interest is a start. Yes, my good man, I can see the universe from there. If my faith is ever tested, I can rekindle it with just one look through my telescope. It's a German make – I bought it through a very good friend who spent many years in Hamburg. Sadly he is long since dead.'

'We're good at manufacturing, Your Grace, but maybe not so good at winning wars.'

The bishop smiled. 'I have some plans for St Michael's, Herr Bauer. They say a fella is mad when he repeats the same actions over and over without success and keeps on doing the same thing yet expects a different result. The poor unfortunate women that came to St Michael's remind me of that fella. We must confront failure, not accept it endlessly. These women gave up their babies for adoption. It is a sad affair. They returned to society scared and crushed by their experience. I wanted to end this cycle, so I closed the convent as a maternity home. We could no longer facilitate these fallen women. Dr Hammond mentioned to you that we have seven abandoned children still within the convent. I want you to work with these children, help prepare them for the life we have chosen for them. Dr Hammond will explain all to you in time. You do understand, Herr Bauer, the need for confidentiality? This project must be protected from prying eyes.'

'Yes, I do, Your Grace.'

'Dr Hammond is a brilliant man. Don't be fooled by his precocious ways. He has this project up and running. It's way ahead of its time and somebody like you will be invaluable to him. Give him every assistance you can, my good man.'

'My good man.' Those words rebounded; the dark faces appeared, faces he once knew so well but which were now long gone. Hugo sat up in the bed, propping up his pillows behind him. He was afraid of waking Addie, but she didn't stir. He waited for a second, trying to clear his mind, but those faces kept on coming. Yes there he was – a young man with Down's syndrome with no trace of bitterness or even protest. The young man looked at him, smiling, and Hugo could feel the sweat build, and with his heart thumping all he could visualise was the disintegration of everything inside him. The Down's syndrome man was laughing and then slapping Hugo on the back, then he pointed to the chamber door that was made of steel. They used to tell their victims they were taking a shower, but others were brought away into the countryside on special buses, then a hose from the exhaust was returned to the vehicle, and the engine was left running. Yes, he was responsible for this.

'My good man.'

He had been the selector, the arbitrator of life and death. This man, Hugo Bauer. He had been God.

Now this Down's syndrome man pleads for Hugo's life, but it is not just his life that he wants. No, he wants Hugo's sanity along with it.

'My good man.'

They gassed people who were normal, gassing them because they thought they weren't right ideologically. Over there through the steel door, in the shower room. Hugo remembered the smell of death, the pong of stealthy slaughter.

'What is it, Hugo? What's wrong?' Addie was awake; she had been watching him.

'Nothing, dear. I'm finding it hard to sleep.'

'You're too tired, my love. All of this is so new, and everything here is so different to Germany. Did I tell you that I found a tutor for Hedy?'

'No.'

Hugo turned to her. She was covered up to her breasts. For a split second he wanted to peel the blanket back further and have a look at her, but he resisted.

'Who is it?' he asked.

'It's a lady from the district. She used to teach in Dublin, but she had to return to look after her aged mother who has died since. She speaks fluent German. She'll stay over, too, so Hedy will get the best of everything, and we can spare her the Irish Catholic system.'

'Don't say that too loudly around here, but well done you!'

'Thank you,' Addie said, rolling over to take more heat from her man.

'And to think I used be an altar boy,' Hugo said.

'Yes, husband, you are a hypocrite!'

'Do we have time?'

Addie looked at Hugo's longing eyes. 'I'll make time. Who doesn't have time for their favourite man in the world.'

He kissed her.

Addie held him close, and after a minute she felt his trembling stop.

'The view would inspire poets, but, Herr Bauer, you may have noticed that I am not at ease with poets – these people who are maudlin' over life and death, a constant muse for them, pondering our birth and our extinction. But they forget how to live, so I prefer the company of fishermen who might harvest the lake or even the lowly sheep farmers from the mountains. They are truer to the world for in their work there lies hope. Don't you see, Herr Bauer, that it is endeavour that rewards both the mind and the spirit. What use is it to me for someone to try and describe differently to me what it is I can already see.' Dr Hammond opened the car door. 'I often stop here. The lake looks big and imposing from up here, and when the boats are out, they look tiny. It allows me to see the world in miniature, don't you agree? I hope you're not too cold. A wisp of freezing air is great for the senses.'

Dr Hammond closed the door and the draught was gone.

'I thought Yeats was a hero?' said Hugo.

'Yeats, yes – if you like that sort of nonsense.'

'He's renowned around the world, no?'

'He is big in Sligo, Herr Bauer. His early work was good. Then he started to take himself and the world too seriously. He became a fool, adopting left-wing ideology and marrying this to his ridiculous theories about the occult. I think he went mad to be honest.'

'You are spoiling so many famous poems.' Hugo laughed.

'He spent some time here in 1923, but if he wrote about this place I dunno, and I don't care. As I say, give me the working man any day.'

***

Dr Hammond started the car and the Bentley set out on the forest road. The trees made a dark tunnel and when they reached open ground the doctor said, 'On to St Michael's, Herr Bauer. I have many things to show you.'

6

I think Mike is going to sit up with me but he doesn't. He is tired and I am exhausted too. Maybe we should lie down together and sleep. I wish! He is adamant that we get some rest and he tells me to meet in the morning for breakfast. I wonder if he is shy; then I think that he must be gay. But why must he be gay or shy? I'm in bed and I conclude that he is gay. I think of his mannerisms, his clothes, the way he expresses himself. I am sure he is gay and that is why I sleep alone. I think I will mention it to him – tell him that it doesn't matter. But sure why would it matter? Pity, but it sort of matters, that's why I am on my own. Sleep comes to the rescue.

It's morning and I chide myself over Mike. He may not be gay at all. It's very possible that he has a girlfriend, or he just doesn't find me attractive. I am attractive – men have always told me so – but the bathroom mirror says different. It's telling me that I used to be attractive but my best days have passed. My chin sags when I bend over the sink and I have dark lines below my eyes. My hair looks better back from my face as my eyes come more into view; they are still my best feature. I am determined to find out about Mike over breakfast, but Mike suspects something. He is uncomfortable; he moves about in his seat, drinking his orange juice down. Maybe he is sly and stayed up for more drinks after I went to bed.

'I was thinkin' – yer man must have been inside the house when we called.'

'Yeah, I never thought of that. Some detective, huh!'

'All this excitement,' Mike says.

His full Irish arrives. I sit back and wait for mine.

'Work away, don't let it go cold,' I say.

He smiles at me and takes a slice of toast. 'I like my toast cold,' he says.

'I'm the opposite. I hate it cold, love it hot.'

'Habit,' he says taking a bite.

'What about your wife or partner? How does she like it done?'

'My partner liked it cold, just like me. She died a year ago. She had a problem with her liver. Went on for years till it finally took her.'

'I'm sorry. Hey, I didn't mean to go on about the toast.'

'It's all right. Most women think I'm gay.'

'My God, why do you say that?'

'It's true. I must look and act gay, if you can act gay. What makes you gay?'

'Gee, I thought that's when men don't go for women – in the biblical sense, I mean.'

'But I do.'

'I know.'

'But I'm not ready, and women think a man should be ready one hundred per cent of the time, don't they? If I hit on them, they go mad, thinking, wow, his partner is barely cold. It's a tough life.'

He is eating a sausage that looked too big and fat to be a sausage. The waitress comes with my breakfast and I catch a glimpse of Marcia pushing through the kitchen door. I see her, but I don't reckon she sees me.

'Anyhow, how come *you* are single?' Mike asks.

I am not ready for his question. 'Have you been to Maine?' I reply, smiling and pretending to be interested in my breakfast.

Mike shakes his head.

'The men are a little too staid for me. I am a very forward individual. I frighten them off. Marriage isn't my goal, and all they see is this private investigator with attitude. That's enough to make them run.'

'Sure, but you are a delightful woman!'

'Even when chewing a sausage?'

'Especially when eating your breakfast.'

I am glad he doesn't spout the obvious, but I am sure that he is thinking it.

'I'm going to Belfast this afternoon,' Mike says, looking at his empty plate dolefully.

'What's the problem there?'

'Interviewing the leader of the DUP.'

'Who's he when he's at home?'

'She.'

'Excuse me. I thought everything was hunky dory up that way?'

'Is it ever? She's trying to change attitudes, to be fair to her, but the old guard are stubborn and she has to play to her constituency. My job is to tease out how far she is willing to go.'

'So, what do you think?'

'I think she must be very careful. There is no saving grace, even if they are all at her rear wielding daggers. She can bring in reform, but she has to be patient.'

'How long will you be there for?' I don't want to sound too interested. 'I suppose you'll go back to Dublin after that?'

'I was hoping to come back here for a few days. It's all happening here – a murder and a girl disappearing. We are right in the middle of a hotspot, news-wise, I mean.'

'Yeah, I guess.'

The waitress returns and starts to take the plates, but I indicate that I am not finished my coffee. Yet she still tries to take the cup, so I put my hand over it.

'Can you bring me a top-up?' I ask.

She moves off with a face on and I shrug. 'The staff in this place stink!'

'It's a yellow pack world.' Mike says, smiling.

I watch him leave. He stops at the hatch to pay his bill and Marcia is all attentive. I guess she likes him too, I conclude. I watch him go out the front door before following him. His jeep is dirty, stained by dead snow and slush.

'So when will you know?' I ask.

He turns to study me. 'What?' He smiles, throwing his bag onto the back seat.

'When you are coming back?'

'A few days, maybe a bit longer. But I will be back. You be careful now – there's a killer on the loose.'

I want to kiss him but I don't have the courage, so I place my hand on his left shoulder.

'You drive safely.'

He laughs as he turns and gets behind the wheel.

* * *

Mary calls it right – her description of the rubble and the darkness. I have a powerful torch but it is cold in here. My God! I am thinking that it can't get any colder outside, but this is a different version of cold, one you get from being too close to ghosts.

I am in an austere hallway. The walls are stained where I guess photos hung. I try to imagine the photos, possibly of children or maybe they were all of sullen nuns, and the biggest stain is where the Reverend Mother would have hung, over the broken door by the end of the corridor. The windows on this side are smashed, broken by kids having rock-throwing contests. There is mould everywhere, its fur lining the ceiling; cockroaches scurry to the shelter of broken slates and brick. The place is huge, with a spiral staircase that was once grandiose, but is now missing steps. A giant leap is needed to progress upwards, and down a corridor leads to a huge room that I imagine was the dining room. This takes up the whole rear of the building and it falls onto a courtyard. Beyond that I see the overgrown mess that was once a manicured lawn. It reaches a pine forest that is desperately trying to expand.

It is snowing again, and the snow falls in a light fine dust, making the trees graceful and the wild grass blow, but all is sadly unkempt. Further on is a battered door and lots of broken glass with more stained walls where photographs and pictures once stood. This is followed by smaller rooms that were most likely offices or classrooms of some kind. My walk seems endless. I am looking at this whole section that is destroyed, with blackened beams that have fallen. The whole roof has caved in, and among the rubble lie the remains of church pews rotting to deadwood.

Now, with my entry to daylight, the snow is falling on my head. I need my torch no longer. All I see beyond the cracked wall is oil stained. These invasive cracks tell me to tread warily, this place isn't safe. I notice the remains of iron frames, one then two and I keep counting till I count six or seven. The interiors of mattresses provide bedding for wandering rodents and other animals, yet all the while I get this dead musty smell and midst the rubble a shining thing. At first, I see a gold coin but then I realise it is a golden strip. I lift the crumbled brick and disturb the wire and rusted metal. There, covered in dust, is a small book. The shining gold is the bookmark ribbon still sewn into the hard cover and what I think is black soon becomes white as I remove the dirt and dust with my finger.

I open it and several pieces of debris fall through my fingertips. I can only watch as it forms a new cloud of dust, but inside the book, clearly written in fountain pen, is the number seven – nothing else. It' is a simple child's prayer book, with short prayers beautifully printed on each page. As I flick through the pages, I stop at a replica of a savage portrayal of the crucifixion in which Jesus is taunted by his tormenters. One of them spears his side and blood oozes from the wound, he is surrounded by Romans while those thieves who are crucified alongside him look on. It is a cruel painting for a child to see, and I wonder who the number seven refers to. I close the small prayer book and place it gently in the pocket of my jacket. I immediately rummage through the rubble to see if there are any more artefacts, but I find none despite my struggles. I retrace my steps and go back along the corridors, my torch burning once more, and when I finally return to fresh air, I see the light is failing because of a fresh fall of snow.

* * *

Marcia Mellon holds the glass up to the measure and I shake my head, so she lifts it up a second time and I nod. She brings the whiskey to me.

'It's the worst year yet. The old people are dyin' from it.'

I nod again. She must think I am mute.

'It's worse than Maine, and I never expected that here.'

'We get it bad every so often, but this year is worse than 1948 – so they say.'

She goes off about her business. Maybe I will go to my room and study more of Professor Black's notes, whatever I might learn from them now! Feeling its weight in my pocket, I retrieve the prayer book I found earlier. It is even cleaner now, but I worry about the state of my pocket and promise myself to have the jacket dry-cleaned.

'Hello, stranger! Are you enjoyin' the cold.' It is Moya Breslin. 'Good to see you're enjoyin' a wee dram of whiskey – warms the bones, don't it. Ach, a wee dram will save your life. Wasn't it awful about poor Jane. Her father used to come in here – a regular, and a gentleman too. Do you know her poor mother died when she was young? Some people never get any luck, do they. It's dreadful to think that someone broke in and murdered her. Jesus, you would hope they are not from around. I won't get a wink of sleep till Sergeant Boyle makes an arrest. Ach no, but maybe they are from some other place.'

'You never know, Moya,' I say. 'It's a terrible thing. I never thought these things could happen in a quiet little place like this.'

'Nah, me neither. No wonder you're keepin' warm. I might join you, but it's a bit early and I have to go talk to the accountant. Wouldn't do to be smellin' of drink. He might shut me down.'

She toddles off out into the hallway, the big swinging door closing hard behind her and the draught invading the bar, making it emptier and colder. Now the prayer book is my only companion. I open it once more just to see the number 7.

I am cold, so I get under the covers. It takes a while, but I warm up gradually and think of home. I wonder do people miss me – not anyone who lives in my apartment block, just Granma and the folk in the office. When you see people every day, they banter with you and get used to your face, and if you go home sick, they text you to see if you're better. But when you move on they wish you well in your new job and soon all is forgotten; you fade into memory. I guess you eventually disappear altogether – out of sight, out of mind. I conclude that nobody misses me; maybe 'nobody gives a rat's arse about me' – except for my granma and she is out of her mind most of the time.

What about poor Mary? She is telling me about another visit to Terence Fleming away out in the woods. He is helping her to understand things in a way that she never knew about before. I wanna shout, 'Be more specific,' but Mary just rambles on. She should have written fiction. She is describing the road out there, with the majestic trees, and she rejoices in discovering the thick ice on the lake and comments on how she was afraid to step on it. I wanna intervene, to tell her about the prayer book I found, but that's pointless, of course. Instead, she tells me that Terence is handsome and soft-hearted, although she found him austere and tough to begin with. After time she says he melted into this vulnerable man with a huge appetite for empathy. This, she confesses, is his lure for romance. I hear her laugh at it all, and it's the giggle of a young innocent girl who is smitten. Oh, how she longs to live out in the woods with him, because the world seems so perfect out there. She tells me that being there with him is the only sense that she can find, that the rest of the world is crazy, so full of hate and evil that she can't stand it anymore.

I can't lie still. I sit up and wait for more revelations from the professor's notes, even though I have read these notes time and time again. Each time I read them it reveals something new. He is presenting Mary with the awful truth. All those romantic notions she had about the world have been dashed. She says they sit up late at night drinking wine with not a sound outside in the forest, and the lake so still. 'I am lost in

time. Nothing exists any more – just Terence and me. We toast our existence. What else is there to do?'
Then she refers to Professor Black directly:

> By now you will be devouring my notes. You will read all, and smile, thinking that I am besotted, but as you read on you will see what I mean, this evil that persists. When I was a teenager, I used to lie awake at night thinking about the devil. What if he took me over, possessed me like in The Exorcist? But now I know that all of that is a misconception of evil. The truth lies in our acceptance of power. Within each of us we possess that power and evil is our driving force. It's like the story Terence tells me of the self-made man who finally thinks he is safe. He has made all the money he can make, he has a beautiful wife and two magic kids, and he lives in a fine big house overlooking the sea. All is great until the workers rise up on his land because the poor want to be fed and the peasants want to be educated. This man runs out into the night screaming, 'I won't share, do you hear me. I worked my arse off for what I have, and I won't share. Hear me, motherfuckers!'
>
> That is our world, Professor, where three quarters of the population don't have enough to eat, where poor people are shot, imprisoned, tortured, put upon and abused. How can we brush over the truth, pretending there was only one holocaust? There are plenty of holocausts. It just depends on who perpetrated them – that's if you get to know the truth about them at all. Terence reckons that most of us live in a kind of fantasy world, with material goods, a nice glass of wine, kids who go to college and marry well. All of this is a denial of reality, and every now and then folk wake up when some disgruntled soul commits an atrocity because it is an assault on our fantasy. You will think I have gone mad, but if you are reading this you are digging. Who knows, you are maybe even here, searching. Whatever you're doing, don't worry about me. Just get to the truth. Please get to the truth.

The notes stop. I missed out on this page before. How clumsy of me. I must go to see Terence Fleming again.

I step out of bed to check the weather and use the bathroom. It is still snowing and Mike has shown me the way up the mountain, but I don't have the confidence to drive in these conditions. To be frank I am still amazed that he did. I will wait until daylight. Perhaps there will be a thaw. The bathroom is cold and I try to hurry what you just can't hurry.

At last I am back in the warmth of my bed wondering if Mary lost it. Was all of that the advent of madness? Terence Fleming – is he responsible for grooming her into his vacant world, this world of stone walls and stop signs, where nothing is good and of any value. Maybe he is a horrible man because he denies hope and sees acceptance as a weakness and the naïve efforts made by folk as ignorant folly. I can sense a deep hatred of the absurdity of women in his view of the world, those women, forever hopeful, having babies, offering their offspring to the universe. He possibly sees this as a kind of arrogance as they acquiesce to what is, in his view, a sick society. In his view, we are all merely striving to be middle-class and to live a complete lie for the sake of self-gratification and expediency.

7

The first bullet hits the fly window and the second hits the windscreen proper in a jagged line, blinding me.

I slam on the brakes and my jeep skids, leaving the road. I bounce into a conifer and stay still, listening.

Then I panic. Why did I risk it? There was a temporary thaw. Maybe I made a mistake. I just burst a tyre. The glass shattering was just pebbles flying upwards from the road. This time the windscreen shatters.

I need to get out fast. I fall and hit the freezing earth with a thump. I hear noise. The sound is coming from the other side of the road. Over among the trees there is someone with a rifle shooting at me. Another shot rings sharp; it pings off the metal bonnet and grazes the side of my face. My blood colours the fallen snow a bright red and all I can do is crawl further into the wood. I want to get on my feet, but I can't bring myself to stand up. One more shot rings out and I hear it whistle in the air just above my head. A dog barks and Bruce comes into view. I am scrambling for my phone. Who do I call? The police are miles away.

The German shepherd is by my side and I see Terence Fleming walking towards me casually, with his rifle resting over his left shoulder.

He sees the blood trickle down my cheek. 'What the fuck …? Who's shooting?'

'I dunno. I think they're trying to kill me.' I try to sound brave but Terence crouches down, pulling me forcibly behind a thick tree trunk.

'Let's not give whoever it is a clear shot. Sssh, sssh,' he whispers, putting a finger to his lips. 'Might give him a taste of his own medicine. Sit, Bruce!'

The dog sits.

Terence points his rifle in the general direction of the wood on the far side of the road. He fires two shots indiscriminately. This is followed by a deadly silence. The only sound I hear is Bruce panting. Bang! This time a bullet flashes past our protective tree and Terence covers me. We are lying flat, our faces in the snow. Two more shots are fired but they land six feet behind us. Then silence.

'Who the fuck is that?' Terence says softly, like he is afraid the sound of his voice might give us away.

Somehow I manage to move my lips and make a sound. 'I dunno!'

* * *

Sergeant Boyle is unimpressed.

'You should have called us straight away. Whoever this was has legged it by now. He was good too. He didn't leave a footprint – not a trace. We found a few empty shells, but these rifles are common around here. There are hundreds of them in farms. They're fuckin' everywhere.'

I am in shock, so Terence brings me back to his place to clean me up and give me some sugary tea. Only for him I might have been murdered.

'You might have been killed!' says the sergeant, spouting the obvious. 'Forensics will examine the jeep. Can you do without it for a few days?'

'I suppose I have no choice.'

'I can bring you back to the village. You'll need to have your wound checked in the dispensary.'

'It's not safe, Sergeant. She'll be better off here with me. That scrape is clean. It'll heal in a few days. You can hardly allow her go back to the hotel – she's a sitting duck there.' Terence stares at the sergeant head on.

'What about my stuff?' I ask.

'The sergeant can get all you need. I have the spare room here, and we have my rifle and Bruce. What do you think, Sergeant? She'll be much safer here, won't she.'

'I suppose.' The sergeant scratches his chin. 'I have to warn you, Avril, this is a very dangerous place right now. We have a team of detectives coming from Dublin later. Poor Jane's murder has them all panicking. I think they fear we have a serial killer on the loose. Yeah, maybe Terence is right – you'll be a sittin' duck in the village. Can you bring your work out here to a halt? The way I see it is if you don't poke your nose in, it won't get bitten off. It could be the right time to throw yer hat in and go home.'

'You said it.' I look at Terence, expecting comfort, but he shrugs and walks off
rounding the kitchen counter, he makes more coffee.

'Bet you thought Maine was dangerous,' the sergeant says blandly.

'Maine is paradise compared to here, Sergeant.'

'I don't want to trouble you now, Avril, but maybe in a few days you might come in, have a look at Jane's papers, see if there's anythin' that sparks off in you. There's probably nothin', but you might see somethin'. Worth a try, don't you think?' He turns to go.

'Sure, count me in on that one.'

I watch him leave, noticing his female companion, Paula, hasn't bothered to get out of the squad car. Perhaps he told her not to get out; who knows, she might have been on the phone. I am sore all over, especially down my knees where I hit the ground. My lower back aches and the left side of my face stings.

Terence hands me a mug of coffee. He has some plain biscuits which he puts haphazardly on a plate. I fear that one is going to fall onto the floor and old Bruce will get it, but Terence takes it and puts it in his mouth; the problem is solved.

'Who do you think is trying to kill you?' he asks out of the blue.

'I've no idea.' I feel stupid. 'If I knew I would tell the sergeant, but I don't. Maybe it's whoever killed Mary.'

'So you think Mary's dead?'

'Do you?' I reply.

'We're going around in circles again.' Terence sighs.

'I'm just saying if someone killed Mary because she stumbled on to something that they want to hide, they probably think that I'll find out their secret sooner or later. So they're coming after me.'

'Will you take the sergeant's advice and go home then?' Terence sits back now, supping his coffee and eating his biscuits like he is having afternoon tea in the Ritz.

'No, I don't think so. I'll be buggered if I don't find out what went on here.'

'Let's hope not.'

He smiles, and I smile too, despite my pain.

* * *

I spend what seems like an eternity in bed. Terence's spare room is small but it is warm. The bed is comfortable and has fresh sheets and pillowcases. I am reminded of home, which is good, but I guess a little sad too. I sleep for hours. I wake to the sound of someone chopping wood, then Bruce barking, but I fall back asleep just as quickly. It is dark when I wake properly, and for a few seconds I am unsure where I am.

My feet and lower back still ache, but somehow they don't feel quite as bad. I struggle to dress and I could use a shower. I'll need to ask about that. Terence is at his desk and I welcome the blazing fire.

'What time is it? I feel like I have slept for weeks.'

'It's seven fifty. Are you hungry?'

I had forgotten about food – until now. 'I'm starving.'

'I've a casserole in the oven. I made loads, so you can help yourself.'

'Is it ready?'

'Twenty minutes.'

'I was gonna have a shower, if you don't mind.'

'Yeah, it's upstairs off the landing on the left. There are clean towels in the hot press. Help yourself. Just leave me one.'

'I will.'

I set off for the stairs. Bruce lifts his head from the mat in front of the fire. I feel its heat and look forward to sitting by it to dry off.

'Have you enough hot water?' I ask from the top of the stairs.

Lifting his head from his desktop, Terence shouts, 'It's electric just press the button.'

'Thanks.'

The shower is lovely and hot. I stay in it too long and only give up when it starts to burn my shoulders. I dry off as best I can. I feel bad putting on my soiled clothes again, so I only put on my underwear. I take his bathrobe from the hook on the back of the door. It's blue and has a towel feel against my skin.

Terence looks up at me as I come down the stairs. The fire is truly blazing now; he has put more logs on and Bruce lies asleep beside it.

'Nice robe,' Terence says walking around the counter to the oven. 'And great timing. This casserole is ready. I took the liberty of opening a bottle of red.'

'You don't do whiskey?' I am ungrateful.

'Whiskey drives me crazy. Red wine I can just about tolerate. It's red wine or beer here, I'm afraid. Sure we can get some whiskey tomorrow.'

I follow him around the counter. He is leaning over, getting plates from a press, and I ease myself on to the single wooden stool.

'You still sore?' He turns to look at me.

'A little. You're very kind to take care of me, Terence, but maybe it's best if I go back to the hotel. I have all of my things there. Surely I'll be safe in broad daylight. Whoever this maniac is, they're hardly going to take pot-shots at me in the hotel.'

'Whatever,' he says, lifting his steaming hot casserole from the oven.

I love his female oven gloves with little flower designs. I say nothing. I just watch him scoop generous helpings onto the plates.

'Come on,' he says. 'We'll have it by the fire. There's a couple of trays in that press beside you.'

I find them eventually, but I must lift a plastic basin out of the way.

Terence leads the way. The fire is beautiful and I feel my hair dry just like it used to when I was a kid, all natural like. He places a tray on my lap and gives me a full glass of Bordeaux. It is strong yet delicate. I like it. it goes down a treat with his casserole, which is delicious too. Terence is an all-rounder, it seems. I watch how he eats slowly, as if he is thinking in between spoonful's. Me, I eat fast, so I stop for a minute so as not to appear greedy.

'The sergeant will bring out your clothes. How about you stay till Friday. That's only a few days. He wants you to go through Jane Watts's papers, so stay till then at least. Maybe you are in grave danger, Avril, but then again maybe you're not. It might just have been some lunatic messin' about, or a deranged hunter who thought you and your jeep were live game. I really don't know, but why not stay a couple of days to let that pretty face heal.'

I wait till I swallow before speaking.

'Sure, yeah, what's the hurry. You make a great mom. Anyhow, the way I'm feeling, a few days up here by the lake might save my life altogether.'

He smiles. 'You have lakes in Maine?'

'Lots of them, and rivers too. It's no secret.'

* * *

Terence brings me out to the lake. The new day is crisp and the snow clouds are gone; he thinks there will be a thaw. He is quiet now, but he was full of chat earlier as he cooked sausages and rashers and made pots of coffee. He lit the fire first thing and the cabin was warm.

'I can't work if it's cold,' he said.

'Hope it's going well!' I offer.

'Very topical.'

I want to pry, but I don't. 'Don't you get lonely up here – just you and that dog?'

'Nah, I had Mary stay over. She almost moved in, but she didn't in the end. We used to walk out here by the lake and chat about the world. She looked at the world in a totally different way to me, but she changed, and then the difference was that she was even more cynical than me. She had this thing about death.'

'It doesn't come across in her notes.' My words fade into the wilderness around me like I'm too tiny and insignificant to matter.

'She got to this point where everything was useless. She used to say there was no value in nothin', like time was only temporary and everything we say or do vanishes into a black hole in space. She said people don't realise that, and if they did, they'd just give up on everything and kill themselves.'

'Do you think she was mentally ill, Terence?' I raise my voice in a vain attempt to sound important.

'If the rest of the world is sane, maybe.'

'Was it because of the stuff she found in her research down in St Michael's?'

'Dunno, but as I said she changed. It was slow at first, but then the change sort of became very rapid. She was questioning everything about our existence. It was like nothing made sense to her.'

Terence unties the rowing boat from the jetty and hands me a lifejacket. I have trouble putting it on, so he helps me. He doesn't wear his and I want to give out to him but I don't. We row out on to the calm waters and for a moment I forget everything. I am captivated by the stillness. A gentle breeze just ruffles the water like a soft brush on a little girl's hair. I see the trees get taller as they climb the mountain, and smaller as they fall down the valley on the other side. Big birds screech in the sky above. They circle above us like they are expecting fish. Terence rows and Bruce sits serenely behind him like it is a regular jaunt and he is used to it all.

'Did you take Mary out here?'

'She loved it.' Terence continues pulling gentle strokes, but the boat has a decent speed. 'She liked to fish,' he says, smiling. 'We went out twice a day if the fishing was good. She wasn't bad at it. She pulled in a good trout one day and a few small ones along with it. Yeah, the fishing kept her from thinkin' too much, you know?'

We go to the far side of the lake and shelter under some overhanging trees. I see he is worried.

'I should have brought the gun,' he says. 'We're cannon fodder out here.'

'We should be safe up here. Tell me, why were you and Bruce down in that part of the woods?' I ask cause I feel I should.

'Huntin' rabbits. That wood is full of rabbits. Too cold up here. We had only started out when I heard the shots. I thought it was someone hitting the jackpot. Nosey me went to see.'

'Some jackpot.'

'Yeah.'

Bruce is getting restless. He sees something move on land.

'Sit!' Terence commands. The dog obeys but growls all the same.

* * *

He feeds me steak from the freezer it has been thawing most of the day. I say no when he asks do I want to watch a movie. I am tired again, and my knees and lower back still ache but my face is getting better. Terence says it looks better so I check in the mirror of the downstairs bathroom. It's no longer purple. If anything it's much pinker, which is a great relief. While I am there, I check to see how I look overall, and I don't look so bad even though I am not the best judge. My hair is too long; it falls into my eyes, but when I sweep it back, I think it looks good. All this stress has made me lose weight, which can only be a plus as I want to look my best. The sergeant never brought my things and I am pissed with him, but at the same time I sort of understand that he is busy. Terence doesn't mess about. He has mushrooms and onions and mustard with the steak, and the most wonderful fries that he says he got from the supermarket freezer. I don't believe him; they are too good. He has more wine and then he tells me he ordered a bottle of whiskey with his grocery order.

'Should come in the morning. They are spot on, these people.'

'You're spoiling me,' I say, smiling.

After our food he invites me to sit by the fire. I sit on the rug with my back resting against the armchair. My feet are touching Bruce's soft fur. He gives me a look, but decides it isn't so bad and goes back to sleep. Terence sits on the hard chair he has procured from his writing desk. It is not as good as the soft chair he swivels on, but he chose it not me. I think he is looking serious, but he is enjoying his wine.

'Professor Black's notes tell all about St Michael's,' I say, trying to shape the conversation.

Terence moves forward to listen more intently.

'They took the babies away, evidently. They were to go to better homes, have better lives. Can you imagine, Terence, what it must have been like to have your baby taken away?'

'They sold them, it turns out – mostly to childless American couples.' He looks at me sadly.

'Yeah.' I try to sit up straight to match his intensity. Bruce raises his head to see what the hell I am at but he settles again. 'How does it happen? You go into a home to have a baby, they take the baby away and you go home empty. How could that happen?'

'Beats me,' Terence says, pouring more wine first into my glass, then into his own.

'In her notes to Professor Black, Mary says she suspects that some women were forcibly kept in St Michael's for over a year after their babies were taken.'

'The only reason to stay another year would be to have another baby,' Terence says and looks at me for a reaction.

'I know.' I bow my head.

8

1948

Addie woke me. I was sleeping like a baby. Maybe the years of arduous work and stress were finally catching up on me. My time in the institutions in Germany continued to haunt me. As I made the selections I filed my reports, but I didn't physically hurt anyone. That was not me, not the way I was brought up. I am from a good family. My Belgian mother is proud; she brought me up to be good. I am a good person.

When Dr Hammond came by he brought me to the convent. The weather was still cold but there was no snow in Lough Lyn that week. The building was very imposing. The Reverend Mother was very nervous. She kept tapping her feet and repeating the same lines.

'It's very cold, gentlemen. Let's get you inside. It's freezing.'

And it was cold, but when we got inside the place was steaming, so much so that I had to remove my hat and coat.

'You're very welcome to Ireland. We are all your friends here,' she said.

She ushered her subordinates away like they were tiny ducklings, and the novices scattered at her command. Inside, the building was even more impressive, with a huge spiral granite staircase. It was grandiose and seemingly led nowhere, but I was dying to climb it to discover what lay at the top.

'Reverend Mother Agnes, do we have coffee?' The doctor wasn't really asking.

'Of course, Doctor Hammond. We have it all ready, and Mr Carroll, the vet, is already here with Doctor Eccles.'

'Eccles! As tiresome an individual as you are ever likely meet, Hugo,' said Hammond.

We followed the Reverend Mother down the narrow hallway. I saw windows with small drapes drawn on my left side. I could only presume they looked out on the gardens. On my right were several photographs and paintings of nuns. At the end of the hallway, face on was a large painting of Jesus with a perpetual light underneath. We followed the Reverend Mother into a large dining room with a long mahogany table. I have never seen a table so wide. It stretched the whole width of the large room. Here the drapes were open. The windows overlooked an extensive lawn punctuated by bare flower beds; in the distance, conifers towered as if they marked a border.

'Hammond, you are late.' Doctor Eccles said. Then he laughed so anyone wondering would know he was only joking.

'I will leave you gentlemen, Sister Dominic will stay by the window. Should you need anything, ask her. I will see you all later.' The Reverend Mother forced a smile.

'Fair enough!'

Dr Hammond sat beside Dr Eccles and gestured me to sit opposite him, which I did. Mr Carroll sat two seats down, sort of isolated from the rest of us. He was a very small man with a penchant for reaching for his cloth handkerchief and blowing his nose every couple of minutes. When he did this he made an enormous sound and I worried that he would blow his brains out, such was the force of his exhalation.

'Tell me, Hammond, is this the nice German man you told me about? He doesn't look German. Whatever happened the blonde hair and the blue eyes?'

Eccles was one to talk. He had red hair that was disintegrating by the day, thus leaving a huge monk-style bald patch in the middle of his head. To make matters worse, he vainly allowed two vagrant strands fall from his forehead to tip the rims of his black spectacles.

'Never judge a book by its cover, Eccles. It's beneath you. You know as well as I do that very few Germans are blonde or blue-eyed. I think Herr Hitler lost the war on that very point. His pigmentation of choice should have been black hair and brown eyes. I declare this coffee is cold! Sister, can you fetch some hot coffee? This is appalling!'

The sister rushed off to attend to Dr Hammonds wish.

'Is that your field?' Mr Carroll asked me directly.

I hesitated as his handkerchief was out once more. 'I studied eugenics in Berlin, during the war,' I said eventually.

'My son wants to study eugenics, but I told him it's all a load of horse manure. Took me ages to convince him. He's studying to be a vet now, thank God.'

'Thank God,' Eccles said in support.

'Did I tell you, eh?' Dr Hammond said suddenly. 'This is Hugo Bauer.'

'Hammond has no manners, Herr Bauer,' Eccles said, going deep red.

The nun returned with a pot of coffee.

'Blessings,' The doctor exclaimed. 'Hot coffee warms the soul; cold coffee takes its toll!'

'Jaysus, I never heard that,' Mr Carroll said looking at Dr Eccles for guidance.

But Eccles, distracted, added, 'Did, I tell you, Herr Bauer, that my wife's maiden name was Hide, rather than Hyde. Old Hammond came to one of our dinner parties one night and after a few whiskeys, christened us Doctor Eccles and Mrs Hide. Get it? It kind of stuck.' Dr Eccles roared with laughter.

'Herr Bauer may not be aware of Doctor Jekyll and Mr Hyde. I dunno if Germans read Stevenson,' Mr Carroll offered.

'No, I do. I've read most of Stevenson's books. I'm a fan!'

Dr Hammond took his coffee cup away from his mouth. 'A truly great work, don't you think so, Eccles?'

'I do. It's a gem,' Eccles said, smiling at me like he was still enjoying his own joke.

'So how did you do today, Eccles?'

'We did fine, Hammond. Mr Carroll has a vast knowledge of bovine diseases. It's over a month now, and we can't find any side effects. One of them has had a bad cold, but besides that, all healthy.'

'Great.' Dr Hammond banged the table, making Mr Carroll reach for his handkerchief again.

'All in good health,' Mr Carroll said before giving his nose a massive blow.

'Damn good. You know we get a grand income from these pharmaceutical companies. They're mad keen to test their newest drugs, but as usual they're delayed and frustrated by red tape. But we don't have red tape here, do we, Eccles?'

'Hammond doesn't do the red tape, does he,' Eccles said.

The doctor was on his feet. 'That bread is stale, Sister. I'm going to complain to the Reverend Mother!' The nun scowled but remained silent.

'Am I missing something? Sorry, but are you testing drugs on someone?' I said.

Dr Hammond sat down again. Eccles said, 'We have a research programme going on here, Herr Bauer, We test all sorts of drugs, from bovine diseases to human scourges like influenza.'

The gaiety dissipated somewhat.

'We have permission,' Dr Eccles asserted.

'From who?' I asked.

'The bishop,' Mr Carroll said confidently.

'The diocese,' Dr Hammond added.

'Who are these subjects?'

'Children of the unwed – the penitents.' Dr Eccles looked at me, astonished to think that I could ask such a question.

'There are children here? I understood that once the children were born they were put forward for adoption.'

'They are, but I did tell you we have seven children here,' Dr Hammond said.

'Some children just didn't make the adoption process – minor ailments – so they came back to us. We got permission from their mothers, and the bishop has given his blessing. All are happy, especially our darling little children.' Dr Hammond looked at Eccles for support, then pushed his chair back from the table aggressively when there was nothing forthcoming.

* * *

'We can take a little detour,' Hammond said.

Night was closing in, and the evening sun was jaded-looking in the western sky.

'Where are we going?'

'You'll see.' Dr Hammond was concentrating on his driving along the darkening country road. 'What you think of power, Hugo?'

'Power corrupts, my good doctor, no matter who is entrusted with it. It's a bitter pill, to be honest with you, doctor. I'm still reeling at the thought of innocent children being exposed to brucellosis and other diseases just to test the effectiveness of remedies and other dubious drugs. That is immoral, no?'

Dr Hammond was quiet for a moment, as if he was finding it hard to see the road, so I decided to leave him be for now, much preferring to battle with my own conscience.

'It may be immoral, Hugo,' he said eventually. 'I'll give you that, my friend. I assure you we don't want to damage these children. All our tests are carried out under the strictest supervision, but on the point of immorality, Hugo, wasn't everything ever done immoral? They have been sterilising women all over the world for years. When I was in the Congo, I heard stories that would make the hair stand on your head, stories of how, under the Belgian colonisation, children had limbs removed because their fathers didn't meet the piece rate on some mining job. Those Belgians were the cruellest of colonisers, believe me.'

'May I remind you that my mother is Belgian.'

'So be it, my friend. What did power lead to in your country? Nearly twenty years of savagery. Look at the world, where one race conquers another, only because they are mightier. They don't have to be more intelligent – no, just mightier. One culture eats up another and makes them slaves. That is power, my friend, and we have this power. But we can choose to use it or not use it. That's the beauty of it. We use it because we can, as you will soon see.'

It took us about ten minutes to reach our destination. Dr Hammond pulled the car up outside what I thought was a derelict cottage until I noticed there was smoke coming out of the chimney. I could see the dark puffs fade into the settling night. I followed Dr Hammond as he walked up to the front door that was barely hanging on its hinges. He opened it and walked inside, beckoning me to follow.

It took me a few moments to adjust my eyes to this new and profound darkness. Over on the far side of the room, partly illuminated by a dying fire, sat a large woman. As we drew near she moved in such a sudden and nervous fashion that I was sure she had been sleeping and we had just woken her. She stared at me trying to fathom who I was in the absence of light, but it was obvious she knew the doctor.

'Where is he?' the doctor asked sternly.

'He's out in de village. In't dat wher ya always fin im?'

'Where are the girls?'

'Sleppin, frum da cold.'

The fire sparked up, catching a small piece of wood. I could see her better now. She was an incredibly ugly woman. She had a nose like a pig and her jaw dropped all the way to her chest. Her hair was like a fisherman's net, all tangled with no shape to it. Her chin was covered with volcanic sores that spread to a plateau around her blackened lips.

'I want to show this man the girls, Maggie.'

'I wan care wat ya do.'

She was bowing her head. I saw the whiskey bottle on the fire place; there was just a drain in it. As we moved across the room I noticed there was no back on the armchair she sat on; the straw stuffing poured out like lava on to the stone floor. I got a sudden smell of cat's urine and when the doctor opened another door, there was a distinct smell of human excrement. I followed him down a narrow hallway. It was brighter here, as a candle burned in a holder on a little table that marked what was supposed to be a kitchenette. I felt something brush against my feet. I thought it was a rat and I recoiled, only to discover it was a scrawny black cat that darted into the darkness like its life depended on it.

The doctor opened the only door off the kitchenette. Inside, another candle lit up a bedroom, but there were no proper beds, just old mattresses. The smell of damp was nauseating. Three girls sat with their backs against the rear wall while above them, trickles of water came running from the damp patches by the ceiling. The whole area was infested with green mould. The girls were young. The youngest was about ten and the oldest sixteen. They were emaciated, and the middle girl, who looked to be about twelve and who was very plain, had paper thin arms that lay drooping across the old blanket covering the mattress. I wanted to speak, but the younger girl let out a cry in pain. As I got closer, I noticed that she was quite plain also, especially when she opened her mouth and exposed her swollen gums and missing teeth. The oldest girl was flirting with me. She was the best looking, but she too had a misshapen mouth and dull eyes.

'Where's Maggie?' the youngest cried out.

'She's asleep,' the doctor replied harshly, and then, as if he thought the girls couldn't hear him, he added, 'There were younger twins, but they had to go away. They were chewing the electrical wires when they were in use. Would you believe it, Hugo! As mad as get up. I'm sure they were the offspring of the older girl here.'

The older girl, listening, pursed her lips and removed the blanket exposing her genitals.

I looked away, but the doctor said, 'See what I mean? Cover up, Biddy.'

The girl, annoyed, spat on to the middle sister's face. The middle sister took it and waited a second before spitting back in Biddys face; the youngest girl moved to the edge of the mattress like she knew what was coming and didn't want to be part of it. Then the two older girls started to pull at each other's hair, with Biddy scratching her sister's face with her long steely nails.

'Biddy!' the doctor shouted.

She looked up at him and smiled while her sister covered herself completely with the dirty old blanket.

Back in the car the doctor told me more. 'The father goes to the village every day for drink and people sell him drink – anything he can get his hands on. Then he gets arrested a lot for brawling or annoying folk – begging – until the guards end up throwing him in the cells for a few hours.'

'Till he sobers up I presume?'

'Well, yes, but they come out here to tell Maggie he's in the slammer again. And, of course, some of them use their power, don't they?'

'How do you mean?'

'They pay visits to that bedroom we just left. All three of those girls are raped a few times a week. They bring Maggie bottles of whiskey for payment. Don't you get me now, Hugo? This is power and what it means.'

'But why don't you do something?'

The doctor looked at me incredulously. 'Do you think I can do anything? This is the law you're talking about. How can I contradict the law?'

'But you know the inspector.'

'Old Whytie?'

'Yeah.'

'He's the one that started the whole thing. The man's a raving alcoholic. You'd see him praying piously at mass on a Sunday morning and that night he'd be instructing those girls on how best to suck his cock. Old Whytie is the instigator. He allows some of his subordinates do it so they stay quiet.'

We drove away into the darkness.

* * *

That night Addie woke me. 'You're sweating, Hugo, and calling out in your sleep.'

I sat up, propping my pillows. 'Do I hear Hedy?'

'No, there isn't a sound.'

'I was having a bad dream, my love.'

'You're not sleeping well in this country. You slept so much better at home. Perhaps we should reconsider. Things seem to be upsetting you. Maybe we should go back home.'

'What, and leave this beautiful place,?'

'A place is only as beautiful as the people who live in it.'

'What are you doing?'

'I'm turning on the lamp. It's too hard to sleep.'

'Germany is in the middle of a desperate change, Addie. God knows what the Americans and British will do. They may not be content to confine their revenge to the ringleaders. They may seek out more junior contributors, people like me. Brack's project has many student names pinned to reports. I'm afraid mine is just one of them.'

'Is that what you're afraid of?'

'No, I'm not afraid, but back home we can never relax. I'll spend the rest of my life looking over my shoulder. I'll be like a rat scurrying away into the night.'

'Okay, let's talk again tomorrow. I'm turning off the lamp. We can give sleep another try.'

'Yes, do. I'll try not to dream.'

But dream I did. I was inside of Hadamar once more, that dark building where I heard the screams of children as they were led to their deaths. What right had I to moralise on what I witnessed in Maggie's cottage? The sweet smell of bodies burning, those lines of Polish workers standing in ridiculous uniforms, how they all looked the same, solemn in defeat. The smiling faces of the children with Down's syndrome as they rushed to meet you when you arrived to assess them. Assess them for what? For Brack's project, or for the death bus or gas chamber. I willingly try not to dream of Hadamar, but its stain is indelibly stamped on my soul. I am beyond redemption. I take the names, tick the boxes. Each entry is the cut of a knife at the base of the throat, pigs squealing, dark blood pumping, while men in white body suits remove the dead. They are the mentally ill, the disabled. I see her, the nurse – that woman was supposed to be a nurse – but I see her clearly along with the faces of the able-bodied Polish men and women she had conquered and then butchered. The doctor speaks of power. I was the link in the chain and without me the engine couldn't turn. That is me, not the good Hugo Bauer whose mother would be so proud to proclaim me as her own. No, me, Hugo, the assistant to genocidal maniacs, those who traded their humanity for a taste of dysfunctional ideology.

9

1948

It was Saturday. Hedy ran on down to the jetty, stopping at its edge. She looked back at me nervously, unsure whether to continue. I wanted to wave her on but Addie did it for me, and on Addie's instruction Hedy stepped forward on to the solid beams. The lake was calm, but when it was stormy it swished up and over the sides and we would have forbidden Hedy from walking on the old wooden jetty.

'I wish it could always be like this here, Hugo.'

I stopped in my tracks to look at her face. She was pale and serious.

'I like this country. It's very beautiful, but these people – the doctor and even the bishop – the complete set up sounds wrong. It's like something stinks. I like it when there is just you and me and Hedy, and we can bring her down to the lake.'

'But those men are paying my wages. We have this house.'

'I know, Hugo, but what price are we willing to pay? We have our daughter to think about.'

'I know. Some tough decisions must be made. But don't worry, with you behind me we can move mountains, hey?'

'Not those mountains!' Addie pointed up to the towering peaks that reigned over the eastern side of the lake.

'Not likely.'

I set off in a trot to catch up with Hedy.

* * *

Noel Wade stuck his big bushy head out of the car window.

'Glad you could join us, Herr Bauer. It's always good to have new blood. The bishop is sick of our stories, and to tell you the truth we're all dog tired of listening to his. Is Meaney coming?' he asked Dr Hammond.

'He's in Galway – party conference.'

'The Blueshirts need to talk, don't they. Sure they'd have the country fucked.' Wade stepped out of the car. He was a massive man. 'They're the party of the business classes, Herr Bauer, whereas we represent the common man – well, everyone really.'

'What is your ideology, Mr Wade?' I asked.

Wade stopped in his tracks and stared at me like I had two heads.

'Ideology? Votes, Herr Bauer, that's the only ideology I give a fuckin' damn about!'

I followed him and the doctor inside. The bishop's hall smelled of fresh polish and everything was gleaming. I was glad to be led by my companions; they seemed to know the drill. The door was open, leading into the dining room. There was a blazing fire on the far side of the room and we three gravitated towards it, though it was unusually mild outside.

'Meaney's the one to ask about ideology,' Wade said. 'He wants to be a minister in the next government, doesn't he, doc? Someone should tell him that your party must get enough votes to form a government first. Meaney's not great on the detail, is he, doc?'

'It makes no difference which one of your pathetic parties are elected, Noel. This country will remain a shithole.'

Wade, suitably chastised, went quiet for a second but then he responded gamely. 'The problem with you is that you're a cynic, doc. We've rescued this state and all in it. If we'd allowed the Blueshirts to rule, the Joe Soaps wouldn't have an arse in their trousers.'

The doctor was about to respond but in walked Bishop Cassidy.

'Gentlemen, not a bad day for it?' Nobody said anything, so the bishop added, 'Dr Hammond, did you arrange a set of clubs for Herr Bauer?'

'Of course, Your Grace. If you want precision planning, then just come to the good doctor!'

The bishop laughed. 'It's your proficiency in the art of skulduggery, my dear friend.'

'Never a truer word spoken, Your Grace.' Wade said. 'I left my clubs in the boot. They're covered with mildew. It's so long since I hit a ball. I hope we won't be wagering on this. If so I must insist on playing with you, Your Grace, as you're the only golfer here.'

'What about Herr Bauer. I hear golf is huge in Germany since the war,' the bishop said.

'I played a few times when I was stationed in Hamburg – a delightful golf club in Hamburg. I think the Fuhrer played there – or so they say.' I was sorry I mentioned the Fuhrer as there was an immediate silence.

'Well,' the bishop said finally, 'we best go, or we'll lose the best of the day.'

It was decided that I would accompany the bishop in the rear of his sedan and the doctor and Wade would follow in Wade's car.

'We only have nine holes, Herr Bauer. We hope someday to expand to eighteen, but for now we must make do with our flat nine. It's basic, but with a stream, there are a few tricky shots over water and we have plenty of trees. God save us from the trees – they have a habit of swallowing a fella's golf ball – but you'll enjoy the experience, I am sure.' The bishop laughed at his own eloquence.

His driver took us through the narrow entrance. The sign read 'Lyn Valley Golf Club'.

'Doctor Hammond brought me to this house, Your Grace. To be honest with you, I was greatly disturbed by what I saw there, and even more unnerved by his description of what takes place there – perpetrated by those in authority too. It's a disgrace!'

The driver pulled into a space under a sign marked 'Honorary Life President'.

'Where was this?' the bishop asked, fiddling about looking for his carry bag, which contained his towel and other personal possessions.

'Maggie's place.'

'Sure that's the devil's house. No good goes on there, and God himself would run a mile. To be honest with you, Herr Bauer, so would I, and I do. Come on, before the day is gone. It's a day for light conversation and all serious matters can wait.'

I followed him into the clubhouse where we changed into our golf regalia, and we all managed to make the first tee in good time. Wade hit first, his ball running low along the ground about one hundred yards.

'See what a lack of practice does?'

The bishop hit next – a fine shot, two hundred yards straight down the middle. The doctor pulled his drive, yet the consensus was that it would be all right; it was most likely on the other fairway that ran parallel to the one we were walking down. The bishop assured him that his ball was safe.

When I hit, I felt like I was in slow motion, my head swerving back with the swing.

'By Christ,' Wade said, 'trust a German.'

And then the doctor said, 'I don't know how you did it, Hugo. You moved your upper body so much, but you cracked it and fair play to you and to Germany!'

Wade and the bishop won the first two holes. The bishop was a tidy player, and he recorded two pars on the basic opening par fours. Wade had two sixes which wasn't bad; I recorded a seven and an eight; the doctor had a seven, then picked up after going into the stream that crossed the apron of the second green. The third hole was a par three, and the green was one hundred and twenty yards from the tee. The green nestled neatly in between two giant trees. The bishop hit a wedge, but though the line was good, his ball dropped short and his second shot required a blind hit over some thick furs. Wade hit his hard and it bounced off the tree trunk on his right. The ball hit it with such force that it almost came back to the tee.

'Fuck it,' he wailed and quickly said, 'Forgive me, Your Grace.'

The bishop held his head in his hands mockingly. The doctor hit a good shot, low but powerful enough to make the edge of the green, but my shot was the best. I hit a nine iron to five feet, my ball sailing over everything and landing perfectly on the green.

'Good man,' the doctor shouted. 'A dark horse, Your Grace, and I can smell the money from here!'

I missed the putt but we still won the hole. In fact, we went on to win the match in the end, by three and two, and in fairness the bishop took it well. But Wade had a sour look. He paid his pound to the smiling doctor, while the bishop got his driver to pay me. It was like the bishop never actually handled the filthy stuff; that was for lesser mortals.

'We'll have a few drinks on the winnings,' the doctor said gleefully.

The bar was empty and the steward was excited to serve the bishop, but he informed us that the kitchen was officially closed as it was off-season. He could make us salad sandwiches and soup, and we all agreed on the salad sandwiches. The bishop instructed that all expenses be added to his tab. The doctor chuckled at the thought of that, and Wade smiled politely. I went to protest but the doctor cut me short when the bishop went to speak to the steward.

'Do you do Robin Hood in Germany, Hugo?'

'Yes, we know about Robin Hood.'

'Then you know that he stole from the rich and gave to the poor, and that his arch enemy was the Sheriff of Nottingham and ecclesiastical types like our bishop here – one can't sympathise with his philanthropy, his Grace robs from the poor and gives it to the rich. He is the classic nemesis to the great Robin Hood; pity Robin was English but here in Catholic Ireland nobody like him could exist.'

'Steady on,' Wade said, but the doctor was ready.

'The winners of our golf challenge get to do the jokes, Mr Wade. While you're at it, don't you people have your collection plates at the ready outside every church in the country? Don't tell me that you two choirboys are not singing from the same hymn sheet.'

The steward served malt whiskey all round and the bishop returned to sit with us.

'Good luck,' the doctor said, downing his.

'May God bless you and forgive you,' the bishop said, smiling.

He only drank a touch of his whiskey and Wade drank his carefully too. I didn't like the harsh taste at first, but it grew on me and soon I began to enjoy it. We drank two more before the sandwiches and soup arrived. The bishop devoured his portion. He ate so fast that Wade offered to donate one of his allocation, but the bishop wouldn't hear of it. Wade reluctantly accepted his will and ate his own slowly, taking each bite in a deliberate fashion.

'Tell me, Hugo,' said the doctor leaning forward. I saw the bishop eye his plate enviously. The doctor had hardly taken a bite and his soup had gone cold. 'How was it during the war? Are the stories from the camps true? Did the Fuhrer have people exterminated because they were gypsies or handicapped?'

'Ah now,' Wade protested, but the bishop awaited my answer.

'Much of it is true. The Nazis had a great regard for Mr Darwin – what you might refer to as Neo-Darwinism, adhering to his theory of survival of the fittest.'

'And do you regard this as pure evil? Didn't they want to make the world better and tried to do their best in their own twisted way?'

I reflected for a second before delivering my answer. 'You should remember, doctor, that these people were fanatics. They wanted to protect the gene pool, cleanse it of imperfection. The idea was to create the perfect human being. In practice, though, it is debatable what success this method would ultimately bring. My own view is that it was flawed. It was cruel and unnecessary, as many of the Nazi projects were.'

'Ah yes, I see,' the bishop said, then added, 'You see, while we in the church believe in the sanctity of life, we respect the right of all to live, even the unborn, but we wouldn't have been a million miles away from some of the Nazi philosophy, such as the abhorrence of communism and all that it brings. On genetics, though, I suppose we are poles apart.'

'We certainly are!' Wade said softly, but the doctor interrupted him.

'We're hypocrites as we attempt to shape our own tiny gene pool at St Michael's. What of the idea that in doing something evil, even if it is morally reprehensible, it weaves its way home to safety, like a blind drunk behind the wheel of a car. Does the end ever justify the means? Look at the bloody revolutions, like the French with their guillotines, or the blood-stained revolutions that have founded some modern states. Were they worth it? Is the bad road always the wrong road?'

I intervened immediately. 'That is a question for greater minds than mine. Perhaps some of the bishop's theologians or great philosophers might have an answer, but me, I'm a social engineer. I'm afraid my expertise is lacking within the power and poignancy of your questioning.'

The bishop interjected. 'St Michael's is your project, Dr Hammond. I just gave you my blessing. To be honest I have no interest in the details of it. What interests me are the results you will bring.'

'Very true,' Wade said. 'The questions you are putting to this man are too hard for anyone to answer. He'll be damned if he does and more damned if he doesn't.'

'Gentlemen,' the bishop said, gaining in confidence, 'let's not get too bogged down in this debate. The good doctor wants another drink, I can tell. But perhaps the question could be simply asked as "Does the end justify the means?" Another round please, steward.'

'So when the black African slaves were freed, the world sits back to say one million Negros were beaten to death by their masters,' the doctor said. 'No, I don't think so. The world just celebrates their liberation. The million who died are forgotten in an instant.'

'That's true,' the bishop admitted dolefully.

Then I offer coyly, 'Except your one million slaves have been documented, so the evidence is there should anyone want to look at it, doctor.'

'Yes, but how many will ever choose to do so?'

* * *

The rest of the evening is still a blur and I will always contend that I was poisoned – that my drink was spiked or that somehow I was administered a bitter pill. I have said repeatedly, it isn't that I have no memory at all, but while I was aware that I was in a place I knew and recognised, I had this constant companion of haziness as if I wasn't really experiencing what was in front of me. To everyone, I am sure, I appeared steady on my feet and looked perfectly normal, but on the inside I was possessed by a cold and callous uninvited guest.

We returned to the diocesan house, where the bishop dished out the whiskey liberally, and then I recall climbing the steel ladder into the tower. The bishop's telescope was unreal, His Grace setting it and naming the stars that it trained on. Whether it was the hallucinogenic effect of whatever had been administered to me or something else, I was suddenly transferred from the barriers of this world. I entered a whole new universe. The stunning colours caressed my senses until I longed to leave this grey world that I had been born into. I wanted to extend myself and kiss this new and vibrant galaxy before me.

Later I was in the bishop's car. It moved steadily in the black of night. There was no moon, so all I could see were shadows jumping up and down. Those dark ditches were alive, and the high conifers were dancing banshee-like in the wind. The car pulled up outside Maggie's cottage. I saw Wade. He was standing by his own car. He wasn't alone. Someone was waiting on him in the passenger seat. A light shone on the car just for a moment and I could see that it was Whytie, I am almost certain. It was his big head stuck up against the pane of glass. I was leaning on the doctor by now, hardly fit to stand on my own two feet, and I felt someone push me through the broken front door. Then I heard the bishop's car pull away, and I was aware of this terrible silence; not one person had uttered a word since we left the bishop's house.

The smell was worse this time. Maggie was there, head bent. She wasn't sleeping, she was drinking. She drank from the bottle and the naggin of whiskey fitted perfectly into her right hand. She laughed at me. It was like she was looking down on me and pitying me, and when she opened her mouth, I could see that she was toothless and her whole jaw seemed set to explode. Two garda stood beside the measly fire. One was younger than the other; he looked uncomfortable and scared. The older one looked too robust to be a garda, and when I say he was older I mean he was probably about twenty-five. I knew Whytie was in the room by his shadow. It flickered against the far wall like he was made of luminous paint. But I didn't see Wade now and the doctor was gone also. All I can recall is watching Maggie, her big face going red, and I felt it come right up to me till I smelled and tasted her foul breath. Then darkness.

When I woke, I was in Wade's car, slumped over the wheel in the driver's seat, and Biddy, the oldest of the girls, was there with her head in my lap. She was semi-naked. I knew it was her even though her head was buried between my legs. My fly was open, but beyond that I don't think I was exposed. Then I saw the blood trickle from her hair and drip onto the floor of the car, splashing against the clutch and the brake. I could make out that the car was in a clearing and I could see now the first light was upon us. The door on the passenger side opened suddenly and the fat garda took three photos. He didn't say anything. I watched him close the door and shuddered at the loud bang. I lifted Biddy to try and rouse her. Then I knew she was dead. All life had left her. Her body was limp, and when I rested my arms for a second, she fell back like a rag doll into her original position. The passenger door opened once more.

'I don't think the judiciary care for Germans – not since all that stuff about the Jews, not that I've anythin' for the Jews, mind. They killed Jesus after all, but Germans, I don't care for at all. We prefer the word Kraut round these parts. Now, son, you're in real trouble here. You got drunk and you fancied a bit. You go down to Maggie's and you abduct her daughter. What is she – sixteen years old? And you take

Wade's car and take her off to the forest to have your wicked way. What did she do – put up a fight? She don't normally put up a fight, son, so you must have got rough, eh? Yeah, Germans like a bit a torture, eh? She wasn't takin it, so you hit her over the head with that wrench that's got her blood on it. It's under de driver's seat. Believe me, it's there. I'll have my man take shots of it right now. Boy, you are in trouble son!'

I wanted to scream at Whytie, but his big head intimidated me as it was stuck fast to mine. Ironically, as hard as I tried, I couldn't smell drink. No, the inspector wasn't drunk; he was stone-cold sober. He withdrew to check that his man was ready to take the required photographs; then, like a long piece of wire, he bent over to face me once more.

'I'm at liberty to relieve your anxiety, son.'

I stayed fixed on him, a little like a rabbit stuck in headlights.

'We do this your way or we do it mine – it's your call?'

'What is it you want?'

'We want your arse, son. You can stay put there and we get on the radio. We'll have those cunts from Dublin down here in two hours. You go with them, tell them what you like, put your fate in the hands of the judiciary. Don't get me wrong, son, I don't care. I don't like Krauts.'

'Or what?'

'I get my man here and his mate, to take her in the woods and bury her and she'll never be found. I get to keep the camera, just in case your wife and daughter ever want see the photographs.'

I went to punch him, but he was too fast. He recoiled like a snake.

'Now, now, what's this? Don't you see where your temper has already got you? I'm your lifeline, son, and you wanna hit me? No, no, you're not thinkin' straight. Just tell me what to do. Bring her to the woods, we'll drop you home, safe and sound. So what's it to be, son, the radio or the graveyard?'

10

Boyle introduces me to Dolan. He is one of these new breed of coppers who is intellectual and educated and doesn't look like a cop. He wears glasses and has this high-pitched voice that is more girlish than my own. Dolan browses through Jane Watts's papers. I see he has subdivided them all and is concentrating on the papers marked 'Lough Lyn's unwanted history'. Lifting a page from the notes, he shows me.

'Something is missing. What do you think?'

'I've no idea!'

He lifts his narrow head and says, 'I thought you were an expert.'

I don't like the screech in his voice. 'Yeah, I'm an expert, just not a clairvoyant.'

'Funny.' He bends over once more to survey the papers. 'I'm only saying, I think somebody ripped something out of here – a photograph maybe or something like a clip from a newspaper.'

'Yeah?' I notice this young man has dandruff or maybe even worse – psoriasis. His scalp is all flaky and has red marks like a kid was let loose with a crayon.

'Do you want to have a look through these then?' He lifts a pile of papers to show me the cumbersome job ahead.

'Sure.' I take the wad of paper from him. 'Don't be expecting miracles, now.'

'Right,' he says. 'Can I get you a coffee?'

I think, no, *in case the loose skin on his head falls into my beverage*. 'I'll get one myself in a while,' I say.

'Suit yerself,' he says and walks out to chat with Sergeant Boyle in the outer office.

The female garda, Paula, comes in. She looks frantic and speaks rapidly to the sergeant and Dolan, who both stiffen as they listen. I am concentrating on the papers but little makes sense. There are a hundred loose sheets; some have only a paragraph or two written on them including the one that Dolan held up earlier. My mind is racing and then it suddenly hits me – Dolan is gay; that's why his voice is so shrill. I was wrong before and I will be wrong again, so what goddamn difference does it make? Who cares? Why do I keep thinking that people are gay? Yes, I now agree with him – something is missing from the page I'm holding, but whatever it is we will probably never know.

The sergeant comes in. 'Witherspoon's gone missing. The wife's in a terrible state. Someone rang the station anonymously. We're to go check the old abattoir. The caller said we'd find him there.'

'The ceramics man?' I ask.

'Yeah … and his wife Susan has had to be sedated by the doctor,' the sergeant added.

'Jesus, can I come with you?'

Boyle stops in his tracks. 'Why not but stay out of the way. We don't want Dolan moanin' now!'

* * *

The old abattoir is a mile from the police station. It is lost down a quiet country lane. The property is guarded by a high wall that must be a hundred years old, and the yard is way below the level of the road. It is rough terrain and the snow drifts are banked to the sides, covering the grass and hedges with enormous ice-blocks and huge pools of water, some over a foot deep. I see at least five Portacabins and a skip full of rusted iron, in the corner, with its steel door and corrugated iron roof, the old abattoir looks out of place. I reckon the stone building is very old too. The sergeant pulls back the heavy bolt and Dolan and Paula watch him heave the door open. It is dark inside. The sergeant searches for a light switch with his torch but he can't see any. Then he finds a single switch, but when he presses it nothing happens. All three police officers train their torches ahead and from the shadows a large rat scurries for cover, causing Paula to squeal.

'Shine upwards,' Dolan says.

Unquestioningly his companions do, but I am sorry I haven't a torch. It is in the back of my jeep, which is God knows where. Paula lets out a piercing scream. Sergeant Boyle is pointing his torch up towards the ceiling and dangling from a rusted rail with a meat hook through his throat is the body of Kevin Witherspoon. I am intrigued, for in the torchlight he looks better than when I met him, despite the gruesome rusted meat hook.

'Jaysus,' Boyle says.

There are frantic screams from outside.

'Get out there, Paula,' Boyle commands. 'Keep her out there, for fuck's sake. This is no sight for her to see.'

Dolan is unaffected. He is walking around shining his torch on the body from different angles. I follow his beam and can't make it out. It's like he was distorting the image with his torch. I realise that the meat hook is through the back of Witherspoon's head. He is like a foul hooked fish, his blood cascading to the floor. I notice that his body is held fast by a steel chain that is secured to an iron ring bolted to the wall.

'Call the team,' Dolan says.

For a moment I think he is screeching at me, but he is screeching at Boyle who is stopping Susan from entering the building. I hear the scurry of rats behind me and I move, but nothing comes out of the darkness.

'A fine mess!' Dolan says, this time to me. It is as if he has suddenly realised that I am there, standing behind him. He flashes the torch in my face, blinding me.

'Hey,' I scream at him.

'What da fuck are you doing here?' He is more excited than angry.

'Boyle told me I could come.'

'Jesus,' Dolan says. 'The world and his wife … and you. Why do you want to see this? I thought you were going through Jane Watts's papers. Jesus, I didn't know you were behind me looking at this God-awful mess. Go on – scram!'

The rats take him literally. They run under our feet. They are big and bold; Dolan aims a kick at one but misses. I walk back out into the blinding daylight. I hold my belly. The vomit is overwhelming, so I race to where the snow is banked. I puke good and hard, the acidic taste burns my tongue and throat. I stand up straight, taking deep breaths. Then I see Susan, half in and half out of her Ford Focus; Paula is comforting her. Sergeant Boyle paces up and down, holding his cell phone close to his ear. He is speaking very fast.

* * *

Terence collects me. His jeep is much older than mine. Some parts of the front panel on both sides have rusted. He is quiet. I think he might have a million questions when I tell him about poor Kevin, but he just nods and grunts as if I am telling him about the weather. Then I see that he is concentrating on the road, as there has been a fresh snow shower. He speaks suddenly, but I realise he is talking to Bruce who sits cosily in the back.

'I can't say I like Susan, but Jesus you don't wish that on anyone!' he says finally.

We are on the mountain road now, with no traffic, and he starts to relax.

'Why don't you like Susan?'

'What?'

'You said you don't like her.'

'Hah, just cause she's ugly – nothin' else!'

'Gees, there's me thinkin' you might say something profound.'

'My books are profound, Avril, not me. It's all a dreadful mess. Where will it end? Two people are dead, maybe three if you count Mary. Have we a serial killer in our little hamlet?'

'I dunno. Someone definitely took something from Jane Watts's papers, question is what?'

'And who?' Terence gives me a funny look before averting his eyes back to the road as we come to a treacherous bend.

I feel better now that I can see the lake. I love it in the evenings as the birds are doing their last rounds. They lose themselves in the darkening sky. I see the ducks disappear into forests of rushes, and when the wind stirs, tiny white ripples dance about aimlessly. I give Terence a hand with the shopping. He is content; he whistles softly to himself, and I know by the way his notes are strewn by his PC that he has had a busy day. The screensaver is on while his computer sleeps.

Terence lights the fire he has already set and Bruce sighs and takes up a warm position.

'Maybe it's someone from outside?' I say.

'What?' he calls out.

I walk over to the armchair, stepping over the dog.

'Wine?' he ask from the far side of the counter.

'Heck, why not. Jesus, listen I owe you some cash.'

'What are you blabbering about cash?'

'You're paying for everything. I owe you for all this wine at the very least.'

He smiles, and I remember what it is I want to say. 'Whoever is responsible for all of this – if he doesn't live here that would explain Mary's absence, wouldn't it? He came here and took her away.'

'Like the government … or aliens?' He walks over and hands me a glass of red.

'I dunno. I'm just bamboozled. It's not a big place. No one could hide from the sergeant for long. He knows everyone and everything that goes on for twenty square miles, yet he has no idea, no suspects, no clues. It doesn't make any sense, Terence.'

'Somebody doesn't want their dirty little secret aired and that someone is prepared to kill to stop folk from finding out. It's local, I'd swear, and I pretty sure it goes back to St Michael's and what happened there all those years ago. I think the answer lies somewhere in the notes that Mary sent your professor. It's gotta be.'

The fire is taking off and I am suddenly warm, which comes as a shock as I didn't realise I was ever that cold. Terence serves up a wonderful rabbit stew. I ate rabbit a few times back home in Maine, but Irish rabbits taste so much better, mainly because Terence shoots them, skins them and does all the hard work. This rabbit, which I had seen hanging on the back of the kitchen door yesterday, tastes so good. I am in a better mood after the stew and Terence keeps the wine flowing. Then he surprises me by producing delicious crackers and soft cheese for dessert. I am not too sure about the cheese until I wash it down with a glass from the second bottle of red wine. Magnificent!

I am stretched out on the rug by the hearth now and Bruce retreats reluctantly. Terence plays some vinyl records. They are a blast from the past, all seventies stuff from Barclay James Harvest and Genesis. The BJH stuff is very gentle and melodic whereas Genesis is more serious and livelier, but I like both. I look up to see what he is at and Terence is staring at me; when I catch him he looks away like a shy teenager.

'I expect Mike will be back soon,' I say.

'Mike is coming back?'

'Yeah, he said he was.'

'Oh, that will be good. You'll have two minders then.'

'Are you a bit jealous?'

'I am.'

'Are you? You are not!'

'I could be. Come on, Bruce, toilet time.'

Bruce is on his feet and gives himself a shakedown before following Terence to the cabin door. I feel drained. I dunno if it is just exhaustion, or the knowledge that a young girl's body lies out in the woods. She has been there for nearly seventy years, not a soul to mourn or grieve for her. I wonder if I told the sergeant what it was that Hugo Bauer alleged would he take it seriously, especially amid all the current mayhem. My mind turns to the abattoir. I can hear the pained screams of the helpless animals queueing for death, but why did Kevin Witherspoon meet his end in that place? Whoever did it must be strong to winch a body up to the ceiling on a chain. And to pierce someone's neck with a rusted meat hook would require real strength. I am finishing my wine when Terence places his hand on my shoulder. He could see that I was lost in thought.

'You look tired,' he says.

'I am.'

He cuddles me close, then we dance to his soft music.

'Be careful what you wish for, Avril.'

He kisses me, but I want him to stop as I think he is taking liberties. I say nothing as I am taken with the sweetness of his lips and the grip he has around my back. He is saving me.

I respond, and I feel him react. He is getting hot.

'Is this wise?' I ask.

He stops for a second. 'What do you think?'

So I kiss him, only this time I am more forceful than he.

His bed is too big even for two – it's king-size to allow a man roll about. When he puts his penis inside me, I wince. It's been forever since I had a penis inside me – well, in my vagina anyhow – and at first it hurts a little and I don't care for it. But after a bit it gets better, and he settles into a flowing rhythm. All the time he kisses my neck and then my mouth; once again I get used to it. I even find it arousing as he is sweaty and manly, and I know he is sincere as his face tells me so. I am no longer thinking of anything. I am starting to beg; I like to beg. 'No please, don't stop,' and he doesn't. He turns me around and he takes me from the rear, doggy style. I know he is almost ready as I feel his penis bursting to let go. I scream and he lets go, and it's over. The pleasure is only temporary. We are left with memories that will evaporate soon enough.

After a couple of minutes he says, 'I knew a fella once. He ran a shop. He was an old guy. He'd been through the ringer a few times, like failed marriages and such. He used to tell me that he had only one dream left in the whole world and that he was working towards it. That's how he motivated himself to keep on working so hard, to keep on going.'

'What dream?'

'He wanted to save enough to retire and his dream was very simple – he wanted to run a deer farm in the Wicklow mountains. Simple as that. He wanted nothing else – no new wife or exotic holidays, nothing. Just the fresh air and his deer. This fella lived in his shop. He ate all of his meals there. He had a little primus down the back, and sometimes when I'd go visit him he'd be cooking rashers and stuff. He'd buy thousands of boxes of matches from me and he probably made twenty cent a box, but he said that one day all the boxes would be sold and his profit would be made. Now there's patience for ya – the slow build-up on the long road.'

'I didn't know you were a salesman.'

'Not a very good one.'

'What happened the shopkeeper? Did he ever get his deer farm?'

'No, he didn't. He died of cancer a few years later.'

11

Mike is on the veranda. He looks tired. He passes no comment on Terence in his dressing gown, or me with just a blouse and casual pyjama bottoms. I start getting these gay thoughts about him again.

Terence offers to make more coffee and Mike accepts.

'Are you hungry? I can whip you up a few rashers?'

'You know I might take you up on that,' Mike says, laughing.

Terence smiles. 'Starvin' Marvin.'

Mike laughs again. He has a boyish laugh.

'I might nip out for a smoke first.'

'Do,' I tell him.

Mike gives me his *I didn't ask for your permission* look, but Terence says, 'Smoke away. There's no law out here.'

'I couldn't,' Mike says, looking at me.

'Feel free. We're fixated with this shit back home. As Terence says, when in Rome.'

Mike lights up his fag but he moves closer to the fire. He doesn't want us to inhale his smoke; it makes a good ashtray too.

'I spent a whole day with Heather Balfour. She's much nicer in real life.'

'Wasting your time!' Terence says, bending over to turn the rashers. 'It's worse up there than down here, if anything could be worse. It's particularly bland – the same old replaces the same old. What annoys me is, you'd think that after thirty years of conflict they mighta got something decent, but no, the same old parliamentary nonsense with devious political game-playing. They make me sick.'

'Point taken, but Heather isn't so bad. She has a nice line in sarcasm. You won't believe me when I tell ya she has the *Cúpla Focail*!'

'Yeah, so the media won't call her a complete bigot!'

The fag is smoked and the rashers are done. Terence makes a pot of coffee. I look on, doing nothing but sapping up the entertainment. I have only a sort of an idea as to the meat of the conversation, but I enjoy it just the same.

Serving the rashers and the coffee Terence says, 'If ever a people were so poorly served by politics it's the Irish, and the Northerners worst of all. Those fuckers fought a bloody war for what – Stormont and Heather Balfour?'

'The way it's gone in our game, Terence, is that we don't ask any more. We just listen to what they choose to tell us and we report!'

Mike wolfs into his rashers and drinks lots of coffee to wash the salty taste down.

'These people do one thing – they react,' Terence says, pouring Mike more coffee from the pot.

I get more coffee too. I hadn't want rashers, but I'd kill for some now. It's always the bloody way. There is a silence, mainly because Mike has his mouth full and Terence is thinking about what to say next.

'So who do you think is behind all of this mess?' Mike says after swallowing his food.

'I dunno.' Terence is still chewing. Then his eyes light up: 'Maybe Heather Balfour!'

'Yeah.'

Terence agrees. 'She comes down south and blows folk away, or strangles them and sticks their heads in ovens, then goes back to her day job.'

'Not bad.' They both look at me. 'And hangs one poor old sod on a meat hook?'

'Grisly end,' Terence says.

'You should warn all the people you interviewed,' Mike says. 'It's like you marked their doors with the blood of the Passover.' He is smiling but deep down he is deadly serious.

I think of the grand old man Mr Tobin. What if he is next? Should I call Sergeant Boyle? Maybe they could place a guard on the old man, or would I be better calling Eoin, his son?

Mike interrupts my thoughts. 'I think it's time you visited the Bauer's.'

'Mary didn't hit it off with the old woman, that's for sure.'

Mike doesn't respond to me. Terence lifts the coffee pot. He is surprised it is empty.

He shakes it once and says, 'The young fella is strange, but his wife is okay. She is popular enough around the place.'

'Do you think I should ask Boyle to keep an eye out for old Mr Tobin?'

'I would,' Mike says, watching Terence refill the pot.

'No harm.' Terence is smiling. He knows I am worried and he is trying to make me feel better.

I ring the sergeant three times in just five minutes, but he doesn't pick up, so I leave a message. I want to ring Mr Tobin's son, but the guys talk me out of it. They think I should speak to the sergeant first.

* * *

Hedy Bauer looks good for her age. She shows me down a hallway into a dining room where she has a good fire going. The sitting room is over-decorated. It is old-fashioned, with a large sofa and rustic armchairs. On the mantelpiece are ceramic pieces and porcelain figures; above these is a picture of the German countryside. I know this because it is the first thing she tells me about. She speaks perfect English in a soft accent that I struggle to identify as Germanic. When she comes close to usher me into a seat, I smell a rich perfume somehow it makes her seem younger. Then I get lost in the armchair; it seems too low for an adult.

I wonder how Mike is doing in the village. He stopped off at the hotel to change his clothes and pick up some of my things. He said he would drop by the undertakers to advise Mr Tobin to be careful, considering the terrible fates of Jane Watts and poor Kevin Witherspoon. Hedy is aware that I am musing.

'You Americans are used to the cold?'

I nod.

'The Irish don't like the cold. They say they aren't born into it, but I've lived here for many years and it snows most winters. I got used to it, so I wonder why the natives have not. But maybe it's my German blood that makes me strong, eh?'

I agree, unsure as to the sense of it.

'Will you have some tea? You Americans like coffee, no?'

'I am coffeeed out. I think I am okay, thank you.'

'Arnold is working from home now. He makes coffee all day long. He has coffee and tea. It'll be no problem to make you one.'

'It's okay. I'm all right for now.'

'I see. I'm not a tea drinker. I like ginger ale. That is my drink. You come and see me just like your friend or your colleague Mary, but I must warn you that Mary and I didn't see eye to eye. I think she took things from this house. She abused our hospitality.'

'What things?' I am abrupt but then I weaken. 'What things?'

Accepting my retraction, she says, 'Notebooks and diaries – stuff I showed her – but I didn't expect her to steal them. I just gave her these books to look over, then I went out of the room to chat with Julia, my daughter-in-law and when I came back, Mary was all nervous. She wanted to leave in a rush, and when she was gone I realised that the notebooks were gone too. I called her and let her have it, but she was just rude and ignored me. She denied that she took the notebooks, so I threatened to send Arnold over to the hotel to retrieve what was ours, but she still denied she had taken them.'

'They aren't among the notes she sent to Professor Black, but she does mention your father a great deal, so I presume that she read them.'

Hedy eyes me suspiciously.

'To be honest, Ms Bauer, I am not a friend or colleague of Mary's,' I say. 'I am a private detective. I'm trying to find her – or at least find out what happened to her.'

'So you think we are all suspicious then?'

I try laughing to ease her angst, but it doesn't work.

'I have learned never to trust the Irish, but you are not Irish,' she says.

'No, I am from Bangor, Maine – in New England.'

'That's interesting, I am sure, but if you find these notes you will return them to me? I am sure you will.'

'I will.' I am sincere.

'Good,' Hedy says, leaning over to put a log on the fire. 'As my ex-husband used say, we will settle for that.'

'Tell me, Ms Bauer, what do you think is going on here?'

She is surprised I've asked her. 'I don't know what you mean.'

'The killings – and Mary's disappearance. It's dreadfully strange for a small place like this.'

'I don't see how my opinion helps any. I am like everyone else. I am shocked and appalled that such a thing can happen on my doorstep, but I know nothing more.'

'Did your son go looking for Mary to get your notebooks back?'

'No, I told him not to. It wasn't worth it.'

'So she should still have them in her possession? I can vouch that while she mentions the contents of some notebooks in detail, she doesn't have any notebooks with her papers. Are you certain your son didn't retrieve them from her?'

'I am certain, Detective!'

Arnold joins us, startling me, as I don't hear him come in from the kitchen.

'I went to see her, but she wasn't there,' he says.

He is unkempt. I think he is about forty years old and has a big head full of broom curls. There is no shape nor care and it all falls on his face, leaving just enough room for his eyes and nose.

'Marcia Mellon said she had left the village,'

'Did she now?' Arnold says.

'That's what she told me!'

Arnold comes closer and I can find no Germanic heredity, but I get no trace of Irishness either.

'My wife reckons the writer did her in. Julia says he buried her out deep in the forest. He's supposed to have killed two women before.'

'Who? Terence Fleming?'

Arnold looks at his mother coldly before nodding in affirmation.

'Where did you get that from?' I ask.

'Julia is the community health officer. She hears things. There are no secrets from Julia. Do you want a drink, Mother?'

Hedy shakes her head, then she looks at me. I shake mine in response.

'It's all true,' he says. 'Just go ask Marcia Mellon. I don't know what she did with our notebooks. They were all in my grandfather's own hand. Maybe the murderer buried them with her.' Arnold goes into the kitchen.

'Terence Fleming hasn't killed anyone.'

'Rumours,' Hedy says. 'That's how it all starts. In a place like this it spreads like wildfire I'm afraid.'

Mike would know if Terence had some criminal past. No, it was ridiculous.

'I wonder who told your daughter-in-law such a thing,'

'I don't know. Julia would never tell, but she prides herself on her sources. Julia has a theory about everything. She is a most interesting individual but she isn't representative of the local type, mind you. Her people were originally from Dublin. Maybe that says it all.'

Arnold arrives back with a mug of coffee. He stands close to the fire, and in this light he looks more like forty-five.

'I used to go out with Marcia Mellon many years ago,' he says. 'Her father was a tyrant. He put me off, to be honest – otherwise I think I might have married her. But then Julia came along. Julia's father was dead. I didn't think much of her mother, mind you, but her brother – he was okay.'

Is this guy for real? Perhaps he had an illness or there had been an accident. He rattles on for a few minutes, not making any sense till Hedy says, 'Is the boat in?'

Arnold stops to think. 'I think so,' but he leaves the room to go see and doesn't return.

'My son has a benign tumour. They can't operate where it is.'

'Oh.'

'We got the best of advice. It might not get any worse, but he goes on and on. It drives Julia mad, but me, I'm more patient with him. On the plus side he has a great memory. If he tells you stuff from the distant past, then you better believe him.'

* * *

I tell it all to Mike as we drive by the lake. He laughs.

'Terence was never married. I just read his bio.'

'Why do you think Mary took the notebooks? She didn't send them to Professor Black, so where are they? Who has them?'

'Young Mr Tobin didn't take too kindly to me putting old Mr Tobin on alert. I think he thought I was threatening him and his family. Funny how a courteous fellow like that can turn nasty.'

We agree not to mention Julia's accusation to Terence because it is outrageous. We also agree that Sergeant Boyle wins the worst police sergeant in Ireland award for his failure to return my call. Not a word.

Bruce greets us as we pull up and Terence comes out the front when he hears Bruce bark.

'Well, how did the meeting with the Kaisers go?'

'Nothing much. All a bit odd to be honest.'

'Odd is the understatement,' Terence says. 'Are you hanging around for grub?'

Mike throws both hands in the air. 'You twisted my arm, but you can explain all to Moya Breslin. She'll go out of business.'

Mike is at the rear of the jeep. He takes out two bottles of red wine and a six-pack of beer.

'Great French wine I bought in Belfast, and some cheap Polish beer I bought in the Spar in the village. Beat that.'

'We gonna have a party?' I feel excited.

'Why not?' he says with his best cheeky grin.

'Steaks all round!' says Terence as he unpacks the shopping. 'I'sssa loves me steakkk!'

I laugh, but Mike just stares at Terence and then says to the dog, 'He's mad.'

I get drunk. Terence has a bottle of Jameson stashed, Mike doesn't drink whiskey and Terence is supping beer, so I guess I drink most of the dreaded stuff. I end up in bed with both of my men, not that I really want that. Maybe it's because I can't pick one over the other. Either way I had my first three-way since Captain Reynolds and Detective Burke on that Christmas party night. That is listed in the forgettable and awkward category, as it cost me my job and a complete reappraisal of my relationship with alcohol, one which alcohol won, hands down.

This, on the other hand, was good. Terence is rough but unintentionally so. He has this rugged hairy body that rubs off my skin like sandpaper, but Mike is pure and slender by comparison. He is feminine in looks and touch; really his maleness belongs to his face with only his beard stubble reminding me of just who he really is. I don't like anal sex and it don't like me is the truth, so I am not that drunk, and I am sure my asshole has more functional uses; it is not designed to receive.

Now both men are asleep. Terence snores gently, but Mike is silent. Maybe I am a slut, but then I get to thinking that I am just lucky to have found two wonderful men all at once. Neither of them mentions 'relationship' to me, that dreaded word. It's all so easy and if I were on vacation, I would be the happiest woman on earth.

Methinks the whole saga must be affecting my judgement. I am scared that's what it is. Do I need two men in my bed to keep me safe? I am running for cover and they are just as crazy. Maybe they are taking advantage of me. Why did Arnold tell me that Terence had killed two women? I listen as Terence gently snores. He does not the sound like a murderer, but what do murderers sleep like? Do their snores have tell-tale pauses? Mike turns over on his side and the moonlight shines through the skylight. He has female skin; for sure a few chromosomes went astray. I am not in love; I am just terrified of what lies out there. I am so terrified of malevolence. Do I fear the truth? Does such evil exist among all the good in the world, evil like hundreds and thousands speckled on humanity? Have human beings evolved with a kind of evil psychosis? Here I am, animal-like, the hater of monogamy, yet I know that wolves mate for life. Maybe I am not as good as the wolf. I am all alone and frightened in my soft bed with two lovers. Is it that I, the female, could really eat these two docile males alive.

Mike stirs like he is getting wind of what I am worrying about, but Terence still snores softly. Now I know the moon has left; it was an all too brief visit. Outside, the first light of day is stacking on the ridges to the east, and soon the lake water will taste the winter sun and my companions will wake bleary-eyed and slightly confused. Then we will each wonder should we engage again? How does one plan these liaisons, and if they are planned does it negate them in some way? Will it be better to ignore all and prance around the cabin like nothing has happened? The boys will behave as I do – they always do – but I feel the day spread its wings. The light clings to the skylight and sleep is interrupting my consciousness. I hear only the sweet music of men sleeping, bodies failing as they are bound both in dreams and by me. I am celebrating my ownership of not one penis but two. Should I wake Mike for more sex? Am I ready to receive his penis again? I stare at it. His is long and flops like a rubber hose. It falls neatly into the gap between his thighs. But Terence lies on his back. He is more robust and his penis is chunkier, has more body.

Maybe we should resume positions in a few hours, but some guys are ready again in twenty minutes. I fail to act, as sound puritanical sleep chastens me; I am exhausted.

12

I keep thinking about Mike and Terence, and when the sergeant puts a coffee in front of me I grunt. I am barely listening to his apology about not returning my call; I don't know if I care about anything any longer. He is obsessed with keeping old Mr Tobin safe and I want to say I don't care. *Do you know I slept with two guys last night?*

The sergeant is in a funny mood, for sure, and I am certain that if I did tell him the truth he wont even comment. I feel his eyes are steelier than usual. He stares at me like it's the first time he has ever laid eyes on me. Then I am thinking, *oh shit he wants to join in the fun,* but I don't say anything because it's the last thing I want him to know. I am still curious as to why he called me so early in the morning out of the blue, coming to collect me, too. It's strange he never spoke all the way into the village, yet I know he has something to tell me, so why not tell me on the journey in and why wait till he swallows half his coffee to begin?

'I can't protect old Mr Tobin, not completely. I don't have the resources, not unless I sit outside his house for twenty-four hours a day.'

He waits for me to react, but I don't. I guess I am still stunned by my actions of the previous night. I am also dehydrated. I scan his office for one of those water dispensers but he has none.

'Dolan says he will send for more people, so let's see how that goes. How are you out in the cabin?'

'Good. Why?'

'Nothing, just thinking of you out there all alone with two men.'

'Both gentlemen, sergeant!'

'Not suggesting otherwise.' He smiles, and I like him when he smiles. All the worry and stress that shaped his face disappears; it takes years off him.

'I want you to take more of Jane's notes with you. You might find something. I don't want Dolan to see them. Look, it's all fine and well coming down from Dublin with these new ideas, but he doesn't know the background of the folk around here. He doesn't get lots of things. If he sends those few extra bodies to mind old Mr Tobin I'll be happy. Anyhow, he's packed up for now, gone back to his mammy in Dublin, but he'll be back!'

The sergeant does a poor Arnold Schwarzenegger. I pretend to find it funny.

'So are you getting anywhere with the investigation?' I ask.

The sergeant gives me a vacant look. He is ready to let me go. 'Do you want me to drop you back out? I have a few things to do around the village. The good news is the snow is melting and the forecast is good, for a change. Maybe you'll get to see the real Lough Lyn.'

'I think Mike is coming this way. I'll call him to see if he's free.'

Sergeant Boyle pushes his chair back and raises his burly body high into the air.

'Well, what about the investigation?' I say.

'Brick walls,' he says painfully. 'Dolan has taken it over. He's gone back to his mammy with the forensics. He's a great believer in forensics. He says if we don't nail the culprit through his swabs we'll never nail him. He says he'll eat his hat if he doesn't solve these murders.'

I am touched by the sergeant's light sense of humour. I am also chuckling as I think of which of my new boyfriends I should call.

'Maybe Dolan will have to keep his promise!'

I leave his office and walk back up to the village as the road is dry for once. In the distance the hills look bigger and nearer in the clear air. I feel a presence and I look back to see the sergeant watching me from outside his office. He pretends to be looking for something in the patrol car when he sees me looking back. I think of whiskey, but then I'm thinking it's just Mr Alcohol and it is far too early in the day.

Mike answers his phone and I feel guilty for not calling Terence.

'Are you coming by here later?' I ask.

'Yup, but I'm going back to the city tonight. Hey, but it's all right, I can drop you back. It's on the way, sort of.'

'You never said. Never mind, how long are you back in Dublin for?'

'A few days at my desk. Dunno, I might get back next week.'

User, I think, but then I argue that I still have Terence, so I just say, 'Cool.'

The sergeant reappears. He walks from the shadows in the hotel bar where I succumb to the hair of the dog.

'Your jeep will be back soon. I'll bring it out to you if I can. I'll get Paula to follow me out if she's around.'

'Or I can just come get it.'

'If you want. We'll let you know.'

'How is Susan?'

'She's holding up, but she took it really bad.'

'I bet.'

The sergeant is right. The snow has stopped and a thaw is prevailing. The white banks of ice stacked at the roadside are melting. Now everything is wet. I wade through the village and on down the steep hill. Soon I am where the countryside meets the village. The primary school stands out. It is all white. To the side is a small sign and into the gymnasium I go. Over in the corner two people wait patiently. The man is middle-aged. He smokes a lot. I can tell by his skin, and his eyes have a permanent yellow look. They hold water, giving the impression that he is always on the verge of tears. The woman sits away from him. She is untidy, but in a way that someone who once had something but lost it looks untidy. The lady gives me a worried *you know I am in this queue ahead of you* look, and the man tries to smile, but he isn't used to it, so his efforts fail. He moves instinctively up towards the woman who moves in turn. Now they are both making sure that I know they are in front of me in the queue. Then Julia pops her head out of the door.

'Next.'

The woman scurries in. She is determined and business like and she almost knocks Julia over in her haste. Julia isn't as I imagined. She is much smaller. Her hair is auburn and long. Somehow I expected it to be short and cropped, like she is all serious. I wait another ten minutes. The man gets fidgety and keeps checking the pockets of his coat as if he has lost something. Then he pulls the coat down from the ends like he is trying to make it stretch; all the while he just stares at the same place on the ground. The woman escapes. She seems content with her work and even smiles back as she closes the main door. Though the snow is gone I am still feeling the cold, like there is a draught coming from somewhere. Now the man gets up slowly. He fixes his coat again, but this time he jerks it from the sides like he is trying to make it smaller. When the door closes behind him, I am alone.

A tractor goes by and I see the driver clearly through this large window. Wow, it's the 'Wild Man from Borneo'. He looks exactly like before – all dishevelled but intelligent just the same. What is it that is happening to me? Why am I sitting here in this primary school gymnasium in the middle of nowhere? I've had folk taking pot shots at me, which seems to be forgotten for now. Suddenly I'm thinking that all my new minders have abandoned me and life sure does move on, even around here. So what is it I hope to achieve and at what cost? My confidence is taking a dent. Moving out to Terence's has saved me money on expenses, but it is funny this poor writer hasn't asked for a cent yet. The door opens and the man leaves, still clutching his coat at the middle, which reminds me to straighten my jacket and remove my hat.

'What can I do for you?' Julia is all business.

I put her at much younger than her odd husband – younger by maybe ten years or more.

'I'm here on other business,' I say and wait, thinking she might be pleased not to be discussing welfare issues.

'Is there anyone else waiting?' she asks, tapping her pen noisily off the desk.

'No.'

'What do you want then?' She keeps her tone even, though I feel she is bracing for a fight.

'Nothing much. Just to ask you a few questions about the girl who is missing?'

'Oh, you're the American detective, right? You came to see Hedy.'

'That's me.'

'Right. I didn't know who you were. I thought you might have been a reporter, what with all that has gone on. All the stuff about welfare reforms and people are always complaining.'

Welfare cuts, I think. 'No, I was just wondering do you remember Mary Ryan?'

'Yes, I do. She came out to the house maybe three times. My mother-in-law really liked her at first. She thought she was a breath of fresh air. My mother-in-law is a great advocate of feminism and she liked the fact that a young girl like Mary was taking on the world.'

'What do you think happened her?'

'It's obvious yer man out in the woods did her in.'

'Why do you think that? You do mean the writer Terence Fleming?'

'Yeah, why is there another man in the woods?'

'No, not that I know of.'

'He killed his first two wives.'

'He was never married.'

Julia laughs. 'In his books. Don't you read his books?'

'Not yet.'

'In both his novels the husband kills the wife.'

'Are they slasher stuff?'

'No, in both novels the husband kills the wife by showing her the pathway to darkness. In *Deep in the Woods* he introduces his lovely lady wife to a decadent group of swingers, and in *The Darkness of Trees* the husband shows his wife where daylight ends and darkness begins. It's all very arty. He's as daft as a brush and I'd say she got in with him too tight. He's a weirdo, living out there all alone. I hear he howls at the moon, froths at the mouth, all of that. She should really have packed up and gone home. Did she think the folk around here are going to wash their dirty linen in public? I have enough to be at with people's rent issues and the squalor around the countryside.'

I am flabbergasted. Could this woman be even odder than her husband? I am thinking *I* have lost it; it is *I* who has gone mad.

'I was sorry to hear about your husband,'

I am on my feet and Julia is pretending to tidy papers on her desk.

'What's wrong with my husband?' She is alarmed.

'Hedy said that he was sick.'

'That was years ago,' Julia says, relieved. 'He was very sick as a child.'

'But he's okay now?'

'Arnold is fine, thank God. Is there anything else? You can see we are very busy here.'

I look around for the royal 'we' but I can't see anyone.

* * *

Terence is quiet. I cook my favourite and his least favourite dish, spaghetti Bolognese. He says he doesn't like it because it leaves sauce in the crease of his chin and I say I like it for that very reason – my sizzling chin. Anyhow, I make it to my mom's recipe – she made it all the time when she was sober – and I use real baby tomatoes rather than those awful tinned ones. Terence isn't hungry but he tries; he likes the wine I picked up in the Spar. He doesn't ask me the price. I tell him that it was very expensive but Terence just grunts and says, 'Doesn't mean it's any good.'

I give him my hurt look.

'But it's good – it's lovely!' he says.

I smile. 'Good, because I bought three bottles.'

'Wow. I thought Mike would be here.' Terence is serious.

'He has to get back to his desk. His boss put out a missing person's bulletin.'

'Pity.'

'Yeah, who wants to be a journo?'

I'm expecting a reaction but there is no mention of our previous night's threesome, no acknowledgement that our ménage à trois is downright odd. No, Terence is at his computer, his head down as he searches for something.

'What did you do all day, Terence?'

He looks up and then around to double-check that I had spoken. 'Writing. All day. My eyes are sore and my bloody neck is stiff.'

'Do you know Julia, Arnold Bauer's wife?'

'I do. I signed some books for her. She could be cute if she wasn't a bit queer.'

'She likes your work but she says weird things about you. She thinks you're telling the truth in your books.'

'Does she now. I'm having more wine. Let's drink to Julia.' He laughs and throws his right fist into the air.

'She says you killed both the wives in your first two novels. She thinks you killed Mary and buried her out here in the woods.'

'Wow!' He opens the wine. Pop goes the cork. 'Maybe I did. In my second book the wife walks into the dark forest despite her husband's warnings. She never returns to the light. I'm writing about another dark journey at the minute. Maybe Julia can read my mind.'

He hands me a glass of red and goes to sit by the fire. I ensconce myself on the mat beside him and Bruce has to move, but the dog shrugs like it's just a little inconvenience. I should be aware of his generosity.

'I have discovered the world is made for middle-class women.'

I like his light tone.

'Here's me,' he says, 'in my middle sixties, male, a studier of the world and its intrigue.'

The dog looks at him, twisting his head this way and that, like he thinks Terence has lost it.

'But don't you see, Avril, the world's morality is designed to suit the tastes and moral standards of middle-class women?'

'Why? I don't get it. Why middle-class?'

'Because poor people don't count, especially poor women.'

'Yeah, but there are loads of working-class women who aren't poor.'

'True, but the value system has to be middle-class. Money has fuck all to do with it.'

'You're losing me.' I yawn and he just laughs.

'Don't you see, they can forget everything, forgive everything, from famine to genocide, all to conform and be normal in the eternal quest to rise in society, to be one step ahead. It doesn't matter what the system does. If it works, they live according to this one single value – that is, to be allowed to proceed unhindered in the procurement of respectability.'

'What's wrong with that? Anything else and you'd be talking of social anarchy. People feel trapped within the system. They are powerless to change things fundamentally, so they do the best they can.'

'That's why nothing ever changes, Avril.' He is serious now. I can sense his frustration. I am learning that he uses my name when he is frustrated.

'Anyhow, don't men comply to everything too – in their business suits and measuring the length of their dicks in accordance with the model of car they drive? Hey, you're letting men off here.'

'Yeah, maybe, but it's women who are the most compliant and vocal about protecting what they have. They seem to be cool with this collective amnesia when it comes to what the boys in white do compared to the boys painted black. Nowadays the media can justify just about anything. They report what they want and omit what they want, even in a little country like Ireland. They rig the vote by frightening people. It's crazy.'

'Maybe you're just crazy, Terence. You can't blame middle-class women for the problems of the world. It doesn't make sense.' I laugh and drink more wine.

'You don't get me, Avril. The world is being feminised right under our stupid male noses and we are too thick to see it. Middle-class women are the world's police on what is right or wrong, and they are more worried about political correctness than solving hunger and poverty. Now tell me that's not true.'

'Again, you're blaming women.'

'Because women are the designers of nature. They set the tone. It's their ladder that is always in place. It's meant to lead to the rainbow.'

'Ah shit.' I am tired now. My brain has stopped turning.

Later, as we lie still before sleep, I ask, 'Do you really believe all that stuff about women, middle-class or whatever?'

'I do,' Terence says. 'It is deeply rooted, a far cry from the "Black Widows". In the first Dáil Eireann they were far more radical than the men, but they got fucked over by Dev, and the rest of them too. It's like all the spunk was washed out of Irish women and thereafter someone dangled a carrot under their noses. I now realise that women live in the present. Everything is nature and nurture and men take advantage of that. Thus women walk away quietly – at least the radical parts do, with a few exceptions, mind.'

He rubs my brow with the tips of his fingers and I respond by rubbing his bald head like I have a dusting cloth. He turns away from me so as I can stroke the back of his head.

'Do you like Mike?' Terence asks.

'I do. Of course, I do.' I take my hand away. 'Are you jealous?'

'No.'

He turns back to me and I see the large creases under his eyes, the strain of constant peering at words on his computer, but there is also pain in there, stuff I never noticed before.

'Why did you never marry?'

'Wasn't asked.' He giggles.

'All the women too fat and middle-class for you?'

'No, I had a few good relationships, but they sort of faded out. Sometimes things don't get better, even when you really strive for them to work out. I had a difficult childhood. I was brought up by my aunt. Then she died and I ended up in care. But I don't remember being abused or ever wanting for much. No, the people who took care of me were kind. I have this recurring dream, least I think it's a dream, sometimes I'm not sure it is. I'm walking up these long stairs in this old rustic house. The lamps are dimmed and all I can hear is this phone ringing in a room nearby. It rings and rings, forever it rings, yet nobody ever answers it.'

13

Detective Dan Steele had a crop of flaming red hair and was six foot two, so when he stood up to Garda Madden, the local guard was intimidated.

Garda Madden hid behind the counter at the reception. The phone was ringing behind him but he ignored it. When Detective Steele pointed towards it, Madden said, 'That phone rings all day, but we're fucked if we answer it.' He laughed heartily, thinking he was funny.

'What time did you say?' Steele waited for him as he seemed to be changing a note he had written.

'He said he would meet you in the hotel around one o'clock.' Madden spoke like he was reading out the details of a speeding ticket before a sleepy judge.

Steele didn't want to give Madden any hint that he might be nervous about meeting Whytie. The rumours circulating in Dublin about Whytie were most likely embellished – at least Steele hoped they were, for if they were true, he was in for some tough grilling. A country guard like Madden wouldn't be used to much more than cattle rustling. It wasn't likely there would be any murders or girls going missing. Steele comforted himself that he was entering 'Sleepy Hollow', a place full of fat guards and eccentric top brass but niggling him was Whytie's reasoning. Why meet in the hotel and not the station? Even if Madden was just an overweight henchman, why didn't Whytie want him around?

Whytie wasn't what Steele had expected. Yes, he was as described – extremely tall, maybe six four or five. He fitted his description and his name, him being pure white, but what was different about him was his demeanour. Steele expected him to be vociferous and rough, but Whytie spoke quietly and with intent. This caught Steele off guard, as it was hard to be aggressive with such a quietly spoken man, even though what he had to say contained considerable menace.

Detective Steele had already booked into the Lough Lyn Hotel, so he felt an affinity for the place. He asked the waitress for soup and some sandwiches, but Whytie cut him short; he was asserting his local knowledge.

'Moya, I'll go the bacon and cabbage. It's no wonder you look half-starved, Steele. Sandwiches – is that what the Jackeens are eating? No wonder you're all fucked.'

'I don't eat my dinner till the evening,' Steele said, going red.

'Sure, you know nuthin'. A fella can go two dinners. In Lough Lyn the farmers have a good breakfast, a big lunch and a grand dinner and their laughin' at you city boys. I used to walk the beat in Dun Laoghaire many years ago. It was fuckin' posh – a fella wouldn't know where he was with the poshness – and then I moved to Blackrock and they were posher.'

'Not all posh now, Inspector.' Steele watched the waitress walk away smartly.

'Tell me, Steele, why did Malone send a rookie like you to see me, eh?'

'I dunno, Inspector. You better ask him some time. I dunno if I am a rookie. You wouldn't say that if you saw my case file.'

'You make me laugh, Steele, with your case files. Down here we don't even have proper filin' cabinets. I think Malone only sent you to annoy me. Once a cunt, always a cunt.'

Moya brought Steele a plate of sandwiches and a bowl of soup on a tray.

'I'll bring yours in a minute, Inspector. I'm just waiting on the vegetables. I hope that's all right now,' she said to Steele.

All the while Whytie stared at the pretty girl. She chose not to notice, but Detective Steele was uncomfortable for her. Whytie followed her across the room with his eyes. He didn't mind that Steele was waiting for him to speak.

'Why do you think I would meet you for lunch, Detective. Do you think I meet all visitin' detectives?'

'I dunno, Inspector. Your people sent the missing persons to us. We reacted. You really should be having this conversation with Malone. As you say I'm only the runner.'

Whytie sat back in his chair. He was smiling and looking around to see if he could muster an audience, but they were sitting away from the few stragglers having lunch down by the bar. Then Moya returned with Whytie's food. It was steaming hot and she warned him that the plate was roasting. He bowed his head and laughed like a child.

'I sent it to Malone because I figured he would have more sense than to do anytin' about it. The family are stone mad, Detective. Do some diggin'. Ye'll see she was runnin' away all the time, every other day.'

'Yeah, but Malone has to look into it, no matter what, Inspector. Eat your dinner before it goes cold.' Steele grinned.

Whytie went to say something but changed his mind and took a mouthful of hot food.

'I don't get what all the fuss about me looking into it is about,' said the detective, trying to play on the inspector's sense of dignity.

'No, I bet you don't. Her family's wild, her father's a ragin' alco who begs on the street. The mother's barkin' mad, like lunatic stuff. She'll be put into an asylum, but Jesus, I don't think any asylum will have her. They haven't a screed an the kids run round in the nude. You see this girl Biddy? She was the oldest, so she fucked off. Our guess is she was sick of the father ramming his cock into her. She was droppin' his babies on the side of ditches and the younger ones were crawlin' the floors bitin' at the electric cables. She just ran, I tell you. There's no need to investigate.'

'Sounds appalling, Inspector. But how come nobody did anything?' The detective watched Moya approach the table to see if everything was okay. He smiled at her, but the inspector grunted like he was pissed at the disturbance.

'People tried to help, but some people are ignorant. This whole family is a mess. The local priests, even the bishop, tried to intervene. We had every charity on the case, even the black army.'

'Who?'

'The Salvation Army.'

'Jesus.'

'Jaysus, is right,' Whytie said. 'This cabbage is very stringy. I'll have to complain to the chef.'

'The sandwich is fine.'

'Local ham in that. The slaughterhouse is just down the road.'

'So you think she ran away, Inspector.'

'She did, of course. You should just belt off back to Dublin and file a report. Don't be wastin' your time, and everyone else's either.'

Steele stopped eating. If the inspector's cabbage was stringy, his ham was excellent. He took a break to delay its inevitable end and the tea was welcome to wash it all down.

'You know, Inspector, I think you're right. I agree. The most likely scenario is that she just upped and ran away. And who could blame her? But I'll hang around for a few days and see if I can find out a bit more. Inspector Malone is very thorough and when I go back to Dublin he'll bring me out for a cup of tea just like this, and he'll want to know the ins and outs. If I tell him this girl ran away, he'll ask me where she went. He's that kind of man. He's nosy. He won't accept that she just ran away into the abyss. If I told him I found the proverbial needle in the haystack, he'd wanna know which haystack and where in the haystack the needle was hidden. That's the way Inspector Malone is and it's my job to please him, Inspector.'

Whytie was quiet for a minute but then he looked at Steele directly, eyeball to eyeball.

'Son, you're not going to find anytin' out by hangin' around here. There are no secrets lurkin' or anythin' hidden. Get in your car and go home. Just file the report. That's not advice, boy, that's an order. Don't forget I can make a few phone calls and you'll be back home in a few hours. So don't waste your time and mine – begone.' He deliberately pushed his dinner plate away from him, chipping a piece of his saucer. The tiny piece flew across the table onto the floor.

Standing, the inspector towered over Steele.

'The lunch is on me, Detective. Now get the fuck outta here before I have you thrown out.'

He was gone. Steele watched Whytie pay the bill at the counter before he left.

* * *

It was Madden who told him that Martin Foley, the girl's father, was dead. He hung himself from a tree out the country. Madden called by about a half an hour after the inspector left.

Steele wasn't sure what to do. He went to his room and packed his case, feeling stupid for he had taken considerable pride in unpacking it earlier. But that seemed like a long time ago now. He had it all packed and he was ready to check out, thinking that maybe the old lady wouldn't charge him as he hadn't even slept in the bed. Perhaps the inspector was right – the drunk of a father had abused the daughter and she had had enough of it and wanted out. She got out and would never return so the father topped himself, realising the truth of his misdemeanours. But hell, though, didn't Steele get a pang of guilt. This wasn't the way it should be. He had been sent here to do a job and here he was running away. So he unpacked again, this time hurriedly and with none of the care and precision of his earlier effort. Steele wasn't afraid of the inspector. Yes, his reputation in Dublin was poor and his drunken escapades were the joke of the station canteen, but who did he know who would take him seriously. If he contacted Malone he would be laughed at and told to fuck off. The inspector was bluffing, but why bother?

* * *

Steele went downstairs and out the back door to the car park. There was just his car and the hotel owner's battered Ford. Lough Lyn doesn't sport many cars, but he saw two tractors parked outside a poky bar on the main street. He tasted snow in the air.

He was freezing so he buttoned up his jacket and headed off. The road out to the west of the village was narrow and winding and soon he was in open country. The car climbed the road wedged between forests of pine and followed it till it reached a T-junction. As per the instruction he had been given earlier, he turned right, then three miles along he pulled up outside what looked like a derelict cottage. The front door wasn't answered despite his knocking hard for five minutes. A mangy cat looked down at him from the roof, and for a moment, Steele was stuck on its glass eyes. The door creaked open but nobody had answered it. The detective leaned against it and then realised that it wasn't locked. An old woman was curled up on a ripped armchair by a paltry fire. Otherwise the room was empty except for the cat, which had followed him in.

'Good evening, Madam. I am Detective Steele,' he said.

She didn't lift her head to look up. She started to hum a dark repetitive sound that somehow grated on the detective's nerves. He wanted to ask her to stop but he didn't.

'Who else is here?'

She still didn't answer.

He raised his voice above her terrible humming. 'Is there anyone else in this house?'

The humming stopped suddenly and she lifted her head. Steele was shocked by her condition. She was bruised and battered all down the right side of her face and she had silent, frightened eyes filled with blood. He deduced that her new bruises were just covering old ones, and when she opened her mouth she had just two front teeth, like a rabbit, with nothing else only swollen gums and a blackened chin.

'Dey took me daughters to see him laid out. I couldn't go meself. I wud only spit on 'im.'

'Who's *they*?'

'Hah, hah, your friends, boy – de guards.'

'Sorry for your trouble, mam. I'm making enquiries into the disappearance of your daughter Biddy?'

'Biddy? Ah Biddy's gone. Dey took Biddy.'

'Who took Biddy?'

'Yer friends, de gards. Dey took her … wit dat German fella. Dats who took Biddy.'

'Are you saying the guards took Biddy?'

She laughed a crazy laugh that was more like a scream.

'She went wit de German … wit the guards an de Fianna Fáiler. She don't cum back, no she don't.'

'When was this?'

'A long time ago – years ago,' she sang like a child.

* * *

'Maggie makes tings up and you won't want to be believin' anytin' she says,' Madden said, his big face bursting into a smile.

He gestured for Steele to sit, which he gladly did. His joints were sore from sitting and the drive. The driver's seat was cramped. Madden took out a file from the battered-looking drawer that had seen better days.

'Here it is, Detective. Meself and Garda Corcoran went out der on November tenth. Foley was bad that night and we fucked him into the cell. If we're keepin' him we go out to tell her. I dunno why, before you ask me. It wus always the way tings wer done around here. It's not Dublin.'

Steele said nothing; he just listened.

'She was bad dat night too, and meself and Corcoran were jus leavin' when along came the inspector with Wade, the Fianna Fáil fella, and this German bloke. I think Dr Hammond wus der as well, but I can't be sure to be honest with you.'

'What were they doing there?'

'Dunno. I think they wanted the German bloke to see what was going on. He was some kinda expert. He wus out of his head though with drink. I thought he looked mad.'

'So what happened with the girl?'

'They took her off. She wasn't right in the head, and Corcoran and me, we just went on home like the inspector told us to.'

'Where is Corcoran now?'

'He's gone from here. He asked the inspector for a transfer.'

'Where to?'

'I dunno, Detective. I tink he went to Galway.'

'Did you not wonder about the girl?'

'I did of course, but she must have come back at some stage and den ran off. God knows what the German said to her. He was some kind of a guru. They had him up in the convent. He was doin' some kinda study for the bishop. Dats all I know, Detective.'

It started to snow that night and Steele was warm in his room. He was even warmer looking out at the snow drifting up the main street. It brushed its way into the tiny gullies that drained into the Victorian shores and all was quiet, all was soft.

Madden was basically telling the truth, yet he was still holding back for sure. But at least he was talking. He spoke like a fella who had been tutored in what to say and what not to say. Steele knew he needed to track down this Garda Corcoran and get his version of events. And he needed to talk to the German and Wade, the Fianna Fáil fella. He wondered why Madden was so hesitant regarding Dr Hammond. How could he not have been sure if he saw the doctor there or not. The detective found it hard to sleep; the springs in the bed had seized and it was hard all over. No matter how much he turned and flustered he found little comfort. Eventually he gave up and sat with his pillows propped up, thinking over what he had learned so far. He was going over the same things time and time again with no conclusion. There were only unanswered questions.

Steele sat down to breakfast. The old lady was in the kitchen – he saw her go in. He was thinking that she worked hard for a woman of her age. Moya served him. She was very thin, as if she needed feeding, but she had a lovely face and she was prim and proper with just enough blush on her cheeks. The detective liked her, for when she smiled it was genuine. He could tell that she was fair even though her hair was tied back. She had soft blue eyes that examined his face eagerly.

Steele gave her his order – a full hearty Irish to banish the cold of the snow – Moya wrote it down in a pad. He thought, *how difficult was it to remember a full Irish*, but then a party of four came in. They were followed by another crowd of six; the second group were nuns and they chatted loudly. Then he realised that his waitress was just being efficient. He tucked into his food and it was delicious; his tea was strong, the way he liked it. Soon he forgot about the snow as he got very warm and cosy and he enjoyed his people-watching. The party of four looked like mourners who had travelled a distance to attend a funeral. They were two middle-aged men, a nervous-looking woman and a boy of about twelve. He was fidgeting with the salt cellar. The woman rebuked him twice, then finally snatched it from him and placed it on the far side of the table out of his reach.

Moya interrupted Steele, smiling. 'There's a phone call for you at reception, Detective!'

How the hell did she know he was a detective. Later she told him that people around the place knew everyone's business. That was the way of things in Lough Lyn.

14

1943

It was a frosty morning in Frankfurt and I stood on the platform awaiting my train. Previously they had seen fit to provide me with a driver and a car, but the war had drained our resources and everything was cut. There were many Luftwaffe and army officers disembarking from trains and arriving at the various platforms. I was early, so I went to the station café for a coffee.

The train journey wouldn't be arduous. In total, it was just eighty-two kilometres, taking just over an hour. I avoided the groups of uniformed Luftwaffe and soldiers and a small group of SS officers in transit, as they tended to sit together away from everyone else. I was, after all, a civilian so I sat in the corner at a table beside a couple and their fourteen-year-old son. The child had bright blue eyes and was Aryan blonde. How unusual for a German! The couple drank coffee from china cups that were patterned with roses. The boy drank lemonade from a tall glass. He laughed and pointed as he identified the various uniforms of the soldiers, and when he caught the eye of an SS officer who left his stool to light a cigarette, he saluted the Fuhrer. But the SS officer ignored him and returned to his companions, who now sat in a cloud of smoke.

I could hardly make them out as they lined the stools by a steel bar running the length of the window. My coffee was warm. That came as a great disappointment as I had suffered from a flu-like condition for over a week – aches and pains and my throat was sore. In general, my mood was contrary, so I resented the summons to Frankfurt as Viktor Brack was holding meetings with operatives from the 'Action T4 project'. It was time to answer to him, time to admit mistakes and seek his guidance on further assessments to be made around the country. I was on my way to Hadamar as a matter of coincidence, but I suppose, on reflection, that Frankfurt was as good a place to meet Brack as any.

I didn't enter the meeting with any real sense of trepidation. I knew, of course, that I had made mistakes – perhaps on some occasions I had let my emotions rule – but overall I had taken my tasks seriously and never erred in my interpretation or practice of the 'Action T4 guidelines'. I was proud of my achievements.

Viktor Brack had taken rooms at the Bristol Hotel, but I had to wait almost an hour to see him. A member of his entourage, a plump woman in her forties, insisted on serving me copious cups of tea till my bladder was full, but I was afraid to up and leave to use the toilet. I was afraid that some other practitioner might jump the queue and I might be relegated, so I stayed where I was with my knees crossed.

Brack was just as austere as I had imagined. Indeed, it is true to say that he was worse than anything I could have envisaged. The man was menacing, even though he stood to shake hands to greet me, yet he didn't smile or introduce the young lady who sat away from his desk taking scrupulous notes.

'Bauer,' he declared, looking through his notes, then taking an age to rethread his concentration till finally he lifted his head. 'We are done. The Action T4 project is done. It comes from the very top, from the Fuhrer himself, in his wisdom, of course.'

Brack stared at me over his desk awaiting a response. Little did he realise that my uneasiness was due to the pressure on my bladder. I tried to concentrate and stare back at him intensely. I stuck on his receding hairline and I was semi-blinded by the reflecting light from his tight-fitting spectacles. I noticed that he was wearing a crude light brown suit with a V-neck jumper, like a college student, and I was surprised that, although the top button of his shirt was fastened, he didn't wear a tie.

'Well?' he said finally.

'I dunno, sir. What are we meant to do?' I kept my tone soft so as not to antagonise him.

'I'm appalled! There are many things here that disgust me, Bauer!'

I shifted about in the chair but was sorry I did, for the movement only tickled my bladder further.

'I see that you have a low rate of signing off on potential candidates. It says you refused to sign off on a boy with multiple learning difficulties. The boy had autism and dyslexia, yet you thought him all right to be excused.'

'I don't recall, Herr Brack. I see many patients, but if I signed off on it, it was because the boy presented as normal, or as near normal, within our guidelines.'

Brack sat back in his chair and the note-taking girl paused too.

'Action T4 will stop in its current model, Bauer. This war continues and it will take its toll on all of us. That is not unexpected, as we have many enemies. However, Bauer, we will continue with our valuable work regardless of Action T4. The Fuhrer has said so himself. Our work continues but in a different guise. We will proceed by stealth. Remember, Bauer, we have no need to contaminate our role with sentiment. The issue is clear. Our mission is to cleanse a generation. Let's look at it like this. Say we have a barrel full of delicious apples. Yet when we dig down among them we find one or two that are imperfect. What do we do? Just leave them there to spread their disease to the rest of the barrel. No, we remove the decaying apples so that the rest of the barrel continue to thrive. Sentiment has no place. We are sworn to this policy and I trust you are at one with me, Bauer.'

'Of course, Herr Brack, that goes without saying.'

'Good, as long as you understand. There doesn't have to be a deficiency. One's racial and ethnic background can be deficiency enough, don't you see, man?'

I made the Gents, which was on the ground floor, with nothing to spare, and my next task was to find a boarding house. I knew my allowance wouldn't stretch to the grandiose Bristol Hotel so I decided to try a boarding house close to the railway station.

* * *

1944

A year later and I was thinking of Addie as I walked the lonely laneway that ran behind the main road and in Frankfurt lodgings still presented a problem. I was on a quicker route to a small hotel as advised by one of the assistants at Hadamar. Addie was so sweet and for now she was safe in Berlin. I wondered if she missed me at all. Did she imagine me in her mind's eye, wandering the busy streets looking for a room for the night, or was it out of sight out of mind? Do I fade from her consciousness as soon as I leave Berlin? Who knows. No, Addie wasn't like that, she was loyal and true. Yes, there was the music teacher from the university, but he was far too old to take her attention and she had certainly given me a good send off. I had been surprised at her; she really shocked me. I wasn't used to her attentions in that way. She had insisted on going down on me and I was politely put out. I wasn't at all sure what to do and in the end, I just sat back on the sofa and let her do the rest. To be honest I found it slightly uncomfortable in the beginning. She used her tongue, though, like she sensed my discomfort. Suddenly it was all soothing and very sensual. Her continuous stroking of my penis as she rubbed her hand up and down the shaft was new and exciting.

The hotel room was plain and cold-looking, but it was adequate. It had a dressing table and a desk and a chair over by the window. But I didn't like the bed, as the mattress was covered with a plastic cover as if they thought I was going to wet it. I thought back to my earlier visit to Frankfurt and Brack, perhaps they had a point. I lay down to rest. My plan was to go out for some food and maybe a beer, but I was anxious to get to bed early and sleep before my train journey back to Hadamar the next day. The view from the narrow window was over the street. The sound of the traffic rushing to and from the railway station was never-ending, and taxies and buses passed constantly; rain-soaked citizens, some carrying suitcases, moved frantically through the evening. Yes, Brack was right. Another year had passed and the war had taken its toll. The citizens looked worried as they went on their way. They wore dark clothes these days, and many of their suitcases were battered-looking. Nobody seemed to own anything new. The taxies and buses were old and shoddy too.

I was hungry so I took a walk. My route took me away from the station through a series of narrow lanes, and I walked slowly down this quiet street. I knew this was the red-light area but my main ambition was to get some food and a beer. I assured myself that I would always be faithful to Addie as she was my love. The thought of a liaison with anyone was out of the question, and the idea of paying for sex was repulsive. The café was darkly lit and the clientele were mostly uniforms, with a few civilians propping up the corner of the bar. I ordered a plate of lamb and the waiter told me that I got potatoes and vegetables with that. I was happy to wash it down with coffee. My lamb was good if a little tough, but the potatoes and the veg were fine and fresh. I went to the bar to pay my bill, but before I paid, I ordered a beer and put it on the tab.

I saw that a few scantily dressed women were laughing with officers in a snug just off the main bar area. These women were peroxide blondes and although they were made up and unreal, I felt a sudden urge. I resisted and chose to just drink a few beers and stay quiet. A grey-haired soldier took a stool next to me. He was in his forties and his face didn't suit his hair. He appeared too young to have such a grey head. He ordered whiskey and drank three down one after the other. He was a corporal from the infantry and told me he was back from the Russian front because he had lost three fingers and two toes to frostbite.

'I would never have got back only my uncle is General Guderian.'

'Yes, I hear no soldiers are returning alive. But victory will soon be ours!'

He looked at me like I had gone mad. 'What do you do?'

'I work for the party!'

'You Gestapo?' he asked fearfully.

'No, I'm working on a special programme. I am a scientist.'

'A scientist. Well, can you please tell the generals that our soldiers can't fight through the Russian winter.' He ordered another whiskey and a beer for me, all the while looking around to make sure that nobody was eavesdropping.

'I am Heinz Weber,' he said. 'And you?'

'Hugo Bauer.'

'Ah, Hugo, you are smart and intelligent, I can see that. A true scientist. I have come to Frankfurt to see this specialist. I need him to look at my deformities. I'll go home soon. I live in a small village just outside of München. Things are quiet there despite the war. I have a wife and two half-grown daughters, but I still come here at night to see Dohman. He's not here yet. Some of his women are, but not he. But he'll be here soon.'

'What is he – a pimp?'

'He's the best pimp in Germany. If you want a man or a woman, Dohman will supply you, or if you want a child or a cripple, he will get you that too. I know a captain who likes midgets. He gets him midgets. He can get anything you like, despite the war.' He whispered the last part.

'He can get you a cripple?' I was disbelieving.

'Oh yes, and any multiples of same. Dohman is very famous. Sssh, there he goes!'

A small bespectacled man passed us by and he took off his wide-brimmed hat. I was shocked to see that he was totally bald. Dohman ordered a beer and looked long and hard at his ladies in the snug. Somehow they became more attentive to the officers when Dohman arrived, with one or two leaving by the side door.

'Where do they bring them? Is it out onto the street or the back alleys in the rain?' I was getting tipsy now, listening to the rain splashing against the roof and the windows. It was a horrible night to be out. I could hear it all above the din and the slushing of the passing traffic.

'Nah, my friend, Dohman has a deal with the hotels and boarding houses. It is all very cosy. You tell him what you want and he goes to the phone booth outside. Within one hour your room is ready. Your chosen partner is in place and all for just a few Marks too. This man is conscious of the war effort!'

'And you, Herr Weber, will you avail of his services this night?' I ordered another beer and him a whiskey.

'I will. It's my vice, I'm afraid, while I am in Frankfurt and while I recover from my deformities. I love my wife and my daughters, but they are so far away and I am a lonely man. I only seek comfort and I love peroxide blondes. It is my weakness. Tomorrow over breakfast I will shed tears of sorrow, but tonight I will be a man and show one of those peroxide bitches that I am a complete man, a soldier of the fatherland, a true patriot. She will know that when I'm done!'

Weber downed his whiskey. He shook hands using his good right hand, and then using his shoulders he bullied his way through the crowds till he reached Dohman. They only spoke for a minute and then Weber went into the snug and sat away from the officers on his own. I saw a waiter follow him with a single whiskey on a silver tray and I studied him. But now and again I had to lean this way and that to avoid the tall servicemen passing by en route to the toilet.

The air was full of white smoke as the soldiers pulled hard on cigarettes. Dohman lit an expensive cigar, which he seemed to enjoy too much, blowing out rings of smoke that made circles above his head before fading as passers-by destroyed his clouds. Weber had company. She was mature, in her late thirties maybe. She was a peroxide blonde and his whole face lit up as he engaged with her. I thought he was like a child opening a birthday present such was his delight. Then he left with her, the side door opening giving me a glimpse of the sheets of rain coupled with flashes of lightning burning the street; I could just hear the distant sound of thunder. I hoped the boarding house or hotel that Dohman used wasn't far away, as Weber and the peroxide blonde would be drowned – hardly the precursor to passion.

Dohman was quieter than I imagined, his voice hoarse, probably the result of millions of cigars, I mused. He gave me the once over but I didn't find him intrusive as he had kind, if serious, brown eyes. Somehow they didn't suit the perfect baldness of his head.

'So you want a blonde, eh?'

'No,' I said nervously. I noticed that the snug was empty. The officers and the women had all left to take their chances with the night. 'I want a cripple.'

Dohman stared at me. He took a fresh cigar from his inside pocket, lit it and blew the smoke right into my face.

'I don't do cripples. What do you want to do – stick the crutch in her arse?'

'No, but I heard you can supply anything.'

'Ah yes,' he interjected. 'I can get you little boys or little girls. I can get you a man or a woman, dwarves, midgets, but cripples I don't do.' He stared at me.

'Okay, I must have been mistaken.'

I went to walk away.

'Hold on, I do have a girl. She is deformed. She can't walk properly. Her whole torso twists this way and that. She's small but she has big tits. Yeah, maybe you would like her.'

'Maybe, yeah. I can do that.'

'Get another beer and wait in the snug. This is a different request, mister. I will charge you ten Marks extra. We can shake on it and I will get you the beer.'

I nodded.

Dohman ordered me the beer and I saw him walk past the snug to use the public telephone. I sat in the snug alone thinking of Addie, how she would never forgive me for this, but for once I didn't care, as forgiveness was out there in the sloshing rain, and guilt was a nothing word on this dreadful night. For now regret lived with the angels, and it was lost in the fantasy of religious morality.

Johana came in. She had cropped hair like a boy, but her face was painfully pretty. She gazed at me with an intensity that was new and refreshing, but when she walked, her waist wobbled like a duck. She wore normal clothes, not the kind you'd expect from a whore.

'It's not far to the hotel. We must hurry to avoid the rain. The storm has abated.'

I knew by her accent that she was Polish. I wanted to interrogate her, but I just smiled to put her at her ease.

'I don't want to get wet, so I'll follow.'

She led me out to the wet street. The drains were like rogue rivers. They were full to overflowing. We swung right down a back alley, which led us by a nightclub where people queued outside. Johana moved fast for a girl with such a disability and I struggled to keep up. Finally she stopped by the side entrance to this tall, austere building and I followed her to the lift.

15

1944

Johana knew the room and she went straight to the dresser. She re-painted her face and, when she turned, the light shone on her so I could see her eyes properly; they were dead calm.

'I was born like this!' she said, anticipating my question as she waddled across the floor. 'My mother is from Hamburg but my father was a Polish sailor. I barely knew him.'

'How old are you?' I felt cheap asking her age like I really cared.

'What age do you want me to be?'

I shrugged.

'I am twenty-three,' she said, lying flat on the bed. She was lying lazily like she was tired. 'What do you do? Are you a policeman?'

'No, I'm a scientist.'

'Oh, are you a doctor?'

'No, not really – not a medical doctor.'

'You can't fix me, no?' She laughed.

'No, I can't, I'm afraid.'

I sat on the bed wondering if I should hurry things up, if there was a time limit, but she beat me to it. Getting to her feet suddenly, she started to undress. Her body looked good when she stood still and it was impossible to tell that she had a deformity. She had delicious thighs and a pert, proud bottom. When she faced me again I noticed that she had significant breasts; they were fat and sturdy like on leaving adolescence. Then she smiled at me, displaying her ruby lips.

'Are you getting undressed?'

I undressed slowly, finding it difficult to undo my pants and then to remove my socks. Johana examined my naked body like she wasn't used to seeing men nude.

'How did you meet Dohman?' I asked.

She sighed turning her head away to find a soft part on the pillow. 'He found me. I was sleeping rough up by the station. He finds a lot of his girls there.'

'What's he like?'

'He's a pig, but he's fair as he is a pig to us all. He doesn't have favourites. The girls sort of like him because he is generous, and he looks out for us. He won't tolerate any fooling around. Sometimes the soldiers get too drunk and they want to beat us up, but Dohman protects his own and those soldiers are taught a lesson.'

'He's a pig?'

'Ah, he likes to try the girls out himself first. Dohman has us all. He takes a different one each day, whether we want to or not. Whatever he decides, we oblige. We don't have a choice.'

I reached out and touched the side of her face. She turned to look at me intently as if she was trying to figure out my motives.

'I don't normally do the rounds. Dohman sends me to the same place all the time. This man is an official in the local government. I think he is connected to the Gestapo. I know because he is great at pillow talk, but I don't like him.'

I am exploring her tummy now and soon settle on those adolescent breasts. Johana passes no comment.

'Do you like the Gestapo? Do you know them?' she asks.

'I don't know anyone in the Gestapo. I am a scientist. I do a different kind of work.'

'So are you helping with the war?'

She looked at me fearfully and I could just about gauge the intensity of her eyes in the semi-dark.

'No, it's not helping the war effort – not really.'

'I don't like the war. I don't like it one bit and the news from Russia is not good. Our boys are being slaughtered out there. I think we are in grave danger, no matter what the radio says. We're losing this war, that's for sure.'

I didn't reply. It was time for the talking to stop. She was restless, and when I went to mount her, she freed her head from beneath me as I had inadvertently pinned her shoulders with my elbows. I was pleased when she gasped at my efforts – I took this as her willingness – so I increased the fury of my stride, but Johana cried out so I withdrew and turned her around. I liked her proud bottom and she stuck it back into me. I took her from the rear and once again she cried out. I don't know if this was as a result of pain or pleasure, but I kept going till I finished. When I did I sensed her relief. I was thinking of Addie in those last moments but I could have been thinking of anyone as the flesh became neutral. I was really just a wild animal. I may well have been a lion with his lioness, and this girl could have been a mannequin. We just had crude sex with no suggestion of love, care or intimacy. This is me, the man. I watched her waddle back to the dresser where she stared into the mirror for at least a minute before getting dressed. I wanted to say something reassuring about the war but I couldn't. How could I reassure this person who almost tripped herself up as she walked? Perhaps an elephant has more grace. Johana left me there, lying naked on the bed.

'Five minutes. You must go in five minutes,' was all she said and she was gone.

The rain had stopped and that was something. The weather was to turn colder overnight; they were expecting frost and snow. Through the window I saw Johana waddle her way back down the dark alley. Would she return to Dohman at the bar or was she on her way to the local government official and his pillow talk? I wanted to sleep but I knew I couldn't so I headed back out into the dark streets. It was the early hours, but people still moved about as they do. When I reached my own accommodation I finally slept. I listened to the sound of cars hum past; their senseless droning lulled me, and my final image was a beautiful one of the wonderful Addie in perfect health, looking over me and smiling.

The train was full of returning passengers to Hadamar and, even though the war was in full flight, parties of young women still made their way to the big city for the weekend. There were a few soldiers too. They were going home for some well-earned leave. I noticed a few nurses in uniform. They must have been returning to the clinic. Medicine still carries on, and despite the torment, we still try to make people better.

I found a compartment with two seats available so I took one by the window. Soon we were passing the grey sheds of factories and crossing narrow bridges over anonymous back streets. I studied the rear gardens of crumbling houses that were once grandiose. Who lived in these houses now?

It was only an hour to Hadamar. I regretted not buying a newspaper and I was thinking maybe an attendant would come selling snacks and drinks and newspapers. After twenty minutes there was no sign of an attendant, so I reluctantly settled on scanning the dark countryside. Here and there patches of frost melted to create small pools, but the fields were bare as the cattle were kept indoors to protect them from the frequent Allied bombers. I knew that further south the fields were planted, but not here, and not now; it was the wrong time of year. My stomach churned as I gazed upon field after field of emptiness.

A soldier opposite rattled a newspaper. I tried twice to read the headlines on the back page but he noticed my efforts and rattled the paper more till it crumpled. Then to complete my frustration he folded the paper and placed it neatly on the seat beside him. I wanted to ask him if I could have a read but I hadn't the courage. Yet in my mind's eye I grabbed the newspaper from the seat and, when he complained, asked if I could see his identification documents. Of course I didn't do that. Then the soldier got bored with me and started to look over my shoulder at the deserted fields. Maybe he was from Hadamar. He had probably taken this train journey since childhood. Perhaps in different times these fields were busy and alive with farmers and their livestock and his journey hadn't always been so bland. I was lost in my thoughts when the train slowed. But we hadn't reached Hadamar yet – there was still at least twenty minutes to go.

Men wearing trench coats and wide-brimmed hats walked up and down the corridor. One was much older than the other and he hadn't shaved. This made his baby-faced companion look even younger.

'Papers,' they asked a plump woman sitting opposite the soldier and she fumbled in her purse nervously before producing her identification which was accompanied by a handwritten letter. The younger man was about to hand it back, but the older man snatched it from him.

'What is this?' he barked.

The younger man spoke for the woman. 'It's a letter from her son on the Russian front, Herr Fuchs.'

Herr Fuchs unfolded the woman's letter, read it carefully and then studied her identity card.

'You are not in date,' he said accusingly.

'I'm waiting for the replacement. I applied six weeks ago.'

'Nah, we don't take six weeks to renew a card. We are German, not English.'

He handed her back the card. The woman was crying with relief.

Then the soldier with the newspaper handed over his military ID and the younger man handed it back to him immediately. Herr Fuchs nodded at the soldier and the soldier smiled momentarily.

Then he took my identity card and read it through. He turned around to the younger man and, speaking quickly, said, 'Hadamar.' His face broke into a positive grin. 'It's arduous work but we need people like you to do it. You are dedicated to the cause just like us, yeah?'

I smiled back at him and, suddenly remembering his business, he turned and was gone to the next carriage.

The train was delayed for more than fifteen minutes and the passengers were none too pleased, many of them giving the conductor an earful as we disembarked at Hadamar railway station. I recalled a conversation from a year earlier:

'This is Nurse Annett. She runs the place,' Conrad Bischof had said. 'We would be lost without her.' Then he told the driver to slow down. 'We are never in such a hurry. Let our esteemed guest see a little of Hadamar.'

The young driver had slowed down and took his chastisement with the ease of a fellow who was thankful that his job was so simple.

'So Brack says we are to stop?'

'For now.'

I could see that Nurse Annett was listening with great interest, so I went on, 'But we will recommence in six months or so. Tell me, how are the sterilisations going?'

'Well, very well!' Conrad Bischof exclaimed.

'We are at over five thousand,' Nurse Annett said. 'But what are we to do now?'

'Wait,' I said. 'The project will continue in the new year. I already have plans to return here. By then we will have won the war, no?'

Conrad had remained quiet, but the nurse exclaimed, 'Of course we will.'

The driver took a sharp corner too fast. Then before me was the big austere building that housed the hospital.

'Tell me about the capacity, Conrad. Do we have much room?'

'We are short of staff but we can manage with greater efficiency. Nurse Annett is nothing if not innovative. Why, do you think we will have more sent to us?'

'Very possible. Indeed, I have no doubt you will.'

I had turned around to see the reaction from the rear of the car. Nurse Annett had smiled, and when she did, it took the natural hardness from her face.

* * *

Father Vogel laughed. He knew I was tired after my walk, but I had enjoyed walking through Lichterfelde; Berlin was very cold coming up to Christmas. The old buildings cheered me up and I was happy in myself as I ventured along the narrow streets.

The church of the Holy Family was impressive. The architects from the early part of the century knew what they were doing. It was all solid and impressive. Father Vogel could have been part of the old brick as he was at least seventy years old but he looked and acted like he was forty. He had solid grey hair that fell lazily across his forehead. He stooped when he was speaking and talked so much that folk thought he had a permanent stoop.

The old priest caught me sitting at the end of my favourite pew. He was on his way to start confessions, but the sight of me stopped him in his tracks.

'Hugo!' He was surprised to see me. 'You look exhausted.'

'Father, you are red like the bricks of this building.'

'My blood pressure is up. This war and all that it brings. I wonder if any of us will outlive it?'

'You are a pessimist, Father Vogel. As usual you are over-concerned with our souls. The war will end soon and we will be the victors.'

'Hey, it's a long time since you rang the bell in the tower. I could slap your fat ass then but now you are not so fat and I am too old. If I lift my arm I fall over. Are you still at the university?'

'I'm on sabbatical, Father. I'm working on a government project.'

'I see. To be honest with you, Hugo, this is not how I foresaw Germany.'

'Patience, Father, the glory days are ahead. You would be the first to remind me to keep faith.'

'I wish. Are you coming to confession?'

'Yes, it's been a while.'

'Better late than never, my son!'

He walked slowly to the confessional and I searched the pew in front of me. Just two older women and a man waited patiently. All this time I was thinking of Addie.

The news of her pregnancy had shocked me to the core, not only for its implications for me, but also for Addie's studies. Any pressure to serve the Reich would now be lifted; that was the only good thing. Should I tell Father Vogel? No, it wasn't Addie's pregnancy I wanted to tell him about. Was it the night with Johana in Frankfurt? I was so ashamed.

I sat thinking as the old man went in first. The women continued to bow and pray. I felt the freezing air of the big open church; it bellowed down from the altar like it was making a statement about God's anger. I was confused.

At first the whole project enthralled me as a scientist. What if removing deformities over a few generations made people well and helped human beings to be happy and healthy all their lives. Sterilisation was the correct approach, but then Brack and his disciples had dismissed this solution because it didn't free the state from the care of what he termed 'the useless and the idle' – those wretches that would suck the life blood from society and never contribute anything, not a single thing. What was the answer then? Brack decided to cleanse us of this problem. The showers were fake. Canisters of gas were dropped in through hatches in the roof. They burned the bodies, sometimes two at a time, and Nurse Annett oversaw everything. She oversaw the removal of brains for further testing and analysis, the taking of gold teeth and anything of value to fund the war effort, and she didn't mind; it was written all over her face. She was convinced she was doing the right and merciful thing.

One of the women stood as the old man took a pew further up to recite his penance, his footsteps making military sounds that echoed and marched in my brain.

Conrad had no scruples either. This was his game, his contribution to the new Germany. He spoke of parties with dancing and wine when death targets were met. I referred to it as euthanasia but he laughed when I said that. He told me that death is death in any man's language. I noticed how excited he was when I warned him about the future, how the plan would extend to able-bodied prisoners and shell-shocked soldiers. That soon they would be included in the project. Nurse Annett took great heart from what I was saying.

The second woman went in to the confessional and her former companion took a seat somewhere behind me. She wasn't too far away as I could hear her whisper her contrition.

Addie was pregnant. How would that change things? I was so sorry about the cripple now. My fear was that I would bring back some disease and give it to Addie and our child.

Father Vogel went through his prayers at great speed. Then he asked how long since my last confession.

'Three years.' I wanted to add, 'Addie's pregnant,' but I didn't. What I said instead was, 'This project I am working on for the party …'

'Yes, my son?'

'It's a research programme on eugenics, Father. I don't know what the church's view is on such matters but I am very confused by it.'

'I see. The church and science have never seen eye to eye, not since the arguments about whether the world is round or not. I have read many things about Darwin and all this survival of the fittest stuff. Yes, I think that's true in the animal world, but then animals don't usually kill each other for sport or for gain – other than for food or access to food. Are you involved in the killing of the weak, Hugo?'

'I am, Father, but I have never killed anyone personally.'

'I see. There are rumours about this. Children are disappearing without trace. The church, it seems, is confused. My German church and the party are not always at one, but the confusion emanates from elsewhere outside of Germany. We take our guidance from Rome. I advise you, Hugo, do not serve this. Find a way to rid yourself of this burden. You must do this immediately.'

'Yes, Father.'

I was contrite, fully believing, in my state of grace, that I would obey his command; in truth, my slavish following of Catholicism was dead. The church had failed the people. It sat idly by and watched as the carnage continued. I decided that my priest was advising me in his personal capacity.

16

Old Tobin died, but there's nothing sinister in that. The old man died in his sleep sitting in the armchair by a blazing fire. What a wonderful way to go. I can only hope that my granma goes the same way. I dunno if he had anything else to tell me, but if he did, well, he took it with him. So that, as the man says, is that.

Terence is sitting outside with Mike and the dog. Today the weather isn't pleasant and the boys have their heavy coats on. Unbeknownst to them I am sitting at Terence's computer. He has left it open on the current page of his novel. His writing is good. It is easy to read, the characters compel me and I'm drawn in. Every now and then I lift my head to check on Terence and Mike; they don't move. Mike is smoking and when he exhales he waves his arms above his head. Terence responds to his gesticulations; it is like he moves his head in response to Mike's hands. Bruce is there someplace, but I can't see him; I just know that he lies there lazily within a safe range.

I continue reading. Terence's creation is a place just like Lough Lyn with the lakes and the quaint village. In this story, the detective is a woman and she is pressing the owner of the hotel, a Mrs Vance, for information. Many of the references are the same – the missing research student and the bizarre journey into the past. I page up and find many similarities to our current predicament. I look up again and the men are still chattering but this time it is Terence pontificating to Mike, who lights another cigarette. The smoke is crystal clear in the freezing air. Terence's murder scene is almost identical to the real life one: the man hangs on a meat hook in the abattoir. So is Terence just plagiarising life, or, wow, is life just copying Terence's book. Was Kevin Witherspoon murdered before or after this passage was written? I hear the shuffle of feet. Bruce is clawing at the front door and the boys' heads are no longer visible through the window. I quickly scroll down to the page I started on. When the lads appear, with Bruce trailing behind them, I am standing by the fire. Terence notices that I'm staring at him. He goes to speak but Mike beats him to it.

'We're thinking of going shooting. Do you want to come along?'

'I can't. I've gotta collect the jeep.'

'I can drop you now – get a few things. Need to get some juice too.'

I smile at Mike. 'Soes you can drop me?'

'Yup,' says Mike.

Terence seems uncomfortable and gives me a funny look.

'Get on with the book,' I offer just to break the awkwardness, but Terence is unnerved by me, he turns away to stare at the fire.

'How long will you be, Mike?' Terence asks.

'An hour max.' Mike pets Bruce, pulling back his ears.

'Grand, I'll make up a few sandwiches. We can wish for rabbit stew!'

'Lovely.'

I am sorry for it all. I must be reading Terence all wrong. He may have written about the abattoir well after Kevin's body was found. Anything else just didn't make any sense.

Mike is quiet on the journey, driving slowly as the road is wet and slippery. I catch him looking at the fuel gauge regularly; the tank is on reserve.

'I shouldn't let it go so low,' he says.

'I do the same. Once I let my car run out. I was miles from the nearest gas station. They say I'm bright?'

'Yeah,' Mike says. He is non-committal.

'What do you think of Terence?' I ask calmly so as not to excite him in anyway.

'Terence is sound.'

I think that Mike is going to add to that and I wait for him to educate me on all things Terence but he doesn't; he just shuts up. I go quiet for a bit and wait till we reach the lower road. Then we start on the bad bends that lead to the village.

'Lonely life though, isn't it, Mike – stuck up there with just Bruce for company?'

'Yeah, but he has us.' Mike looks at the fuel gauge again and smiles over at me. 'Spit it out, Avril. There's something you're dying to tell me.'

'Nah, it's just some stuff that Julia was going on about.'

Mike is disappointed the first of the Lough Lyn garages has closed its doors. 'What? It looks like they're closed down.'

'Don't worry, the other garage in the village is always open.'

'What did Julia what's-her-name say?'

'She's odd. She says Terence kills off all his female characters in his books. I think she was trying to be funny. Then she says he killed Mary and buried her out in the woods.'

Mike laughs heartily. 'Terence, a killer?'

I smile back not wanting him to see how worried I really am.

'He feels bad for shooting rabbits.'

'It's just that …'

We pull into the garage.

'… he describes a killing in his book. It's a replica of Kevin Witherspoon's and I don't know if he wrote it before or after Kevin was killed.'

'Jesus, Avril!'

Mike gets out and goes to the pump. I hear the diesel tank fill and imagine it is grateful for the top-up. In my mind's eye, I see the sediment drown within the new wave of fuel and the dirt sinking to the bottom of the tank where it belongs.

* * *

Sergeant Boyle hands me the keys. 'Sorry it took so long.'

'It took an age!'

'Those Dublin boys do nuthin' now. It's all the cutbacks. What's the word? Demotivated. They're demotivated. Most fellas are just seeing it out till retirement. There's no pride in nuthin' any more. A fella will earn his pittance either way, so nobody gives a flyin' fuck.'

'So how's the investigation going?'

He gives me a funny look. 'What da fuck do you think? We have nuthin' and Dolan and his smart-assed Dublin crowd haven't a clue. As far as they're concerned the matter is done. Whoever is responsible is either gone or they've done all they had to do and have gone quiet. That's what we think just now. It's what I am tryin' to say to you. We don't expect any more killings. Whatever reason they had for doing what they did is done. What do you think? As a detective, do you think you'll find anything new?'

I want to say, 'Yeah, I've several leads. Sure I've almost cracked the case.' but I don't want to lie.

'I thought Dolan was good,' I say, 'but I get what you mean about the city boys. It's the same back home. Our guys hate the dudes from Portland.'

'Dolan is a prick, forgive my language, but that's where we're at. I don't know why someone would do what they did to poor Jane. She was a harmless soul. Kevin – well, you either liked him or you didn't, but he didn't deserve to die like that.'

'How's Susan?'

'She's not good – barely holding up, to be honest. The doctors have her drugged up. They say she may never get over it.'

'I see Paula coming. I best be going. Thanks for the jeep.'

'You're welcome. Sorry it took so long.'

I am delighted to get my jeep back with the bullet holes and damage repaired. Then I wonder if I will get a bill, but the sergeant didn't say anything about that. I catch up with Moya Breslin at the hotel. She is looking over forms and doing her usual – drinking whiskey slowly but surely.

'We miss you,' she says, peeping up from her forms.

I think this woman is a wonder. She gets younger-looking by the day. I must start drinking more whiskey. It seems to be good for the skin.

'I was thinking of taking a room again, maybe for just a week?'

'Are you askin' me if I have rooms now?'

She makes me smile.

'We always have rooms here!'

I laugh. 'Yeah, I need to get back into the village. That mountain air is intoxicating!'

'Ah yes, the upper lake is like that. Terence won't mind?'

I guess she is fishing. 'Terence will be busy with his book and looking after his dog.'

'That dog goes everywhere with him. What about Mike? He pays his room in advance but he hardly sleeps here.'

'I dunno, Moya, you best ask him when you see him.'

'Sure, can I buy you a whiskey?' She beseeches me with her one good eye.

'Ah, go on then.'

'Good. They say it's the saddest thing a woman can do – drink alone.'

'I can only have one. I have to go and get some stuff from Terence's.'

'Okay, just have the one, so.' She asks Martina Mellon for two whiskies. 'I might as well join you, dear.'

I am glad. She refills her glass.

'What do you think of Terence?' I ask.

Her eyes light up. She remains composed. 'He's shy, a bit beaten up, but he seems decent. Probably a bit mad. I've met worse.'

She waits for me.

'I'm wondering about him. I guess I'm just interested in what other folk think about him.'

'I think most people around here think he is a stranger living all alone out in the woods. His books are popular enough. He's well-liked by the intelligentsia. Maybe some ordinary people don't get him, but hey, Avril, live and let live.'

She raises her glass and I go, 'Cheers!'

'Cheers, dear,' Moya says, smiling with her eyes.

* * *

I think about many things on my drive back to the lake. Sergeant Boyle has the look and feel of a man who wants to forget it all. I get no real sense that he is frustrated by the lack of a breakthrough in the case. I guess the folk of Lough Lyn are moving on and so is he. It seems he is just a defeatist by nature; after all, he is a sour sort. I wonder if he has the hots for that Paula, though they both wear wedding rings. Stranger things.

The road is dry. Whatever snow remains lies embarrassed in patches in the fields. Suddenly the woods appear. Up here there is no slush, nothing now, just the chilly air and I think about Mike and Terence. Have they shot any rabbits? Will they mind if I don't join them for a stew? I feel strangely worried for Mike. What if Julia is right? Maybe Terence has turned the rifle on Mike deep out in the woods and he's lying wounded waiting for help. I try to dismiss my racy thoughts, but they return and each time they are somehow worse. I guess I have a lot of my granma in me. Now how unkind is that! Just where did I steal my morality from to sleep with both men. My granma isn't like me; she isn't promiscuous. Me, I made up my own mind but I was always a good girl.

My granma paid for me to go to a good Catholic school. We were taught manners. Those nuns taught us how to keep our legs crossed. So what influenced me? Where did that singular Catholic ethos disappear to? I don't recall ever rejecting it outright. What led to me uncrossing my legs? Doesn't mean I am no prize, mind, but what the hell made me sleep with two men? It wasn't the first time, but you couldn't call the Christmas party 'sleeping'. No, I just had sex with two men in the captain's office. There must be something badly wrong with me. I can go years without a kiss and then I do that. The common denominator is whiskey, of course.

The cabin is empty as I expect. I smell Bruce. That makes me laugh as it's dogs that smell humans, not the other way around. Terence left the place clean and I start for the bedroom. I see the computer is turned off; Terence normally leaves it on standby but this time the power light is off. Mike must have said something. Shit! I go to get my clothes and I pack all my night attire into my travel bag, but I am missing knickers and bras. They are out in the utility room in the dryer. I remember my coats and one dress are in the wardrobe in the spare room. Jesus, I have shoes and boots up here too.

I reach into the dryer to retrieve my knickers, but the machine slides and I curse, 'What da fuck?' But when the dryer slides, I notice what appears to be a hatch in the floor underneath. A trapdoor to where? I slide the machine back further till it scrapes along the wood. Then I lift the trap door. A small ladder leads into the dark; I'll need a torch. Terence keeps a torch where? Beside his computer, it's in the tray beside his computer. So I run to the living room. I check out the window. It is getting dark but there is no sign of Terence or Mike. I stop for a second and I listen for any sound. Bruce always barks incessantly when nearing home, but there is nothing.

The tray beside the computer is full of old batteries and felt markers with red, blue, and black tops. The torch, when I find it, is tiny. I nearly miss it lying hidden under a yellow-handled screwdriver. Just the job. I go to the utility room and shine the torch down the ladder. The floor below is carpeted. Is this another room? I go down the four steps of the ladder and find myself in the basement. It takes up the whole area of the cabin. Terence has never mentioned it. That's weird. I flash the torch around the room to get a better view. There is a single bed away in the corner. There must be a light switch somewhere. I search the walls but I can't see one. I notice there is a lamp beside the bed on a bedside table. I go over and press the switch. Miracles! It works and the room floods with light.

Over by the far wall there is a bookcase but it is empty; on top of it are some framed photographs. Then I notice an annex leading to a toilet and shower. Does someone live here? Did somebody stay here recently? The bed is freshly made but a musty smell makes me think not. Why didn't Terence tell me about this place? I go to the book case and look at the pictures. They are old. One is of a child and the other is of a woman. The child is about five years old and the woman is in her mid-twenties.

I know I must get out of there, so I switch off the lamp and the torch guides me back to the ladder. I pull the dryer back into position, then bend over to make sure I have retrieved all my smalls.

'You are leaving us?' Terence says calmly. He is holding a dead rabbit on each arm.

'You scared the shit out of me!'

'You didn't hear Bruce? He barks the place down when we get near the house.'

'Nah, I was away in my own head. Where's Mike?'

'He's lighting the fire, opening the wine.'

'I think I should go back to the village, you know?'

'No.'

'Well, the case is at a dead end. Even the sergeant says it's useless. I got the jeep back, so I think it's best if I go back to the hotel – maybe stay a few more days and then go home.'

'Okay, is it me or is it Mike?'

'How do you mean?'

'Which one of us pissed you off, Mike or me? Or both. Do you want to make a choice?'

'Nah, it's nuthin' like that. Look I came here to find Mary and I don't think that's going to happen anytime soon. Best I make plans to go home – tell her family that I failed.'

'Cool. So like the stereotypical bad man, you find 'em, fuck 'em and leave 'em?'

'Fuck off, Terence. I'm not in the mood.' I brush by him.

My travel bag is on the bed. I sling it over my shoulder. 'I still have some things up in the spare room but I can drop by for them. I might just take that old rain mac off the hook by the doorway. It will do for now.'

Mike appears. 'You not staying for wine and food? Terence needs to hang those rabbits, but we had some defrosting from the freezer, so stand by for rabbit stew!'

'Nah, I gotta go Mike. I'll see you around the village. Should be here for a few more days.'

'I'm nearly finished my article on the whole affair and I wanted you to read through it.'

'Okay. Drop by the hotel tomorrow with it. We can look at it then.'

'Okay.' Mike sounds disappointed.

Terence goes beyond the counter to hang the rabbits. I think I should warn Mike about the room down below but I don't want it to be too obvious.

'Can you bring my travel bag to the jeep while I say goodbye to Bruce?'

'Sure,' Mike says, taking the travel bag from my shoulder.

I kiss Bruce above his eyes. His forehead is warm from the fire. When I stand up I am aware of Terence's stare. I choose to ignore it and walk to the door.

'See you around,' I say, glancing back at him.

'Hope so!' He stops looking at me and grabs a dishcloth.

Mike puts the travel bag in the passenger side of the jeep. 'Hey, what's up?'

'I gotta go, Mike. Did you know there's a basement in that cabin with a bed and carpet and a lamp?'

'Yeah, Terence showed me. It's not his place. He rents it from the lady who owns the hotel. He doesn't know what she used it for. She just told him to keep it clean and fresh for her.'

I am stunned. 'Anyhow, I better go. I need some space.'

'Sure, that's cool. I'll drop by to see you with my article. Safe drive, Avril!'

I drive into the night.

Moya Breslin never told me that she owned the cabin. I had specifically asked her about Terence and all she did was pour scorn on his isolation up by the upper lake. She owns the cabin where he lives?

***

I drive slowly because of the darkness. The trees leap out of their roots to clash with the headlights of the jeep. I slow to a crawl around the familiar bad bends. Funny thing is, I think Terence is more upset by me leaving than Mike.

17

1949

Inspector Malone said that Whytie had been giving out yards to the powers that be in Dublin, that he had made calls to high-ranking TDs – some fella called Meaney, along with a few councillors and even a renowned barrister. Steele grimaced. He awaited Malone's verdict and anticipated the words 'Get the hell out of there', but they didn't come.

Instead Malone said, 'They're hiding something, Steele. Find out what the fuck is going on. I don't care if you stay there a month, just get to the bottom of this and good luck.'

Steele asked him to find out about Garda Corcoran and where in Galway he might find him.

'No need,' Malone said. 'Corcoran is back in Lough Lyn. His wife tried to top herself and he is on leave looking after the kids. You can ask locally for the house, but all his information came to me when he applied for a transfer to Blackrock.'

'When?'

'A month ago.' Inspector Malone hung up.

Steele was alone.

'There you go!' Moya said. 'Your jacket. It's freezing out!'

'Thank you, you are very kind.'

Her face went red. 'I better go back and clean up, so.'

The detective watched her go back through the open door to the dining room.

* * *

The freezing air woke him. It negated any lazy dreams or fantasies he might have harboured for her. Hell, he mused, she will think me slow. Maybe she likes detectives – that might be good. Then the car took an age to start; his battery was frozen. He pulled out the choke, but nothing, and then he flooded the thing. Eventually, when he had almost given up, it suddenly burst into life. His efforts thawed its inner workings. She revved up, the engine soon heated the interior of the car and he began to feel warmer.

His choice: he could go and seek out Garda Corcoran or go out to see this Hugo Bauer. It was a Saturday so it was possible that both would be home. Steele knew where Bauer lived. He couldn't miss that big house. He should have asked Moya about Corcoran but he didn't, and he wasn't up to stepping out in the cold again. He could always stop by the station on his way back and ask Madden.

He took a drive out by the lake to clear his head. Finding a small lay-by, he parked the car. He had a fine view over the choppy water. The detective planned to stay ten minutes but when he checked his watch he found he had been there for nearly an hour. How time passed in a beautiful place like this. Finally setting out for Bauer's, his car skidded to the other side of the road twice. Each time he managed to steady her, only to feel the grip loosen again. He had to concentrate or he would end up in the ditch. For a short stretch between a line of conifers the snow had dug in. It was funny that the car was happier on this surface and that allowed him time to breathe.

The Bauer residence was uphill half a mile further on but visible once he reached the main road. There was a black Ford parked outside. A tall unkempt man was hammering nails into the roof of a shed to the side. He stopped working and stared at Steele coming up the drive. The driveway itself had been cleared of snow and ice, and the detective was glad of that. The door was answered by a stout middle-aged woman wearing an apron. She had lots of hair down the sides but very little on top.

'Who is it, Mrs Rooke?' a woman's voice called from the rear.

'Detective Dan Steele.'

'Come in, Detective,' Mrs Rooke said calmly. 'It's coming up nice. I don't think the snow will last.'

'I hope not.'

Mrs Rooke showed him into the sitting room, which was bright and airy. A fire blazed and in the corner a young woman was dusting the sideboard. He was astonished to see Moya, the waitress from the hotel. She turned and smiled.

'My daughter says she met you this morning at the hotel?' Mrs Rooke said.

'We did indeed!' Steele smiled back.

Moya turned away and resumed cleaning as the lady of the house came in.

Mrs Bauer said, 'Hello.' She looked him up and down.

Though Steele didn't know many Germans, to him she was very Germanic. He thought she looked aristocratic with her auburn hair and sharp chin. She had strong intelligent eyes.

'Madam. I was looking for your husband.'

'Is he in trouble?'

'No, I'm investigating the disappearance of a young girl. I just want to ask him a few questions. He was one of a party of people who were the last to see her. I just need a chat.'

'He's not in the house, Detective. He goes down by the lake to walk on Saturdays, but I can send Moya down to fetch him if you like. Or maybe you fancy a stroll yourself. He won't have gone far.'

'I can take a walk down that way – clear the lungs!'

'Come this way. It's quicker out the back way.'

Steele followed her, admiring her female shape; she was firm and womanly from the rear. She left him by the steps leading to the lawn. All beyond that was wild meadow. She pointed to a distinctly battered path running down to a boathouse. It met a rugged jetty stuck fast in the choppy waters of the lake. Steele saw Mr Bauer standing at the end of the jetty. He was lean and dark, with hair that was too long for the current fashion. When the detective got close, he swung around suddenly, the footsteps startling him. Bauer looked at him wide-eyed.

'Who are you?' he asked nervously.

'Detective Dan Steele … from Dublin.'

'Yes, what do you want with me?'

Steele could feel the freezing air choke his voice. 'I want to ask you about a missing girl, Biddy Foley?'

'Yes, I know her. A dreadful business.'

'Can we go somewhere out of the wind, Mr Bauer? I'm finding it hard to talk.'

'Yes, follow me.'

He brought the detective around a narrow path to the boathouse. Two small boats were resting on wooden beams. 'I'm not much of a sailor, Detective, are you?'

'Nah, never been on a boat in my life and I grew up by the sea.'

'Yes, that is often the case.'

Hugo sat on a bench by the window and Steele took the only chair. It was a workman's stool.

'I was wondering if you can tell me about the night you visited Biddy's house?'

'What? Oh yes, we went there to examine her.'

'Why so late in the evening?'

'Because she tended to wander during the day. As you know, the father was a raving drunk. Biddy went off during the day and wandered the countryside. Those that know say she was trying to avoid the old man. Rumour has it that he impregnated her several times – a dreadful case!'

'Do you remember who was with you on the night in question?'

'I do. There were several people present. You have to remember that I'm a stranger here and I needed local advice. You see, it was on the bishop's instigation I went to see the girl. He asked his friend Wade, the politician, and Doctor Hammond. Let me see … yes, that was it – just us three.'

'There were no policemen there to oversee the whole thing?'

'Yes, of course. That's right. There were two guards there when we got to the house.'

'Would you remember their names?'

'No, I would not.'

'Anyone else present? Was Inspector Whyte there?'

'No.'

'Are you sure?'

'Yes, I'd remember if he had been. I know him. I met him on several occasions.'

They were interrupted by Moya. She was holding a tray with two bowls of soup.

'The missus sent these down because of the cold,' she said, removing two cloth napkins to reveal slices of buttered crusty bread. She smiled warmly at Hugo Bauer before placing the tray on a barrel lying idle beside the boats.

'Don't worry about the tray. I'll collect it later.'

She smiled at Steele. He felt a sudden pang; this girl and her simple beauty was stirring something within him.

'A fine specimen, Detective. She will do well in life, and she has the cheer to go with the good looks.'

'Specimen is not a word I'd use, Mr Bauer, but I take your point.'

Steele tried the soup; it was delicious. Hugo took his bowl and used his spoon sharply like someone who hadn't eaten for an age. He consumed his bread in three bites, but the detective ate slower and Hugo slowed considerably in respect of that.

'I'm an expert in eugenics. The bishop wanted me to study this girl. I guess he mistakenly believed that I had the power to change what is already in existence, despite me telling him more than once that my work was in preparing for the next generation or generations to come. For example, if we can eradicate some diseases in this generation, it might lead to better health in generations unborn. Anyhow, the bishop seemed to think I could help. He wanted my opinion on the girl.'

'The mother says that you people took the girl away?'

Bauer stopped chewing the last of his bread. 'That isn't true. We took her outside to the car, just to speak to her in peace.'

'So the mother is lying … or mistaken?' Steele tried to sound friendly, not hostile.

'No, Detective, the mother is mad. She is not a credible witness. When I finished my initial analysis of the girl, we left. She stood outside the cottage and watched us leave. I presume she went back inside once we were gone.'

'Credible or not, the mother says she never saw her again.'

Bauer swallowed his bread. 'Whatever you say, Detective.'

'I'll cross-check with the other witnesses. I've plenty of people to see. Thank you for your help, Mr Bauer. I'm sorry to take up your valuable time, particularly on a Saturday.'

'No problem, Detective.'

'Oh, one more thing, Mr Bauer. I keep calling you mister, but are you a doctor?'

'Mister will do fine, Detective.'

'Great, and what were the results of your analysis?'

'How do you mean?'

'Did you make a diagnosis on Biddy?'

'The time we had was too short. I would have needed to see her again – possibly a few times – but then she went missing.'

Bauer followed Steele outside, and they walked together up the path to the lawn and on up to the house.

'So what do you think of Ireland?' Steele asked as they entered the kitchen.

'I dunno. That is a hard question to answer. Things are very different in Berlin.'

'I'm sure they are.'

The detective left, the car starting first time. The tall dishevelled man had finished repairing the roof on the shed; he saluted as Steele passed by. Funny to be dressed in an old suit when doing manual work, but that's country folk for you, Steele mused.

* * *

He was pale. Steele thought he was very nervous but that might have been down to his family situation. His wife stood behind him, using him as a shield. She was dark-haired and petite. Steele wondered what made Corcoran desire her; she was so flat-chested and thin that he wanted to go get her food. Yet Corcoran was protective of her. She grunted in disapproval when he ordered her to go make tea, and suddenly she was sour towards him. Two little girls played by the fire. They were full of curls and startling screeches. Steele knew that his visit disturbed them. Then Corcoran gruffly ordered them to the kitchen. They went politely as they were used to his growl. The smaller of the two smiled at Steele and, for a moment, he was touched. Corcoran showed the detective to an armchair by the fire, but his feet found themselves planted on the small wooden toys the girls had abandoned and a doll stuck her legs out from the cushion behind him.

'I heard you were about, Detective.'

'News travels fast!'

'It does around here.'

'How's the missus?'

'She's coming around slowly.'

Corcoran took the armchair opposite. He didn't quite know what to do with his long legs. One minute they rested on the hearth and the next he let them flop lazily on the lino.

'It's her nerves.'

Steele could see that Corcoran had once been clean-shaven but was making valiant attempts to grow a moustache. It had the look of one that could have grown fuller but he had shaved it off in the hope that it would grow better the second time.

'Her muther suffered with her nerves too.'

'Did she? It runs in families.'

'It does, so they say.' Corcoran was trying to act and sound much older than his years.

'I was wondering about the night that you and Garda Madden were at the cottage – the night the German fella was there. Do you recall that night?'

'I do and I don't, Detective.' He looked at Steele, waiting for a reaction. 'With all this stuff at the hospital with Jenny my mind is in a jumble. Nothing is clear. I can't wait to get back to work to be honest.'

'I heard you applied to Blackrock.'

'Did you? News travels fast in Dublin, so.'

'I'm stationed there.'

'Oh!'

Steele stayed silent, observing Corcoran as he shifted uncomfortably in his seat. Then Jenny brought in two cups of tea on a small wooden tray. The older of the two girls followed her.

'Milk and sugar?' Her accent was more rural than Corcoran's.

The detective said no to the sugar but yes to the milk. Corcoran was delighted to wet his drying mouth. He gasped when the tea hit the back of his throat and the girl followed her mother back to the kitchen.

'Who was there?'

'Madden and myself, obviously. They sort of came and went, so it's hard to say.'

'I've already confirmed with Garda Madden that the German was there, along with Wade, but there seems to be some kinda confusion whether Dr Hammond was there or not. Was the inspector there too – at some point at least?'

'Yeah, that's right. You're right about that.'

'So in your own words, can you tell me about that night? Just tell me what you remember.'

Corcoran drank the rest of his tea, then glanced towards the kitchen as if he was expecting his wife to reappear; she didn't.

'It was ages ago. I've been to Galway since and then Jenny had her nerves. She very nearly succeeded this time so, you know, my own nerves are kinda shot too.'

'Yes, I know, but all I'm trying to find out is what happened on that night. A young girl has gone missing. She may be dead.'

'Is that what you call her, Detective? A young girl? She wasn't like any young girl I've ever known. She wasn't normal. Biddy must have been driven mad by her father and mother, but my guess is she was born mad, just like her sisters. She knew what she was doin', Detective, believe me. She was dishin' it out goodo. She knew what she was doin'. Don't be fooled for one minute.'

'You've lost me.'

'I dunno what you know, Detective?'

Steele said nothing and waited for him to continue.

'The inspector wanted it to stop. That's why he called in the German. We used to call to the house regularly to tell them the father was locked up for the night. The oul wan would act mad and I always said to Madden she was a con, but the young one, Biddy, she might come on to you, offering to do stuff for money. She offered the younger ones as well.'

'What did you do?'

Corcoran went silent, looking at his empty cup; then he looked at the closed door to the kitchen. 'Is that what this is about? I thought you wanted to know about that night. I wasn't thinking of nothing else, mind.' Corcoran's tone changed. A hiss of aggression marred his words. 'They were all there at some time or another.' He softened once more like a fellow who was full of remorse. 'The German came in but he looked dazed, like he was full of drink, and he went into the back room after a few minutes. Then he came out with the girl. They left and that was it. The place emptied and Garda Madden drove me back to the village.'

'You never saw the girl again?'

'No, that was it. She left with the German.'

The detective waited for a second just to see if he would retract what he said, but he didn't.

'Seems a right crowd to arrive at someone's house late at night and take the daughter away.'

'It does sound funny, but that's the way it happened.'

'Okay.'

Steele was on his feet when Corcoran placed his left hand on his shoulder. He had big hurlers hands and Steele felt the weight of them press down on him.

'You can put a good word in with your inspector now, can you?'

'I can.'

Steele lied, thinking that he might need Corcoran again.

18

1949

Steele was exhausted when he got back to the Lough Lyn Hotel. He got a strong musty smell, so he held his nostrils tight going up the stairs. Outside the snow was falling. The roofs opposite were painted with a fluffy white finish and some kids down in the street threw snowballs at a passing tractor. The village was ready to seize up and so was he. He didn't know what he was going to tell Malone. He had asked many questions, but he still had to talk with a few people like Dr Hammond and Wade, the politician. Maybe he should seek permission from Malone to have a chat with the bishop. Malone was no Holy Joe but he knew where to draw the line. So did Steele. He didn't know much but he was certain that they were all lying. Ironically, the only one telling any truth was the German, even though evil oozed from him. But perhaps he was just playing on his own arrogance, like he didn't care if Steele knew the truth. After all, what could an average detective from Dublin do to a man who was appointed by the bishop?

Steele went down to the lobby to phone Malone but realised it was after six. Malone was like clockwork: he left his desk at five thirty hail, rain or snow. He could try him at home, but his home was sacrosanct, not because he had a wife and kids but because that was where he kept his bottle of whiskey. The man didn't touch a drop-in bars or anywhere else; home was where he kept his baby. Home was his sanctuary and Steele wasn't about to disturb him with lots of questions and not many answers.

Moya was serving behind the bar and the detective ordered a pint of stout. He wanted to nurse it and allow the dark creamy pint to soothe his thoughts. Maybe it would put some shape on them. Moya smiled as she handed him his pint.

'We keep meeting,' Moya said.

'You work hard.'

'I need to work hard – I have a family to keep.'

She laughed and went quickly about her business. The detective watched her go through the swing doors. She returned a few minutes later carrying plates of food. Steele's eyes followed her all the way as she served a table at the rear of the room where a distinguished man sat pontificating to his companion. Then he realised that the companion was none other than the German, so when Moya returned, he whispered to her, 'Who is that with Bauer?'

'That's Dr Hammond.'

'Oh good!'

'What?'

'Nothing. Thanks.'

He turned around on his stool to study them further. The doctor ate furiously while the German talked too much to eat his food. He tended to play with it rather than eat it. Every now and then the doctor would stop – it was like he was egging his companion on to eat his food before it went cold – but the German kept rabbiting on. At first Steele thought they were merely engaged in friendly banter, but after time he concluded they were in fact having a serious discussion, if not an argument.

Moya went to their table to collect the plates and take orders for dessert. The doctor ordered something from the menu but the German shook his head. When she came back to the bar Steele ordered another pint and asked Moya what the doctor and the German were drinking.

'Whiskey,' she said with a twinkle in her eye.

As she went through the swing doors Steele noticed her firm behind and was struck by the gracefulness of her carriage. When Moya returned, she looked even more beautiful, if that were possible. She had pinned her hair back, which allowed him a full view of her face. Steele ordered two whiskeys to be delivered to the table and when Moya arrived with her tray, both men looked over at him. The German simply stared but the doctor raised his glass and nodded in a gentlemanly fashion. This was the permission he sought.

Steele brought his pint to their table. The doctor looked the detective up and down in a bemused fashion, but Hugo Bauer scowled as if he thought the detective's interruption was rude.

'I notice you've finished eating. Do you mind if I join you?'

'Thank you, Detective. Any man that sends two glasses of malt to a table is always welcome in my book. But my young German companion is not used to our Irish hospitality. I'm afraid he has a dislike of all things police – memories of the Gestapo, you know. It's very understandable in the circumstances, don't you think. So out of politeness I shall allow Hugo decide whether we will become a threesome. What say you, Hugo?'

The German was shocked by his friend's arrogance and candour. His face reddened and he drank most of his whiskey down.

'Of course, Detective Steele. You're welcome to take a seat. It's bitterly cold and three is warmer than two.'

Steele was surprised at the ease of his words; his face was saying something very different.

'Gentlemen, it is after seven in the evening and detectives need time off too. It's not an interrogation. I wish to join you for the pleasure of your company and to pass a little time as I'm a stranger here.'

The German gave him a 'you hardly think that I'm not a stranger' look.

Steele took a seat opposite the two men.

'You like the common man's pint. I like that!' the doctor said, laughing at his own attempt at humour.

'It is mother's milk!' Steele was making sure not to apologise or explain his pint drinking.

The German drank his whiskey down and then called a round from the passing Moya. She smiled at him, which made Steele feel uncomfortable until he remembered that she also worked for him. They know each other well, the detective comforted himself, but his efforts were in vain as the bitter taste of jealousy settled on his tongue. Moya returned with the drinks.

'You're most likely wasting your time, Detective, not that I want to dwell on your investigation, nor do I want to appear obtuse. To understand this affair one would need to be familiar with the plight of the poor in this parish. Some of these people are so poor and afflicted by madness that your investigation will run dry in due course. I am, of course, like any good doctor, fascinated by the factors that lead to such impoverishment. That is part of the reason that Hugo came here. It's a long way from Berlin. I suspect you may want to interrogate me about this matter very soon, so why not save yourself the trouble. Come, ask me whatever it is you want. You'll find that I have an open mind and an honest disposition, so fire away!'

Steele was a little unnerved by the doctors tone but on balance he decided to take him at his word. No more than the German had exuded evil at their earlier meeting, the doctor was now just as menacing in his expression and delivery.

'Why did you go to the cottage that night, so?'

The doctors eyes moved in their sockets. It was like his brain was speeding down a steep hill and needed assistance to slow down.

'I was only there in an advisory capacity, my good friend. Hugo has excellent English. However, the local dialect can vary from quaint to indecipherable, as can the local habits. I was there as his guide, so to speak. I had no other interest, I can assure you.'

It was the doctor's turn to down his drink. He immediately searched for Moya but she was away from the bar.

'Gentlemen, we must slow a pace as I will be drunk. I am consuming volume and you men are merely swallowing shots. It's an unfair competition. If you insist on ordering another round, Doctor, make mine a whiskey too.'

The doctor did as requested. Moya took immense pleasure in carrying the drinks to their table. She rested the tray on the edge beside Steele's right elbow before placing a glass in front of each of them in turn.

'Cheers all.' Dr Hammond raised his small glass.

The German raised his and Steele did likewise; all three glasses touched with a distinct chink.

'I'm interested to know more. What did you hope to achieve and why go to the cottage so late at night?'

'What we hoped to achieve was very little really. What we actually achieved was even less. The point of the exercise was for Hugo to see at first hand the degradation, to study this girl in her natural environment. It was all a waste of time, mind you.'

'Why do you say that?'

'Because we didn't learn anything, you see. My friend here had too much to drink, and in case you think he has a problem, I can assure you that my learned friend has no such thing. I'm afraid he was a victim of the bishop's poteen that's kept for medicinal purposes only, so it was all just a bloody waste of time.'

'And none of you left with the girl?'

'No.'

'Why the crowd, so?'

Dr Hammond glanced at the German who had emptied his glass. 'The tide has gone out, Detective,' he said finally.

Steele called Moya. She didn't acknowledge him, but then he saw her go to the whiskey dispenser and knew she understood.

'The *crowd*? This is a small village. Don't you think someone like Wade would want to know everything? He's the TD for the area – one of two – and his opponent is just waiting for a ministry in the Dáil. Wade needs to get the once over on Meaney. That's why he hangs around the bishop like it's his passport to greatness. When the cat's away the mice will play. While Meaney is stuck up in Dáil Eireann trying to get the Free Staters back into power, Wade stays at home looking for ways to make headlines. The inspector was there because I invited him. You see, I wasn't sure whether Foley was around and I didn't want trouble, but most of all, the inspector, despite what the gossips say, has a thing about the disadvantaged. What's more, the man is willing to do something about it. So that's why there was a *crowd*.'

Moya set down three more whiskies. The German was slower to take his this time. Steele could see why a fellow like him might succumb to the drink; he was a light weight, for sure. Then the German surprised him.

'I did learn something from the girl that night.'

'What was that?' Steele watched Dr Hammond's worried face as he tried to anticipate whatever it was the German might be about to say.

'I learned that she was mentally deranged but she had held on to some basic survival instincts. These insulated her from the world, Detective, a little like a wetsuit protects a deep-sea diver. I found her to be an excellent manipulator. She knew how to get whatever it was she wanted. She was like an actress playing roles.'

'Really?' Steele looked at Bauer contemptuously. 'You gathered all that information while full of poteen?'

The German returned an icy stare.

'Now, gentlemen,' the doctor interjected. 'Let's keep this clean.'

'I fully intend to.' Steele, warming up from the whiskey, suddenly felt he was ready for anything.

'You're questioning my professionalism?' Dr Bauer said.

The German was serious, which sort of irked Steele as Dr Hammond had made some efforts to bail him out with the bishop's poteen excuse.

'I am not, sir. I was just reiterating your colleague's statement on the consummation of poteen.'

'I assure you, Detective, the good doctor overestimates the effect of poteen. In fact I was simply overtired and fatigued that evening.'

'Yes, but then can you enlighten us with your diagnosis?'

Dr Hammond looked at Bauer like he, too, was expecting an explanation.

'You can think what you wish, gentlemen, but as my colleague will testify, it wasn't the first time I had met the girl. I'm afraid I must take my leave now. More heavy snow is forecast for later and my wife has agreed to collect me during the lull. I don't want to delay her, so I bid you both good evening.'

Bauer left just when the conversation was getting interesting.

The doctor waited for Steele to speak.

'A bad night to be on the roads?' was all he could muster.

'Indeed, that's why I had the wisdom to book a bed for the night.' Dr Hammond was pleased with his self-congratulatory utterance, but the detective was taken aback by his sharp mixture of arrogance and wildness. 'It's my round, Detective.'

Moya brought the drinks. She was still her cheery self, throwing her eyes to heaven when the doctor changed the order to doubles.

'You'll both sleep tonight. We'll all be housebound with the snow.'

Steele watched her leave the table, her womanly hips curved to perfection as she crossed the room.

'She is a prize,' Dr Hammond said. 'To be honest with you, Detective, I can take or leave females but she is a joy. Anyone can see that.'

'She sure is!' Steele wanted to press the medic further but he didn't, not just because the doctor had become too drunk, as he expected, but because he felt light-headed himself and none of his questions made any sense. While the doctor was patient with him, he soon became disinterested and seemed to delve into a world of his own.

'Are you a fan of Casement?'

'I'm a true republican!' Steele was, and he was proud of it.

'But you probably don't see the contradiction in Casement. I'm not arguing that he wasn't a true patriot. No, that's not what I'm saying at all. He was a patriot through and through. He has proven that and history has proven that, hasn't it, Detective? Are you aware of Casement's liking for boys? I'm not judging him in anyway, remember, nor am I trying to dilute his contribution to Irish freedom. Oh no. But did you know that he viewed young boys as the ultimate in the aesthetic and this fascination led to some wonderful liaisons? When he was in the Congo he had a wealth of beautiful young boys at his disposal, so to speak.'

Steele wanted to tell him that he had little interest in Casement outside of the known history and Banna Strand and all of that, but Hammond was once again in talkative mode.

'Lots of great men have a penchant for children. Some love little girls and others, like Casement, have this thing for boys. Did you know that in Lewis Carroll's time girls could marry at the age of twelve?'

'No, Dr Hammond, I didn't, and personally I find that disgusting. I have a niece who is only ten. She's a child and she still plays with dolls.'

'Yes, we're talking about different times and, in some cases, a different culture altogether. You see, I mention all this to you because the bishop to whom I am a personal advisor, he is an exceptional man, way ahead of his time. He's an expert in astronomy, among many other things, and is extremely well-read. Don't you see, Detective, it was he that invited Hugo Bauer to come to Lough Lyn. Hugo is an expert in eugenics.'

'I'm not sure I fully understand the term. Yes, it has been explained to me but in a vague fashion.'

'I'm afraid I have run out of steam this evening and eugenics would keep us up all night, my friend. I just want you to know that Bauer has expertise in this area and the bishop has a quest to eradicate poverty and ignorance. It was on the bishop's orders that we visited the cottage that night. Don't make the mistake of thinking there was anything funny going on. There wasn't. It was all down to Bishop Cassidy and his quest.'

Steele thought it best to keep quiet. He had his own theories about it all. This bishop was mad, according to those in the know, and Malone said that much of the hierarchy thought him clinically insane. Of course, Malone would remind him about the many conversations he had had with the elite within the church. The man had friends everywhere, but the common denominator was that they were all powerful people. Above everything he was a policeman, and a damned good one at that. He continually reminded Steele that everything he was told about the bishop was off the record and none of his confidants were prepared to go on record, no matter what the circumstances.

Steele bade the doctor goodnight. Dr Hammond smiled at the detective graciously. Moya offered to deliver a hot water bottle to the doctor's room.

Steele jokingly said, 'What about me?'

She smiled and said she would oblige.

'Age comes before beauty, Detective. I'll deliver the doctor his first,'

After a wait of ten minutes she knocked on his door.

'Come in.'

She entered the room, cautiously looking around to make sure he was decent. Steele took the opportunity to look out on the deserted street. The snow was drifting and its accumulations were making ice mounds outside of people's front doors.

'It's bitter out,' she said, placing the hot water bottle under the blanket.

When she leaned over, her back was exposed for a few seconds. Steele marvelled at the smoothness of her skin and the way it hugged tight around her waist. He had this sudden longing for her and didn't want her to leave.

'Moya?'

'Yes, Detective? Is that all? I'll be heading to my own warm bed.'

'Yes.' He took a step towards her. 'I hope your bed is warm.'

She smiled at him as she reached the bedroom door; Steele got closer still.

Moya kissed him softly on the lips. 'Nighty night, Detective.'

Steele wanted to ask her to stay – both his body and his bed were roaring hot for her – but Moya, smiling, said, 'Sleep well,' and the door closed on his hungry gaze.

19

Dolan looks at me like I have ten heads, and the sergeant is embarrassed to see me. It is like his cover is blown. It's obvious that when Dolan is around, he is no longer in charge of the investigation. I see him cooperate and capitulate in equal measure and he knows that I know, so he barks out silly commands to Paula. She knows too, but she is very loyal and sound and says nothing.

The hotel bar is dark. I guess Moya turns down the lights to hide the dirt. She waves at me from behind the counter but I am reluctant to wave back, as it may compromise conversations yet to come; I need to talk to her very soon. Dolan isn't sure why I have gate-crashed his party. They're using the bar as an incident room. Boyle has an area map laid out across a table; Paula is pointing to specific areas marked with an X. One of Dolan's assistants is disputing something with her, but Paula is adamant and the young Dublin woman eventually backs off.

'Can I help you?' Dolan says finally.

'I came to see Moya.'

'Can you come back later?' he squeaks.

'I sure can, but hey, you act like I don't have a stake in this. I was nearly killed, remember, and Mary has been missing so long now.'

'We found a body in the woods,' Paula says.

Dolan's underling gives her a vicious stare.

Dolan is less dramatic; he just says, 'We don't know what we found yet. Some hunters came across bones. We're waiting for the team to arrive from Dublin.'

'Where is it?'

'Out beyond the lower lake,' Moya says. She is ghost like in the shadows.

'The Hogan brothers found bones about a mile from their place.'

I want to ask who the Hogan brothers are but I am too tired to care.

'They go that way regularly, so they think it was the melting snow and the rain that disturbed the ground.'

Moya comes forward and I see her better now. She remains attractive for an old woman. I try to picture her as a young woman, but the shadows return as people move about. She goes to lean against the shelf by the till.

'I'll take my old room back.'

She smiles. 'We're all but empty after the thaw, dear. Take your pick.'

I am relieved.

Dolan seizes control. 'You can sort all that out later. We have a crime scene to visit, so begging your pardon.'

I move to one side and he walks by bullishly, followed by his assistant who is growing in confidence. I learn her name when Dolan says, 'Bring the map, Georgina.'

Boyle and Paula follow, but the sergeant doesn't bother looking at me as he passes.

'Don't I get to see if it's Mary?'

'You can't,' he says, looking back. I see the watery remains of ice trapped under the collar of his coat.

'We can't stop you following us,' Paula says kindly.

'That's not an invitation!' Sergeant Boyle says.

I forget about Moya and the lodge. I am concentrating on Paula; she is a fast driver. She skids around the sharp bends on these treacherous wet roads and I stay as close as I dare, not wanting to make a mistake, and slam the jeep into her rear. We go five kilometres beyond the lake. Moya might count them as a few country miles but us city girls look at miles differently. When we come to a stop, a sign says the lake is five kilometres back so I'm happy that my guess is a good one.

Dolan is there already. Further on a van is parked and at least six people disembark dressed in white protective suits. Georgina and Paula are busy fastening tape from one pine tree to another and Sergeant Boyle looks on sadly. Right now I'm thinking that he is a broken man.

Dolan speaks to Bolton, the leader of the crew in protective suits. This man is portly and engaging. Obviously he has been to many scenes far more gruesome than this. He is relaxed and in jovial mood. I watch as the white crew slip into the darkness. I see the pine needles are a bright red and the soil is damp, especially around the butt of the tree trunks. It is odd to see the white figures move through the trees and for a second I await the arrival of a spaceship.

'It will take an age!' Dolan declared, walking away to chat with his crew.

'It always does,' Boyle says to nobody in particular.

'I brought a flask of coffee. Would you like one, Detective?' Paula offers. Her face is bright red from the cold.

'Love one!'

'Sarge?'

'Yeah, go on!' Boyle says gruffly.

Dolan is back. He gives me a filthy look but says nothing, like he knows better.

'We hope it won't take too long. I want to get it all to Dublin for a full examination.' Dolan sounds knowledgeable.

The sergeant ignores him, so I am tempted to do the same.

'Early indications show that the body has been there for some time but how long?' Dolan says.

Georgina watches Paula hand me a coffee and then the sergeant. She is disappointed that Paula just brings back a plastic cup and there is none for her or Dolan. I see a brief look of resignation engulf her face, Dolan acknowledges it too, but he is too busy talking to care.

'He thinks it's been there for years, but he needs to more time to examine it.'

Bolton gets up from his knees. He walks back towards us, his big jolly frame sinking in the soft pine needle earth. 'It's been in the ground a long time,' he says.

The sergeant shrugged like he knew that was the case all the time.

Dolan was trying to be intelligent. 'How long, would you have a guess?'

Bolton swallowed hard like it was a preamble to deep thought. 'Years,' he said. 'Fifty – sixty years – even more. It's a child's body, maybe a young teenager, possibly a girl but I can't be certain. We need to get all this back to the lab for further examination.'

He is gone and once more he joins his alien friends within the magic circle.

* * *

Back at the hotel the incident room closes. The bones are on their way to Dublin, with Dolan and Georgina keeping them company. Dolan's parting shot was that he would be back soon with the full results. The sergeant looks miserable. I see him place a gentle hand on Paula's shoulder; she glances at him gratefully. Moya is asking him questions but I am too far away to hear their conversation. I strain to listen but then I don't bother. What's the point? Paula is carrying papers to and from the jeep and the sergeant sits up on a high stool beside me. He orders two whiskies, one for himself and one for Paula. I offer to pay but he won't hear of it.

'It wouldn't be right.'

Moya serves him as Marcia Mellon is busy elsewhere. Moya eyes me warily, like she knows that I know something but I haven't yet revealed it. I sense that it is both worrying and frustrating for her. I can smell the scent of her deliberation. I guess she is on the cusp of blurting out a question and any second now I expect her to scream, 'Okay, what the hell is it?' But she doesn't. She continues about her business quietly as the village is in mourning. The sergeant is in such a low mood he carries us all into the abyss and Paula goes out in sympathy. She drinks her whiskey in two goes.

'I'm going home,' she says. 'Will I take the jeep?'

'Why not?'

Boyle is just as pissed with her. Paula smiles wryly and leaves. He doesn't turn to watch her go. Now I know there is something deep between them. Just by him not looking around the sergeant has betrayed everything. Moya takes the empty whiskey glass away and the sergeant nods, so Moya fills his glass again. I sip mine in solidarity with his mood.

'So what do you think?' I say, holding my glass in the air deliberately.

'Doesn't matter what I think.' He is staring at the ceiling, his eyes scanning the rafters and the webs that hang lazily from the wood.

'It's old, so it isn't Mary.'

'No, it isn't.' His head was straight once again.

'Thank God it's not your girl,' Moya offers.

'It's someone's bones though.' The sergeant looks at me, but he is chastising Moya.

I watch him knock back his drink. He shivers involuntarily, then thanks Moya and leaves. I imagine him going home to a ruffled wife and noisy kids. He will be expected to act like Daddy and to act like a good husband. I fear that he will be quiet there also. He is a soured man and his life appears to be without redemption. To him all is mundane and all is failure.

'So you've come back to us,' Moya says mischievously.

'I have. I'm glad to – makes more sense. It's very lonely out in your place by the lake.'

She smiles like she is thinking, 'so that's what's up with her!'

'My husband bought it – well, sorry, he didn't buy it as such. He bought the land out by the lake but I built the house. Sorriest thing I did. It was empty for ten years. Terence Fleming is my first and only tenant, so God knows, but I can't very well raise the rent.'

'No, the poor writer factor?'

'That and other things – people around here wanting to know your business.'

'Why the room in the basement?' I say casually.

She is stunned; she almost says, 'You know about the room?' but she doesn't. She just pours herself a glass of the hard stuff and then tops mine up.

'That's on the house!'

I want to protest. I don't want to be compromised for a glass of whiskey.

'You're quite the detective but it's a long and complicated story. You know about the room but that's all you know and that's all you probably need to know.'

'Did Mary know about the room?'

'I dunno, Avril. What did Terence say?'

'He didn't say.'

'I dunno if Mary knew, but it's no big secret.'

I must be looking at her incredulously, so she goes on.

'My husband drank, like really drank. Not the odd wee drop of whiskey. He would lock himself away in rooms, just him and a few bottles of this stuff. In fairness he was quiet about it. He didn't make a fuss or cause us any harm. I suppose he just wanted to be on his own, so when I built the house I put that room in just for him. A place where he could just sit and drink and think – do whatever it was he did. But he never got to use it, not really. He was sick. Soon after the lodge was ready he was taken to hospital and died.'

I go to say something but she cuts me short.

'No, hear me out. Then Terence Fleming comes along and all is going well till he tells me one day that I am his mother. Can you believe that? He tells me he isn't sure but he thinks I may be his mother. I'm eighty-seven years old now and this is what life dishes out!'

'Can't you do one of those DNA tests?'

'Yes, I know that.'

I see her hands are trembling.

'But there's no need. Don't you think a mother would recognise her own child?'

'You are his mother then?'

'You don't understand. When I was young I was raped by a man and I also had a lover. He was married and when the wee child was born I didn't know.'

'How do you mean?'

'I didn't know which was the father. Terrible things were going on here back then – awful disgusting things. I sent my baby away. I went to see him a few times. I made the trip to Dublin, but then the people who were caring for him asked me to stay away. They said it wasn't good for the child to see me, so I got on with my life. Then one day he came back to me.'

The tears wet her face, small pools forming in the dark crevices beneath her eyes. I want to cross the bar and hug her.

A voice within pleads with me to stop interrogating her, but I shout back, 'Is your son murdering people?'

She is stunned. She wasn't expecting a charge like that.

'What?'

'Is Terence responsible for Mary and the rest of them?'

'Jesus, what the hell!? Terence wouldn't hurt a fly. Are you mad? He's is my son. He's innocent! My God!'

Her terror is infectious. I want to withdraw my interrogation. I have got everything wrong. How can this writer in his mid-sixties be responsible for all that has happened. Terence wouldn't have the physical strength to lift a man onto a meat hook. He is fit and well – his hunting treks require that level of fitness – but Terence doesn't have what it takes and it's about time that I accept that.

'Do you still want a room?' Moya looks at me pleadingly. 'Marcia is getting your old room ready.'

'Sure, hey look, I'm sorry. I didn't mean …'

'No, I'm sorry. I should have told you more when we were chatting before. It's just that around here you keep things close to your chest. I learned that as a very young girl. How's about you join me for dinner. I have many more things to tell you. Best told over a nice meal and a wee bottle of Bordeaux, don't you think?'

* * *

Marcia Mellon leaves my hotel room in spanking shape with fresh sheets and pillowcases. She even puts a new duvet on the end of the bed all rolled up like a tent. I look out onto the street and hope I will see Terence or Mike walk out of the Spar. But the street is empty except for a single car that turns and drives back down the road from where it originally came. I let go of the yellow stained lace curtain, still thinking that I want to go home. Maine is the place to be. I am tired of Ireland. I have no wish to spend a minute longer in this backwater. the police are no closer to solving this case, nor am I. Mary is gone and will stay gone. To hope for any other conclusion is within the realms of fantasy. She is dead, or gone away forever, which is the same thing. The murders are inexplicable, that's presuming that one person is responsible for them and for Mary's disappearance. Possibly the deaths of Jane Watts and Kevin Witherspoon are connected to Mary's case, but there are no leads right now. The best possible solution to these crimes is that someone from outside came to the village and left after committing these vile atrocities. But that, too, is unlikely. It doesn't seem to bother anyone, including the sergeant, that the murders just stopped. Has the killer satisfied his lust for murder? Did he choose me also and failed in his attempt? Or did this killer just give up, retire from his heinous pastime?

I lie on the bed. The mattress is soft. I fall asleep.

* * *

'The convent was due to close,' Moya says, passing me a glass of wine.

I'm struck by its molten red colour and am surprised that it is cold when I drink it.

'The babies had all moved on. The young mothers should have been free to return home but at least ten were made stay put.'

'Lovely wine!'

'Thanks,' Moya says. 'The war was still raging across Europe. We had some troops nearby. They were doing exercises in the area. Everything is hazy, Avril. Remember, I was still only sixteen years old. I am only repeating stuff that my husband told me but he was an honest man. He always told the truth. He told me that soldiers came to the home and the nuns gave them access to the women. The remaining women were raped many times over. This happened randomly for three weeks on end. That was it. They were kept locked up in that place for nine months. All told seven wee babies were born. Some say there were nine babies but only seven survived. In the end the mothers were allowed to leave but their babies stayed.' Moya empties her glass of wine, then she licks her lips.

'So what happened the babies?'

'What babies?' she says seriously while refilling her glass.

'The seven babies?'

'There were no babies. No babies were recorded as having been born. Even though those poor creatures were baptised into the Catholic church, no records were kept. The nuns gave them instruction. They never spoke to anyone outside of the convent. It was all a terrible secret that only a handful of people were privy to. According to the state, these children were never born. They didn't exist.'

I think of the prayer book I found with the number seven written on it. I hear the voice of old Tobin as he sits by the fire, the sound of children's voices screeching, the voices that carried from tree to tree, the echoing sound lost in the undergrowth, children that were never seen. Who were they and what purpose did they serve? Why did someone think murder could hide this secret all these years later? Is this what Mary discovered? Is it this that upset her so? Did this discovery cost her life?

Moya stares at me. She expects a reaction. I drink my wine like it's lemonade. It saves a little on the horror and quells the screaming inside me. Moya signals to Marcia to fetch another bottle. For once I am speechless. She says it for me.

'Seven children who were never born. What happens to them? Anything their masters want, that's the answer.'

'Surely people knew. Did none of the mothers speak out? If not, why didn't they?'

'They were terrified. Most of them emigrated. Others wanted to forget. They were sworn to silence for fear their babies would suffer. My husband knew only because he was an officer in the army. It disgusted him but he had no choice. To speak out meant losing his job and he hadn't the will to fight them. That's the way it was.'

20

1949

Addie had taken Hedy back to Germany to see her mother, so I had the house to myself. Mrs Rooke was unwell, but Jennings popped by. I saw him digging a small trench over by the garden hedge. It was too cold and he was wearing the wrong clothes. The ground was too hard after the frost and snow. His spade bounced off the ground and I could feel the vibration from the window. But Jennings was a law onto himself, which was good as I never had to tell him to do anything. He was always way ahead of me, moving from one job to the next, and he never complained. When he called to the back door for a cup of tea, he respectfully removed his cap; I saw him remove his cap again as Moya was coming up the drive.

She looked hurried and her clothes were wet. I could tell as her dress was soaked from the splash of slush. When I opened the door, she greeted me in a state of exhausted paleness. She wasn't due to make lunch for another two hours, but she was in a state of complete distress.

'Mr Bauer, I'm so sorry. Oh my God!'

'My dear, why are you sorry. You look dreadful! Please, come warm yourself by the fire.'

She followed me to the fireplace, but she wouldn't sit, so I chose to stand close to her with my back to the hearth.

'I don't know how to tell you this,' she said.

She was shaking, and I was in two minds as to whether to take hold of her to comfort her.

'Please sit down. Can I go to the kitchen and get you a tea or a coffee? Does your mother leave any spare clothes here? You're soaked to the skin.'

'I walked from the village through the slush and the remnants of snow.'

'Maybe something of Addie's might fit you.'

'I am drying here by the fire.'

'Look at your poor fingers! They're blue!'

She stopped shivering for a second to stare at me like she was suddenly suspicious of my kindness. I could sense the doubt enter her head, then she stepped away from me.

'Whatever has happened?' I asked.

'I was taken advantage of, Mr Bauer. It was the strangest thing. I was working at the hotel and the inspector called by. He wanted to speak to me in private, so I brought him to the room. We use it to change clothes and such. It's private, for staff only. He starts askin' me questions about you and Addie and this house, and what it is I do here now that Mother's sick. He asked me had you done anything to me … you know. And he was askin' me about Detective Steele. He wanted to know had I done anythin' with him.'

'Yes, and what on earth happened?'

'He kept on at me askin' the most intimate questions and I was really scared, Mr Bauer. I could smell the drink off him, and then he went to the door and turned the key. I cowered away to the corner of the room. He just stood over me, tellin' me that I would have to do certain things to gain your trust, and he was going to show me what I had to do. He's a big man, Mr Bauer. I was helpless against him. He dragged me across the floor and lifted me onto the bed and raped me over and over till I was sore. Anytime I cried out he hit me hard with his fist across the side of my face, then he told me that if I told anyone, he would kill me, and ruin the good name of my family. He kept slapping me and all I could think of was my poor sick mother.'

'I'll call the doctor and the police.'

'Jesus no, Mr Bauer. Please no, the shame of it will kill me. Whytie *is* the police, remember.'

'But he can't just do that to you and get away with it.'

Moya was staring into the yellow flames of the fire. Dolefully she said, 'He can, and he will.'

'I'm shocked!'

I wanted to hold her and protect her but she was too fragile, so after due consideration I agreed with her that she couldn't go home, not now with her mother so sick and she so hurt. I offered her Hedy's room for a few days, or at least till she got some rest. I was thinking that perhaps after a few days she might gain some perspective on the issue. But how can a woman get perspective on something so terrible as rape? I wanted to take the car and drive into the village. Whytie was most likely still hanging around in the hotel sobering up. I imagined myself standing up to him, though he was a bigger man than me. During the war I have done some routine self-defence. Now, I am not saying that I fancied myself in a fistfight with Inspector Whyte, but I could take care of myself if it came down to it. She agreed to stay and went to Hedy's room. I gave her some old clothes that Addie had put by for charity and Moya was grateful. She sat rigid on the bed, her youthful face ghostly white. Her lips had turned a soft pink against her paleness. I wanted to touch her but I didn't; I just didn't have the courage. I told her of my plans to go see the inspector and have it out with him.

'Please don't do that, Mr Bauer. It will only make matters worse. We must keep it a secret, for now at least. Please?'

I left her sitting on the bed and told her to sleep, that she may well feel a little better later as she was exhausted. I left the house and Jennings tipped his cap as I drove past. Normally I salute him back, but this day I hadn't the heart. I saw him stare after the car with his poor sad expression so clear through the rear-view mirror, but my mind was firmly fixed on the road ahead. I had to meet Dr Hammond down in St Michael's. There was something that troubled me greatly, so much so that Addie had grown tired of my complaining and began disputing things with me. In her mind we were doing so well with our big house, and we had good and mannerly servants. We had the lower lake as a backdrop to perfection, so why wasn't I happy in Ireland? Of course, I couldn't tell her of the blackmail, the lies, the deceit, though I did try to broach it with her, but she refused to listen, thinking it trite and somehow unusual. She had formed a liking for Dr Hammond, and though she wasn't overtly religious, she also had an affinity for Bishop Cassidy, thinking he was unique and clever.

At a house party in the bishop's residence one dark evening, the bishop insisted that he had found heaven. He made Addie accompany him to the loft to search the skies with his telescope. He contended that he had found a new planet. The bishop assured her that he named it heaven and went so far as to send messages to Rome about his discovery, but nobody cared a damn. The bishop kept the story going, and all the priests of his diocese read a specially written piece on his findings at Sunday mass. The parishioners were very respectful, but the word was out and the bishop became the subject of many jokes.

The doctor remained adamant that his project had to continue as it was in the children's best interests. Sure wasn't it the stuff of Casement and perhaps Pearse, but either way it wasn't anything to him because he preferred teenage boys with dark skin. He argued that if one took a mere moral stance, it could be argued this project might save thousands of normal kids from good families. The bishop, of course, had from the word go insisted on Catholic instruction. These children were welcomed into the church and their isolation was from the outside world only. My role was to examine them at regular intervals and write reports. I was responsible only for their mental and cognitive advancement. Their physical maturity was left to the nuns. The children, numbered from one to seven, consisted of two girls and five boys, but my information, if accurate, was that there were originally nine children. Two died early into the project; the doctor assured me that they were stillborn, and they were one of each sex. The world went on regardless, and I was to examine the children.

But Dr Hammond was in a dark humour. He was drinking his tea by the fire and he was sour. I could tell by his red face.

'You know, Hugo, people are funny creatures,' he said. 'We set this project up and we all agreed it was for the good. That's why we did it – for the common good. Let's take it as a given that our bishop is cuckoo, but back then he was no more cuckoo than either of us. Now some of them are full of doubt apparently. The bishop has gone too far. They're concerned about the children, saying it's no life, but for fuck's sake, Hugo, that's what it was all about! The idea is to groom children from birth to serve the needs of society and us men like we agreed – Whytie, Wade, Meaney, all of us. I knew we should never have trusted Meaney, fucking Blueshirt toe-rag, but the others! This is the danger when men start looking at the world through emotions, instead of their heads, my man. They're using this.' He pointed to his heart.

'You know I was compromised, otherwise I have grave doubts as to whether I would have stayed here. Ireland is not what I thought it would be.'

The doctor looked at me incredulously. 'Do you think I had anything to do with that?'

'I don't know. You were there.'

'I *was* there, but that was Whytie. They didn't trust you. You can see for yourself, Hugo. We have seven children here that don't officially exist. That's not something these people want made public. I have a scientific interest. I saw things in the Congo that would take all your hair out. I have no interest in the emotions. Personally I think now that maybe they're right. The project has run its course, what with the bishop's madness and Whytie pushing his weight around. I suppose it was never going to work, but you tell me what science project works straight away. How many trial runs does it take? Things couldn't be much worse. That idiot Witherspoon and his son took the children for a ride in the back of their meat truck. Seems they just took a notion. It hasn't gone down well. The children were terrified, by all accounts. Remember, these kids have never seen anything – not a sheep or a dog. They've not laid eyes on another child outside of their own group. It must have been torture!' Dr Hammond swilled the remains of his tea in his cup.

'So you expect me to trust you?'

'My dear Hugo, can you trust anyone else?'

'Maybe not, but why should I trust you?'

'Because I know these people were the wrong people to embark on such a project. They're a mixture of madmen and reactionaries. They don't understand the basic rules.'

'And what might they be?'

'Death, my German friend. If the Gods can give and take away life so cheaply, then what does the citizen do? He is forced to look at life coldly. There can only be morality within the frames of paradise, nowhere else. To be alive one day and be dead the next is the greatest stealer of liberty. Those who profess to retain morality are all followers of God – God, Hugo, this God, the murderer, the arbitrary killer of billions. He is the designer of morality after every mass murder. The victims are replaced. They die unknown and unremembered outside of their own kin. This is a random spread, Hugo, but all told it is mass murder, and for spurious reasons too, like lack of food, disease, malnutrition, accidents, war, and acts of God. You want to talk to me about morality? The world is designed for immorality, so why bother? What is it you don't get? Us in this tiny pocket of the globe reaching out – we are endeavouring to produce children for whom sexual activity is as normal as going to the toilet. Why other than to save the chosen children from the same fate. Is that worse than death, Hugo?'

The doctor bothered me, not because I agreed with him but because his logic was plausible. I had seen it with my own eyes in all that had happened in Hadamar. I was the least qualified to question his morality or that of his co-conspirators. I had disintegrated as a human being. Secretly I knew that Addie hadn't just taken Hedy to see her mother; she was getting away from me and from the countless nightmares on those cold nights of sleep disturbance.

Addie had urged me to go seek psychiatric help and confided in me that she feared that I was on the edge of a serious mental breakdown. What had I to do – own up about Biddy, admit that I had foolishly and in a weakened state succumbed to blackmail? Or was it a return to Germany that I feared most – a return to the domain of Hadamar? Just who was I to judge morality?

I examined the children both cognitively and neurologically. They were well. I was reassured, and they communicated just like any other children that I had encountered. Some were quiet and reserved, but others were loud and more exuberant. I felt the boys were more vociferous and willing to talk; the girls were sullen. Yet maybe they had the sense to realise that having a number and not a name was not normal. I performed some simple IQ tests and the results were above average. In all cases the girls outdid the boys, but it saddened me to see these children numbered one to seven, for they acted like normal children from any family. I wondered would they ever find contentment or the love they required. But all the while the events of Hadamar chastised me, scourging me, this little devil in my head whispering obscenities. I wanted to run away, yet I had no hiding place in my head. If only I could find a hiding place, one as far away as possible.

* * *

When I got home, I was perspiring. It turned to cold beads of sweat, which stuck to my forehead. All was quiet. Jennings had gone home. He had left a good fire and the house was warm and welcoming. I presumed that Moya was still upstairs and asleep, so I made myself some coffee. I could not stomach food.

I knocked gently on the door of Hedy's room. There was no answer and I was just about to turn and go when I heard her call out. She sat upright in the bed with her head propped by two pillows against the headboard. I thought she was looking better. Her face was starting to shine again, with the dullness of earlier receding.

'You are back early, Mr Bauer.'

'I came home to check on you.'

'You didn't go to the hotel?' she said fearfully.

'No, I did as you asked.'

'Good, I'm glad. Best left.'

I noticed a single tear race down her right cheek, so I went to sit on the bed in front of her. I took her hand to give her comfort.

'You are so kind,' she said, and the tear dissolved.

111

Her eyes were bright red around the edges, so I knew that she had been crying for some time.

'Hush now. Let me make you some tea. I'll whip you up some food. I make a mean goulash soup.'

'You're always talking about food. Why are Germans so interested in food?'

'No … well maybe, but this German makes a good goulash, and you are in dire need of nourishment. You get dressed. You can eat by the fire.'

She laughed suddenly, and it was so out of place with her general demeanour that I couldn't help but laugh too.

An hour later we sat downstairs by the fire. My goulash soup was good – I surpassed myself – Moya was full of compliments. I opened a bottle of French red, but she got tipsy after two glasses and kept apologising. I felt this sudden peace. It was something I hadn't felt for so long, not since I first met Addie, but that seemed so long ago now. The heat of the fire reignited Moya's skin; long gone was that pale look that was so debilitating. In many ways she was like a flower now, a flower that had been damaged by a storm, wounded but not dead, her petals becoming robust and full of colour once more.

Later, we walked upstairs together. I bent over to kiss her softly on the head, but she raised herself to meet my lips. I was shocked, so much so that my knees trembled. Moya pressed herself against me and I held her shoulders firm, holding her away from me like you would when chastising a child. But she leaned forward and kissed me again. I succumbed, my manhood was aroused. I was so hard and she was so soft.

I brought her to Hedy's bed and I concentrated on kissing her gaping mouth. She caressed me with her tongue. It ripped through mine painfully like she was using a blade and taking slices of my heart, but all through this she whispered, 'You are my love, my precious.' She lifted her hips and bottom so I could enter her more freely. When I gave her my sperm, she changed face. She was Addie for a second, and then she was someone else and I was lost. I didn't know if I was alive or dead, as the other face did not have a body like Moya. No, she was hideous and deformed. I stared into Johana's eyes and saw nothing but kindness that was replaced by a sudden terror.

21

'My father was a very complex man,' Hedy says. 'To understand him you need to research the times in which he lived. Even in his own notes and papers he admits to being an enigma. Part of his thesis was that human beings are neither good nor bad. He reckoned that all of us are a mixture of the two. He said we were products of our environment and that our experiences will dictate our behaviour in all our actions. You see, my father was neither a good nor a bad man. He was just a human being.'

I am stunned by her candour. I see she is old now. The lines on her neck continue down to her flat chest. I see her skin disintegrate before me. I want to iron her to make it better for her. I imagine the results. I imagine her all taut and healthy, just as she was long ago, and I search her eyes for signs of light, but they are dull and passionless. Is this the legacy of her life? Maybe it has scrubbed away all hope with a rough-toothed brush. I think she has the spirit of a charlady, though she lives in a house fit for a queen. So where is the justice in that?

When Arnold walks in I think he looks younger than before. He has lost weight, for sure. He eyes me contemptuously and in an outburst says, 'Did you check with Marcia Mellon?' I am stunned. I didn't, as it completely skipped my mind. There is no excuse, as Marcia is always around. There is no missing her face, but any conversations we have had are trite. Marcia is just plump and pleasant. I see no more to Marcia.

'What does she have to tell me?' I ask.

'You haven't spoken to her? Of course you never speak to anyone you should. You waste time on those useless types, Detective, the ones that can't help you. It's so long ago since my grandfather died. You want to destroy his reputation, but you don't want the truth. When I tell you to go see Marcia Mellon you don't, but then you come here on his anniversary to destroy him.'

'That's enough, Arnold.' Hedy says. 'The detective is trying to find out what happened to the girl. She has no interest in destroying my father. Anyway, by his own admission your grandfather's reputation was already ruined.'

'Why is that?'

Hedy looks at me. 'You didn't read his notes then?'

'No, I just read Mary's research.'

Arnold takes a seat. He acts like a spoiled child who has just felt the wrath of his mother.

'Julia read them all. I didn't read all them – just the important ones, like the one about the bullet he shot into his brain,' he says venomously.

'What has Marcia to tell me?' I ask.

He looks at me blankly like he doesn't get what I am saying.

'Marcia hears lots of stuff. She is good at her job. If people say anything, Marcia hears it.'

Hedy looks away from me and into the fire. The heat goes all around the room. I see the flames light Arnold's face, and when he turns away all goes dark. But Hedy is the opposite; the fire flicker shows her skin to be as pale as I have ever witnessed. She is devoid of blood and only her deadly eyes support any flicker of life.

'I was nine years old. His feet were still lying inside the boathouse, his head on the frosty path leading to the jetty. My father's blood was still pumping, so dark and thick, and not like you would think blood should look like at all. His hand was solid from the bitter cold and the gun was stuck fast to his fingers. I think the frost acted like a kind of glue. He had no expression, Detective. There was, as the Irish might say, 'no look on his face'. He was dead and that was it – like those deer that Arnold shoots. As dead as that.'

I want to go to her and give her a hug, but Arnold's presence stops me. I am hesitant now. For me this is a strange place to be, not knowing what to say, as I am never stuck for words.

'Marcia Mellon knows all about Terence Fleming and she will solve your case.' Arnold isn't looking at me as he speaks; he is staring at his mother.

'He killed his two wives, so Julia says, and Julia knows. She told Marcia, but Marcia knew already.'

'I'll speak to Marcia.'

'I shoot deer in season. I never shoot deer outside season, not like Terence Fleming and other people I know. I was there when your jeep got shot up and I saw who shot at it. They shouldn't have been hunting deer – the season hadn't started yet. But that crowd are always up to no good. I saw them as clear as day, Detective, just like I'm looking at you now.'

'Who?'

'That day I saw Terence Fleming and the sergeant shooting deer when the season hadn't started. The sergeant breaking the law! That's this country for you.'

'You saw who shot up my jeep?'

Arnold was looking at me again. 'Yes!'

'Who was it?'

'Really, come on.'

Hedy pleads with me. She is indicating that Arnold isn't reliable.

You told me before he was reliable.

'The sergeant shot up your jeep. He was very careful just to shoot up the jeep and not you. He's a crack shot, Detective. If he wanted to shoot you he'd have got you right between the eyes.'

'Why would the sergeant wanna shoot up my jeep?'

'Dunno. Go ask him. I bet Julia knows.'

I think he is done but then he says, 'Ask Marcia Mellon. She knows all about it.'

'Go get a coffee!' Hedy commands and Arnold, obedient as ever, does what his mother asks.

'His long-term memory is great, Detective, but you can't rely on anything else he says. He is perpetually confused. He most likely thinks the sergeant shot up your jeep only because he saw him out in the woods that day. He saw Terence Fleming too, and is just associating everything that he saw that day.'

'I agree.' But, I think to myself, the sergeant never said he was in the woods that day.

* * *

Marcia Mellon sticks her robust face over the counter.

'I think that cold spell has passed now.'

'They say it has … for now anyhow.' I am easy with her.

'Whiskey?'

'Nah, I'll go a beer.'

'Yeah, too early for a whiskey.'

'Depends on the day.'

'Yeah,' she says, getting me a beer from the cooler.

'Is Moya around?'

'No, she's gone to Longford to see her niece.'

'Oh, is that a regular thing?'

'It's not. They don't get on, but apparently her niece phoned her out of the blue. She wants to see her and make up, like.'

'Was their fall-out serious?'

'I dunno. Moya didn't say. She's quiet about her business.'

'I guess.'

Marcia gives me a glass with ice, but I empty the ice back into the sink.

'Annoys my teeth,' I say. 'I really need to see a dentist.'

'John Cadden, here in the village,' Marcia says, swanning away with a dirty cloth in her hand.

I am idle, so I drink the beer. It's already very cold from the cooler, so I am doubly glad I got rid of the ice. I think about John Cadden, the dentist. Why am I surprised the village has a dentist? It isn't big enough to support a dentist *and* a doctor *and* a hotel. It is, as the hinterland stretches for thirty miles in any direction; to many locals this place is the centre of the universe. Many people set off down muddy tracks and trek up hills and down dale, and these lonely souls see Lough Lyn as the place where it all happens. Yes, this tiny village, with its Spar and small hotel and few grotty pubs – this is their Mecca.

Marcia is back. She is scrubbing the counter with her dirty cloth.

'I was talking to Arnold,'

'My ex?' She smiles.

'Yeah, he's a funny fella, isn't he?'

'Only since his diagnosis. He was a fine chap when I went out with him.'

'I'd say he was.'

'He was. We went everywhere together. We took his boat out on the lake and I went with him when he was shooting in the woods. You know, we were going to get married, but then my parents sold this place to Moya and my father died and things sort of changed after that. Hedy never took to me either and then he met Julia. I think Hedy thought Julia was something, so Arnold and me, we moved on, like.'

'When did he get sick?'

'About a year after he married Julia. It was devastating. She was expecting then.'

'Really?'

'Yeah, she lost it. They say it was due to all the excitement – all the worry.'

'Sad.'

'Yeah. What about the sergeant and Terence Fleming. Arnold was rambling on about how you could tell me lots about them.'

'Really? So he still talks about me? When I was with Arnold he was strong and athletic but since his illness he has weakened. He was once a big bull full of muscle, but now he's made of cardboard, he has changed that much. Arnold would go shooting in the woods and try to outdo the sergeant, then Terence Fleming when he came here. He has a thing about them, you know. It's just competitive stuff between men, harmless. The sergeant is always good to him, but Terence just keeps to himself. That's Terence. He's quiet and enigmatic. Women love him because he is sullen and rude. Terence lives in his own secret world. He wouldn't be good to the likes of poor Arnold, like he might pass him by without a word if they met in the woods.'

115

'Poor Arnold!'

'Yeah, not that he was a saint in his day either.'

'So how do you regard Terence?'

'I just told you.' She laughs and pretends to clean by the cash register, but her heart isn't in it. Marcia turns back to me slowly. 'I had a fling with him when he first came here. It didn't last long. To be honest I found him a bit weird. I think Terence spends too many nights alone out by the lake and likes to try things, you know?'

I want to say yes, I know, but I don't utter a word. 'What do you mean?' I say.

'He's a writer. All of those writers have no morals. He is very persuasive and controlling, like in a subtle way.'

'Why do you think Julia says he killed both his wives?'

'Does she say that?'

'She does.'

'Why would she say that? Sure Terence was never married. Maybe Julia is coming out in sympathy with Arnold.'

'Maybe she is.'

There is a pause and Marcia pretends to clean the counter again. She lifts her head slowly, and now I see her not as she is but as she once was. I remove her plumpness and swollen eyes, and I see that Marcia was once very attractive. I feel the surge of her youth as it reappears; it is accompanied by a wave of desperation. Her hands are outstretched; they grab hard to recover what was lost. It is as if her fingernails are scraping at my soul.

'You know about the room?' Marcia asks.

'Yes, Moya told me her husband used to drink down there.'

'Terence used to go there and cry. Many a night I woke in his bed only to feel the empty space and I could hear him sobbing. He just sat down there for hours crying. When I asked him about it, he just laughed it off, like he was in denial. He used to make me feel like those tears never happened.'

We are interrupted by the arrival of a crowd. The sergeant and Paula are followed by Dolan and Georgina. And they, in turn, have a posse of underlings in their trail. Dolan orders pots of coffee for his troops and makes it clear to Marcia that the sergeant and Paula can take care of themselves. The coffee is on him but only for his crew.

'It's the body of Biddy Foley. She vanished many years ago. We got her through dental records archived from the county mental asylum. She just went missing, never to be seen again.'

Dolan checks to see if Marcia has the coffee numbers right.

'How did she die?' I ask.

Dolan gives me his usual 'what the hell are you doing here' look. I am anxious to calm his screeching voice, so as to return it to some normal decibel range.

He goes on, 'She was murdered by a blunt instrument over the back of the head. She was just a child, but we suspect that she was sexually abused for some time as her father killed himself some months later. I expect he was responsible – but we need to do some more research. You'll be glad, Detective Swan, that it's proven now – it isn't your Mary.'

Indeed, I am glad, but that good news is tinged with sadness. What had happened to Mary and would the truth ever emerge? It had gone on so long that folk no longer cared. Poor Biddy. So the research was true. It certainly wasn't Biddy's father who killed her. Mary had opened a can of worms with her work.

The sergeant interrupts. 'We'll keep looking, Detective. There's no way the case is closed.'

'Keep looking? I think you people stopped looking some time ago!'

The sergeant hesitates and gives me a foul look. Marcia serves him a whiskey and Paula a coffee.

'We have lots of other things to do, but the case is still open.'

I go for it. 'Arnold says he saw you shoot up my jeep.'

The sergeant stops in his tracks. I expect his face to go a glowing red, but it stays white and calm.

'I was one of the people who argued that Arnold should keep his gun licence after he got sick. Fishing and shooting were his life, but some others wanted to take it off him. They said he was a danger to himself and to the public. What you just said makes me think I was wrong to argue on his behalf. A man hallucinating when carrying a rifle is a dangerous thing.'

The sergeant moves away and I look over my shoulder as he chats to Paula. I can barely hear, but they are not talking about Arnold or anything that I am familiar with.

* * *

I take a drive up to the lake and enjoy it for a change. The slush has gone and for once the road is dry. The jeep takes the bends and curves confidently. I think the lake is happier too. Gone is that dour grey look and today it has hints of blue. The birds are scratching its white foamy surface as if they have just found a new floating runway. The normally dark islands look fresher and complete, and even the roadside foliage has shaken itself down, readying itself for the advent of spring.

The cabin looks good. Has Mike treated the wood with stain? He did say he might. Bruce hears me coming and barks. Mike is cleaning the windows. He is using a chair and a stepladder for the higher bits. He smiles all the way to the jeep and opens the door.

'How's it going, stranger?'

'Good,' I say sheepishly. 'Have you heard? They identified those bones they found.'

'Oh!' He is alarmed.

'It's not Mary. Some poor kid from years ago. She was murdered by the police, but Dolan thinks her old man did it.'

'Wow! I best get back to Dublin – it's much safer!' He laughs.

Bruce joins us and sniffs around my boots.

'Where's Terence?'

'Where do you think.' Mike winks.

'Cooking?'

'Got it in one. He's doing a rabbit stew. He's going to pack some supplies for tomorrow. We're going on an adventure in the upper forest in the morning. He thinks he'll finally shoot a deer up that way.'

'Let's hope he doesn't meet his wives up there.'

'Who?'

'Nothing.'

Mike laughs and puts his arm gently around my shoulder to guide me inside.

Terence is glad to see me. I know because he beams at me from beyond the counter. Bruce takes to the fire, even though it is abnormally low and only one big wet log hisses all lonely like.

'Coffee?' Terence asks.

'Nah, I fancy a beer.'

'Beer's in the fridge,' he says and continues working.

Mike is back outside scrubbing the windows.

'Moya was tellin' me about her husband and that room of yours,' I say to Terence.

I go to the fridge and take out a beer, but Terence can't hear me with the buzzing noise of the open fridge and I can't hear him with the sizzle of the cooker. We are a right pair.

'I said Moya was telling me about her husband – him drinking in the room down below,' I say again.

Terence stays quiet, concentrating on stirring his food. He must have lots as he is using a huge pot.

'Moya tells that one well!' Terence says.

He walks around the counter and I see he is wearing a man's apron – at least it has male designs all over it, bits of metal and wheels and hammers and axes.

'It was Moya who spent her time down there, not her husband. He drank all right, but nothing like Moya drank.'

'You serious? Moya built that place for herself?'

He is at the fridge taking a beer.

'Yeah, Moya is what we'd call a functioning alcoholic. Her husband was a saint by comparison – that's according to those who know, like Marcia Mellon.'

'I see.'

'Move that jacket off the stool, Avril. Rest your bum.'

I do, and I see he is pleased. I am relaxing. Suddenly all my doubts about Terence are lifting. He is acting normal, as if he has nothing to hide.

'Marcia Mellon was talking about you too. She said you dated for a while.'

'Dated? We had sex, she means.'

'Whatever.'

'Women always dress things up. That's why it kills me. We had sex three times, maybe four, but we never, as they say, *dated*. It must make it sound better for her.'

22

1949

She was pushing hard against his chest, pleading with Whytie to release her, to let her go. Moya wanted him to tell her that he was only joking, but it was too late for that. She had a scrape about an inch long on her right cheek, just where Whytie had slapped her. She felt it stinging. She felt his nail catch in the groove of her skin. Moya was mortified, but Whytie seemed drawn by her terrified look. She kept on pleading with him to stop.

'This is what I want you to do – make Bauer beg you for it.'

Whytie was on his knees. She could feel his breath. He was panting like an old dog in need of a drink. Moya, dazed, thought Whytie looked odd without his clothes. His naked torso didn't match the gravitas of the overall man. If anything he looked wimpish and immature. The whole of his body was without hair, and he was strangely aware of his shortcomings; he seemed very concerned for himself. She tried to reason with him, but Whytie stopped only to remove his pants from his ankles. She was convinced his legs were made of rubber.

'You're wastin' your time, girl. There's not a sinner will believe you, invitin' a man to your room. Sure it's not a thing a good Catholic girl would do.'

'I'll say nuthin'. Just go now and I'll say nuthin'. Nobody need know. Please go before it's too late. I promise, Inspector. Please.'

But Whytie pinned her down, bruising her arms as he took her without mercy. Moya's screams were muffled by his power over her. Each time she cried out he slapped her harder.

'This is the way that Bauer likes it.'

Whytie thrust deeper, making Moya cry out; terrified, she awaited another slap.

* * *

Dan Steele ate his cereal. He was disappointed that Moya wasn't there. The old lady did her best, but she couldn't compete with Moya. Detective Steele was bold enough to ask about his new muse.

'We're short-staffed this morning. Poor Moya has gone home sick.'

'Really? I hope it's nothing too bad.'

'Women's issues!' She gave a nervous giggle. 'You're late, Detective. I thought you were lying in due to the snow,' the old lady offered.

'The snow isn't a problem for me.'

'Now, full Irish. No point in standing on ceremony. You're the last for breakfast.'

'Full Irish, mam! Sounds just the thing on a such a wintry morning.'

'Great,' the old woman said. 'I'll get you the *Irish Independent*.'

Steele watched her walk away. He knew that all was fine, so he started to organise his day.

He was thinking the gods were against him as he skidded twice, the second time on the long road that led to the diocesan house. It looked a picture in the snow, the tower pointing to the sky like an illuminated Christmas tree. Getting out of the car, he shook himself like a wet dog. Water was still dripping, seeping onto the mat, as he stepped into the hall. The butler couldn't have cared less.

Steele thought he was rude for a butler. He was an old guy who had been butlering since the year dot. He had the attitude of a servant but the pomposity of a master.

'The maid will mop it up,' he remarked before beckoning the detective to follow him through a heavy oak door into the huge library.

'His Grace will be with you shortly,' he announced.

He closed the doors and the detective got this cold feeling of being alone. It was funny. He was thinking of Moya. One bright smile and a sneaky kiss on her way out of the room was enough to warm him for the night. He hadn't needed the hot water bottle in the end, such was the steam she aroused within him. He missed her when she left and when he woke that morning, he missed her even more, which was most unlike him as normally he didn't give much thought to women. But there was something about Moya that made his stomach ache. He wondered should he call Malone and make an excuse to go home. Yes, maybe that was the thing to do. He knew that his heart was instructing him to run away before he got hurt. After all, what does a girl's kiss and smile mean. She was most likely just being friendly. These folks weren't going to release any secrets, not to him anyhow. It was all a waste of time, but he promised himself to ask Moya for a date before the day was out. He imagined himself asking her, only to be refused at least twice, but on the third go, in his mind's eye, she said yes.

Steele got back to the job in hand. The girl went missing; she was probably dead and she was murdered by these people for sure, so what was the point. Malone only went by results. He didn't do long stories. There were no hard lucks for him. It was always 'get me a result' at all costs. Steele decided to call him with a plausible get-out story when he got back to the hotel.

Cassidy didn't look like a bishop. He didn't look much like anything at all. Steele looked down at this small man. He was out of uniform and looked as if he had been disturbed while he was painting a room.

'I'm cleaning the lens in my telescope, a challenging task, Detective. Make one mistake or scratch and then we have problems.'

'Very delicate work indeed.'

'You're a brave man, Detective. This weather wouldn't entice you to be out. The roads are treacherous. So what pressing matter brings you to see me?'

'I'm looking into the disappearance of Biddy Foley.'

'Aah, sad case – sad family, I'm afraid.'

'Yes, so it seems. I'm informed you drove a man – Hugo Bauer – to their cottage on the night the girl disappeared.'

'Yes, that's right. Sorry, I never offered you a drink. It's freezing, will you go a brandy? Come on, I'll join you. They say a brandy heats the senses. It'll help me remember better. Now, Detective, you're right, but you are also wrong. Here, get that down you. I don't drive, but yes, my driver did drop Hugo off at the cottage that evening and I went along for the ride. I often do – it kills the boredom.'

He drank his brandy straight down. Steele nursed his but was glad of its heat. The bishop was right – it warmed him up and he viewed the world with greater clarity.

'Why did Hugo go there at all?'

The bishop poured himself another brandy. 'Because I asked him to go visit. You see, the Foleys had serious issues – mental illness, poverty, lack of education. The father and mother were illiterate and Bauer is an expert in eugenics. I wanted him to observe. There would be no point in sending him over in the light of day, as Bram Stoker says. The vampires only come out at night and I wanted him to see the family at their worst.'

'And did he?'

'Yes, he did. He spoke to me in great detail about his observations later.'

'Oh, I see.'

'I'm eternally grateful to him for that.'

'I see. So what did he find that was so enlightening, considering that this girl went missing that same night?'

'Steady, Detective. I don't see that Bauer's report had anything to do with the girl going missing. She just ran off – she ran away.'

'Where did she go? She had no money, no clothes. You say she was mentally ill. How far would she get?'

'I'm beginning to sense some malice in your tone, Detective, which I do not like, I might add. The girl ran. Perhaps Bauer unnerved her. She just ran. Maybe she got lost in the woods. Maybe she died of the cold or hunger. Who knows!'

'Did you order search parties to look for her?'

'Me?'

'I thought it would be your responsibility considering you sent Bauer to see her.'

'The police do search parties, Detective, not the church. We don't do stuff like that.'

'Okay, thanks for your time – oh, and thanks for the brandy ... Hey, I have another question.'

'Yes?'

'Why were other people at the cottage that night. I get Hugo Bauer and all of this eugenics stuff, but why was Wade, the politician, there, and Dr Hammond ... and why were two garda there and the inspector?'

'I dunno, Detective. You should ask them.'

The road back was full of snow. The heavens opened and the entire world turned white. Steele was a mile from the village when the lights went out. A vehicle came up beside him and ran him into the ditch. He didn't know what was going on, but soon he knew he was in deep trouble. It wasn't like anything he had seen before. He knew by the way the fellas took him from the car that he was on a hiding to nothing. His mind racing, he knew these boys wanted him for something, but there was no way they were gonna tell him what they wanted, not at least until he was tired and sore. There were two of them, big burly sorts. One was a horrible country fellow with an agricultural accent. He kept laughing like he was taking part in a game. They put a sack over Steele's head and he hadn't a clue where they brought him. It wasn't that far from where they picked him up, maybe ten or fifteen minutes from where they bushwhacked his car. He kept telling himself to keep calm, to remember everything he had ever learned. He could call on everything that Malone had taught him, all he had learned over the years. They tied him fast to a chair and Steele tried to speak. Then they ripped the sack off his head and he was blinded by a light. Another man stood in the shadows. It was Whytie. Steele knew it was him by his profile but when he spoke it was a dead giveaway. The detective went to speak but one of the men stuffed a bandage into his mouth. Steele thought he would choke and started to gag, but the man removed it partially so he could just about breathe.

'Naughty boy, Detective. An if you try ta speak again I'll have your mouth stuffed. You'll smother and die. You're such a naughty boy. It makes no difference to me if you live or die. I just want you to know that.

Malone will get a message that you were killed in an accident – the car skidded in the snow – and by de time help arrived you were dead. Are you with me? Just nod if you understand.'

Whytie came closer till at last Steele saw his ghostly face. It was distorted by the lamplight. Steele was reminded of a child holding a torch to their chin under the bedcovers, making monsters.

'You come here askin' daft questions, eh? And then you decide to eye up one of our prized women. That, I'm afraid, Detective, is an act of war – an act of the aggressor. The pesky commies raped half of Europe five years ago. You come here wantin' to do de same. That makes you our legitimate prisoner.'

Steele tried to nod his head to appease Whytie and buy himself some time.

'See the bucket over here behind me?' The detective nodded in its direction. 'What do you think is in it?'

Steele rolled his eyes to indicate that he didn't know.

'Easy, Detective. It's bleach. It's a bucket of bleach, beautiful cleansin' pure bleach. Do you know what you're goin' to do? You're goin to drink it. Joe here will feed it to you timble by timble. Just think of it as a measure of the hard stuff.'

Steele struggled, but the man closest stuffed the bandage back into his mouth till he couldn't breathe. On Whytie's instruction the man partially removed it again. The detective was shaking. He felt like his brain was about to burst.

The man called Joe went to the bucket and filled his whiskey measure with bleach. Steele could smell it as Joe brought it to his lips, the hypnotic fumes powering up his nasal passages and into his brain. Steele shook his head violently like he was having a seizure.

'Drink it!' Whytie said. 'There's a good boy. Drink it.'

The bleach scorched the detectives tongue and he screamed. Joe stopped pouring so he didn't swallow any.

'Come on, Detective. There's a whole bucket and I won't be happy till it's gone.'

Steele's tongue was burnt raw. He went to speak but he couldn't shape the words.

'Now, if you were to change sides, Detective, maybe I'll get Joe here to mop the floor with that bleach instead.'

The man with the agricultural accent laughed, but Whytie turned on him and told him to shut up. The man stopped immediately.

'Can you change sides?' Whytie asked.

Joe went to pour the bleach again.

'Yes!' The words formed miraculously.

'Good man. So we can count on you to fill out a good report on Lough Lyn?'

'Yes, if you want me to.'

'I need someone I can trust, Detective. I could have other jobs too – like I might need you to do somethin' that I wouldn't trust any of these yokels to do. But you must do what I tell you. No argument or conscience, do you hear me?'

'Yes.'

Steele's tongue was sore for days, he had great difficulty speaking. He was cold and damp tied to the chair. They only released him to use a makeshift toilet in the corner of the dark room.

Whytie hadn't come by since the first day. He left Steele guarded by Joe and his agricultural crony and, sometimes, just Joe on his own. They brought him food that was pretty decent. He begged them for ice cold water to try to reduce the swelling on his tongue. At first Joe laughed and said no, but then he relented and brought him a cup with water and ice cubes. Steele held the ice cubes on his tongue and, despite the intense pain at first, the after-effect was soothing. He could feel the swelling reduce each time they brought the water to him.

The detective tried hard to think, to plan. What would Malone do? Surely if he hadn't made contact Malone would smell a rat and send someone to look for him. Joe obviously had other things to do and the door was locked for hours, with Steele sat tied to his chair in the darkness. But Moya was his saviour; he saw her face in his mind's eye. If she knew of his fate, how distraught would she be? Maybe she wouldn't care. In her world horrors like this didn't exist. Her mind was full of the things of spring, full of life and growth and positivity, not the murky world that Whytie threw his dark cape over. They had killed Biddy Foley and now they were covering it up.

For the first time Steele came to a realisation: his only hope was to make an exchange with Whytie. They were all involved – the German, the politicians, the doctor and even the bishop. What was it that Whytie wanted him to do? Sell his soul? This sad fact came with the realisation that it was most unlikely that Whytie would allow him to live no matter what deals were struck. Steele began to see the full picture. He was, in all reality, a dead man. It would only be a matter of time before Whytie pulled the plug. The detective knew too much, and the world outside couldn't know about it. Their lives and reputations depended on it. No, his only realistic chance was to escape. He must get out of this room by hook or by crook or he would end up in a body bag. His tongue burned once more. Steele listened for any sound outside but there was none. How could he overpower his captors when he was tied so tight? Outside of Whytie, the others were amateurs, but how could he wrestle free from these ropes that cut into his skin like chains?

23

1944

The view from my bungalow was not impressive. There was a small grass garden and a pathway leading to the road, but the interior was clean. Basically it had all the mod cons, but the kitchen was too small for me. I didn't like the sink as the porcelain interior was chipped; I could imagine germs breeding in the cracks. Elsewhere, I thought the tables and chairs were cheap. I got the feeling that my landlord had gone shopping for bargains. There was low-grade furniture everywhere filling countless useless alcoves.

I was mad. I didn't come from much. My people were not rich, but they were proper. We didn't like waste, and my mother kept our home very clean and tidy. I suppose that I just wasn't happy here. Sometimes I must admit I enjoyed looking from a height, so maybe it was all down to this ground-level bungalow, as all was neat and flat – and boring. My neighbours were old. Mrs Schmitt was a big fat woman and she and her husband were very happy with their tiny lawn. They had a small poodle that crapped and barked all day long. He could have used their garden but somehow my lawn made a better toilet. He crapped on my lawn at every opportunity. One day, on my way to the hospital, I stood in it and all that white goo stuck to the sole of my shoe. I had to wet an old mopping cloth. I removed the outer crust easily, but the goo had stuck to the grooves at the base of my shoe. I was half an hour cleaning up, with that awful smell wafting up my nose. I wanted to be sick but there was nothing to vomit – I hadn't eaten for days.

* * *

Conrad Bischof sent a car for me around midday and I was driven slowly and lazily to the hospital. The driver stopped at the same place, just beyond the railway bridge in a little siding on the left. He told me he was drinking some coffee that his mother made, but I could smell the whiskey.

'Coffee keeps me awake, Herr Bauer.'

'Yeah, and whiskey puts you to sleep.'

The driver laughed, like he was trying hard to break my silence.

The hospital was busy as the train had brought some German veterans. Most of these men were suffering from shell shock while others had amputations. I saw lines of children, too. Many had amputations to their arms or legs – a bleak picture! Then the grey buses arrived and they went directly into the garages.

The reception for these people was indoors and out of sight. These were mainly people with intellectual disabilities, but it also included those with natural deformities. It was in this area that I was to oversee and consult. Nurse Annett showed me to her office, which was just a small functional room; the corridor leading to it was unusually long. Through its tiny windows I could see the plumes of smoke from a large chimney that was spouting thick clouds of dark gas. I noticed the passing white clouds were annexed by these cumulus black predators. The air was sweet, yet poisonously so.

Nurse Annett met me at the door.

'Heil Hitler!' She released her right arm. Her salute was solemn and true.

'Heil Hitler!'

She studied me to test my conviction. Satisfied, she said, 'Welcome back to Hadamar. Conrad sends his apologies. He has some personal business to attend to. His daughter is getting married. She is, as they say, excitable.' Nurse Annett smiled and when she did, she was very attractive. I knew she was older than me, but not by much. I kept searching her face for traces of wisdom that never materialised.

'I see you are receiving many new patients' I said. 'Will you cope?'

Her face got serious. 'Look at that photograph, Dr Bauer. No, the one on the wall by the door. See how we celebrated! We had reached a figure of ten thousand, so we celebrated by drinking beer and wine because we have shown these people the ultimate mercy.'

'Yes, I see.'

I got up from my chair to study the photograph. I saw the hospital staff wearing their white coats. They were laughing and smiling. Nurses were pouring wine into glasses, and white-coated doctors were cheering on as they frolicked in the sun. It scorched the grassy area outside the building where I stood.

'The people outside just now – they are Jews, no?'

'No, they are German, but they are beyond help, Dr Bauer. The war has destroyed them and their families. Those children are the same. Some have had their legs blown off and others have no arms. Even worse, many of them have lost hope. Their families are dead, so they have nobody to care for them. These children live in this awful state of madness.'

'So what is our plan for them, Nurse Annett?'

'We don't use the gas chamber for our own, Dr Bauer. We will put them to sleep mercifully. As you know, we have the drugs for it. I administer the drugs myself usually. I feel it is right for me to set an example. I must show my subordinates what it means to serve your country.' She beamed at me proudly.

'And the others on the grey buses?'

'They are your concern. They're the handicapped and the disturbed. Many of them are Jews, so they are the enemies of the Reich. The fitter-looking ones are Polish labourers who we have no need for now. We can't afford to feed these people.'

'So I am to oversee your work?'

'Yes, Dr Bauer, that is the plan.'

'So tell me about the procedure?'

'We examine each one on arrival. Our doctors check their overall health, then we use one of three stickers like this.'

She showed me three different coloured rolls of stickers lying side by side on her desk. The first read 'KILL', the second read, 'KILL AND REMOVE BRAIN FOR RESEARCH'. The third read, 'KILL AND EXTRACT GOLD TEETH'.

* * *

Conrad invited me to his house for dinner. He owned a large house in a leafy area in the outskirts of Hadamar. The street was lined with chestnuts and oaks. Many of these trees were very old and had fat trunks. His house sported a huge garden to the front, but down the side the lawn narrowed and linked to a small orchard. I was thinking that Conrad would be glad of such a large garden when his grandchildren came along. He was expecting a posse of grandchildren after his daughter completed her nuptials.

'It's what makes a man!' he informed me. 'To me this is why we fight this war – to preserve the German way of life. The Americans and the British are into divorce, but Germans still believe in family, isn't that right, Hilda?'

His wife looked at me painfully. She had heard Conrad rant many times before and he was becoming tiresome.

'My daughter is everything to me,' Conrad continued. 'I say to her, I say *Anna, if the Lord wishes, you will marry Eric and you will be blessed with the most beautiful children*. Yes?'

'Yes, Father,' Anna said. She was small and petite, and not particularly well built for child bearing but I wasn't about to burst Conrad's bubble. 'When Eric gets back from the front, we will marry, Father, and that will make you happy at last.' She ate her bread like a child, taking only tiny mouthfuls to chew.

Hilda, however, was heifer-like in comparison to her daughter. Amazingly, a woman of her size had borne just one child. She proved that she had the appetite of a cow, too, as she was on her main course already.

'So tell me, Dr Bauer, what do you think of our operation?' Conrad asked.

'Oh dear,' Hilda said, 'I don't think Dr Bauer wants to talk about work.'

'On the contrary, Hilda. Isn't that why I invited him along? I need to get his opinion. He will be reporting on us to Dr Brack. I am so looking forward to a sneak preview.'

Conrad poured water for himself and his wife, but Anna helped herself to a bottle of beer. She politely passed one to me. I was pleased that she had chilled a few bottles in the ice bucket.

I hesitated. 'It's a very efficient operation!'

'See, I told you,' Conrad said, turning to Hilda who shied away from him to stare at her plate of food.

'But in view of the official status of the T4 programme, I think it's better not discussed at the dinner table,' I said with authority.

'You see.' Hilda glared at Conrad who was having none of it.

'Dr Bauer, we are all friends here, my wife and daughter are as committed to the cause as anyone and we are working so hard in the hospital to comply with the aims of the T4 programme, your opinion is vital to me. I'm anxious to keep my workers motivated and what better way to do it than by bringing back a good news story about our progress.'

I stopped eating and took a sip of my beer. It tasted good, and it eased the dryness in my throat.

'I'm not making myself clear, Conrad. It is forbidden to discuss the workings of the T4 programme outside of the business environment. All of us could be severely reprimanded by the Gestapo for breaking this rule. But I will certainly visit your office tomorrow when at the hospital to discuss this with you further. I hope you won't take offence.'

Anna smiled at me. It was a smile that said thanks rather than that she was taking anything humorous from my tirade.

'Yes, well all right. When you put it like that,' Conrad said, yet to be convinced by me.

'Indeed,' Hilda remarked.

'Dr Bauer is correct, of course. We don't want to be annoying the Gestapo now, do we?'

She laughed but nobody else did. They all just continued eating.

* * *

I was thinking of Addie in my pitch-dark room. I turned on the bedside light, wondering if she was sleeping or if she was lying awake deep into the night. Were her thoughts as dark as mine? What was it we hoped to achieve? We were systematically murdering human beings, and why? Because they weren't perfect. But they could never be perfect. Just because we decided, through some weird and obscure formula, that their offspring couldn't be one hundred per cent normal. What was normal anyway? Yes, there was part of the scientific me that could equate with Darwinism and the survival of the fittest, but did Darwin want us to manually intervene. Had he intended us to suppress nature and the natural environment? Why were we branching out? Was it partly retribution? Why were we murdering prisoners of war after years of forced labour when their bodies were spent? We were gassing them, pulling out their gold teeth, and worse still, removing their brains, Kill, Kill and kill again. What insane world was I not only a part of but actively engaged in the continuance of? I should have reported back to Dr Brack and told him of these despicable murders I was witnessing of men, women and children, and all for what? For Hitler and for the Reich, for Germany.

I made myself tea and I sat by the window, watching the daylight arrive. It came quietly, like it was bored with its repetitive self. These countless days returning to burn brightly, before dying out. Perhaps night was just a pause in the inferno. My thoughts said that some bright day I too would die, that I would be at the mercy of God. Nurse Annett was convinced she was engaged in acts of mercy, so much so that she injects the patients herself. She administered the dark, evil capsule and watched on as the children went to eternal sleep. There would be no more days for them. So why had Nurse Annett assumed the role of God? How could she be soulless and without conscience? I was worse than she was as I sat and observed. Could I redeem those lines of broken spirits that stole by in the hope that I wouldn't see them with the death stickers pinned to their coat lapels.

I watched their grey, ashen faces move into the dull light, while some handsome young doctor shouted, 'Next.'

I watched the poodle shit on my side of the tiny fence and wanted to go see Mrs Schmitt to complain, but her husband limped out to collect the dog. He picked up the poodle and kissed it warmly on the cheek.

My driver arrived.

'Today, my friend, I'm in a hurry so don't stop for coffee please,' I said.

He didn't answer properly. All I heard was this gruff sound, but he didn't stop either.

I was brought directly to Conrad Bischof's office and was not surprised to find that it was much nearer the main entrance than Nurse Annett's. Conrad was busy sorting papers. I don't think he was too pleased to see me. He looked hurt.

'Dr Bauer.'

'Yes, Conrad. I apologise for interrupting your busy day, but I thought I'd drop by to continue last night's conversation.'

'Oh yes, of course. Here, do take a seat. I'll order you tea or coffee.'

'No, that's not necessary.'

'Ah, but you will. I know you, Dr Bauer. You are too polite.'

He got up, went to the office door and barked out his instruction to a passing nurse. She didn't reply. She just raced off at speed to meet his request.

'I'm leaving this evening on the seven o'clock train. I'll visit the depot once more before I leave, but I intend to include this in my report. You know, Conrad, whatever way we treat our own who have met with misadventure or through accident or birth defect, we have no right to murder innocent civilians or, indeed, prisoners of war. I intend to write this in my report to Dr Brack.'

Conrad looked at me horrified. Somehow he suspected I was playing a terrible black joke. He settled himself in his chair.

'You can't do that,' he said.

'It is my intention. I'd take photographs only that is expressly forbidden.'

'Nah.' Conrad gave a nervous laugh. 'You must have coffee. It will help you to realise that all you say is wrong. Wrong! We are being merciful here at this institution. This is not, as you say, murder. Look at me, I am a family man. I would not stand over murder. We are putting these people to sleep. They are no longer any good for themselves or for society. In a hundred years people will say that what we did at Hadamar was a good thing – a good thing for Germany and for the world.'

A nurse arrived with two coffees.

* * *

This young doctor wasn't so handsome. He shouted just the same.

'Next!'

A little old man with a grey head came forward. His eyes were dull and partially closed. He was bent forward. Not fully lifting his head, he remained in a stoop.

'Name?'

The grey old man gave his name in Polish.

I searched the line beyond him. My attention was caught by two older women. They were followed by a younger woman who was missing an eye and had a nasty twitch. Behind her were two sullen young men. One was almost completely bent over. I couldn't be sure, but I had never seen such a massive defect before. Then I concluded that he had actually broken his back doing hard labour. I was amazed at their civility and their acquiescence to their captors. But then many of them were completely exhausted, having travelled hundreds of miles; most looked malnourished and dehydrated. When they dismounted from the grey buses, the stewards allowed the women to use the toilets, but the men had to wait. All told, there were five lines with about twenty people in each; the ratio of men to women was about two to one. I counted what I believed to be about seven minors in all.

I heard a voice.

'Hey, it is you! I know you! Please, no, I know him!'

A steward blocked this woman from breaking the line. She was forced to stand where she was, but she still shouted: 'I know you. Do you remember me?'

The doctor dismissed the grey old man and said, 'We will give you a shower, then a nice warm bed!'

His assistant stuck a sticker on his coat lapel with, 'KILL AND REMOVE BRAIN FOR RESEARCH' printed in German. It was impossible to read upside down. The man left and formed another line to go to the showers.

'Next!' the doctor shouted.

'Hey, it's you. I know you,' the young woman continued to shout.

The doctor's assistant gave me a dirty look, like I was somehow infected if I knew someone in the line. The line was moving forward, and the voice was becoming louder.

'It's you!'

She was now third in line.

'I know you!'

'Next!' the doctor shouted.

'It's me! It's me! Remember me?' Johana shouted, her voice dying within the overall din.

'No, I don't remember you,' I said.

She waddled up to the doctor. 'What do these stickers mean, 'Kill, Kill, Kill, eh?'

I wanted to run away.

She broke from the line and grabbed hold of the buttons on my shirt.

'I know you. Remember me? I am Johana. You must tell them!'

The buttons came off in her hand. They dragged her away to the line awaiting showers.

'Bastard!' she screamed. 'You dirty bastard!'

* * *

On the train leaving Hadamar I thought of her and wondered what if the situation had been reversed. Would she have saved me? I doubt it. My last sight of her she was waddling into the shower area. The sticker on her shoulder said, 'KILL AND EXTRACT GOLD TEETH.' The journey back to Frankfurt wasn't long, but the landscape was dark across the ink-filled blotting paper that made up the fields. I thought I saw the gods reach from the cloud. They were sapping up humanity, but I was free to continue. I was free to return to Addie. We would live on, despite what I had witnessed. This was our world. We had made it this way. The train travelled on. The sound was monotonous and mechanical, just like the world I had left. Hadamar lent insult to the name 'hospital' and to those in charge who imagined they were somehow assisting humanity. But this dark night sent me into another place, a place where there was just me and Addie and our new baby.

When I reached Frankfurt, I thought about Johana again and the night that I rented her body. But now her body was still, burned to cinders minus her gold teeth. Never again would I hear her voice call me a dirty bastard. Never would I see her waddle across the room, her hair cropped short like a man's. She was gone forever now.

24

We eat, then Terence wants to work. Mike puts on his jacket and we walk down to the lake. He brings some cold beers and an opener. The dog follows us but then changes his mind and goes back to this master.

'Will you be warm enough in that? It's very lightweight.'

'I'm plenty warm. I bought this back home, sure. It's made for the cold.'

Mike opens the beers. He has an opener on his key ring. The breeze is gentle, but it still raises the water, and the lake water is enjoying a splash against the small wooden jetty. I search the dark sky for some kind of light, but the moon and the stars are someplace else. I only know where Mike is by his voice.

'You going home then?'

'Soon.'

'You found nothing?'

'I found loads but could prove nothing.'

'Same thing really.'

'Did you know that Terence had a fling with Marcia Mellon?'

'No.'

'He did, but he says it wasn't a fling. I think he just wants me to know that he had sex with her.'

'This place is some love nest!' Mike says. 'There's something about wildness and water that attracts women. Terence is a good bloke, but he's hardly God's gift. He's nearly seventy. Maybe women love the idea of the lake and the isolation. I wrote this piece once about male artists and their women. I was sort of saying that women find the enigma of the artistic man to be irresistible. It's not that they like them in particular, they just like to be with them through association.'

'Street cred.'

'Something like that.'

The moon makes a sudden appearance over the west side of the lake and I salute God for visiting. I see by the rolling clouds that he won't be staying long, but for now I can see Mike as he sips his beer. I can make out by his expression that he is enjoying our chat.

'What about you, Mike? I presume you're going back to work.'

'Yeah, I'll head back at the weekend or the papers will keep piling up. I bet I'll have about a hundred unanswered emails since last week, but that's life.'

'Do you like Dublin?'

'I do, but many don't. I love Dublin, but then again where I live we're not too far from Wicklow, and Wicklow is as wild as here, so I'm well used to the treks.'

'Yeah, sounds great.'

I can still see his satisfied expression, but the clouds have almost chased the moon down; the complete darkness returns.

'Do you think Terence is involved in any of this? Moya doesn't know if his father was Hugo Bauer or that creep of an inspector.'

'Terence is a good man, Avril, even if he is a little eccentric. I mean, would you lock yourself away in this cabin twenty-four seven? Weird isn't the word, but he's a good man. Don't you get that sense?'

'Yeah, I do, but it must be dreadful not to know who your real father was.'

'Don't think it bothers him.'

'Nah, it doesn't seem to bother him much.'

The breeze is turning nasty, with a wintry blast shooting up through my jacket.

'Maybe we best retire back to the fire,'

'How much research did you do on this Detective Steele?'

I am surprised by his question.

'A little. All I know is that he was sent here to investigate the missing girl. He was making some headway before he ran into old Whytie.'

'I did some work on him myself, mainly because Terence asked me to check him out. He wanted to find out about him. I think he was going to base a character on him.'

'Well?'

'He was a single man and very handsome – and honest by all accounts. He had a fancy for Moya, but she says she wasn't really aware of that. She liked him just the same. Whytie had it in for both of them it seems.'

'I know. I cringe when I read what they did to the poor man. Do you think that Whytie could have more offspring around here – besides Terence, I mean?'

'I dunno. I suppose he could. The man was a serial rapist, so no surprises if he has.'

I follow Mike back to the house, holding on to his jacket till we reach the outside lights.

I sleep alone, and morning arrives with the screeching of birds over the lake. I don't eat breakfast with the men.

* * *

I feel that Terence is sullen as I prepare to leave.

'We're heading up the woods. There's a herd of deer up to the north. We might not be back for a few days. You'll have the place all to yourself, if you want to stay and chill.'

'No thanks. I have things to do in the village.'

'Okay, come on Bruce, it's time to pack up.'

Bruce follows his master outside.

'We're going to climb,' Mike says pointing to the slopes of granite rock. They look slippery and are most likely bigger than they look from a distance. They stretch into the upper forest.

'Can't you drive around, Mike?'

'Yeah, there's a forest track, but Chris Bonington here wants to use his ropes.'

'What about the dog?'

'Terence has made a hoist for him. This is professional stuff.'

I laugh. Terence is not impressed. He sulks as I start the engine. Mike waves and Bruce barks, but Terence turns his back. That's what I get for sleeping alone.

* * *

Hedy Bauer is down by the boathouse with her son and daughter-in-law. Julia has a heavy cold. They have brought her down to the water to get some fresh air.

'She should be in her bed,' Arnold says boldly, 'but her bed is too hot. Do you believe that?'

'Poor Julia gets a very bad chest,' Hedy says.

'I'm not so bad!' Julia declares bravely.

She wants me to know that she is still alive and kicking, but she does look pale, though the lower lake is doing its best to help her as downwind it is sharp. It is making grey therapeutic waves that venture up and around the small stones beyond the jetty.

'I was hoping to speak to Hedy.'

Julia, clearing her throat, says, 'We are a very close family, Detective Swan. You can speak freely.'

'Actually, I can't. It's a delicate matter.'

Hedy looks decidedly uncomfortable. Arnold was having trouble thinking, at least his expression said so.

'Okay, look, we can go get some tea. Arnold, I'm parched,' Julia concedes.

'Yes, we'll get some tea,' Arnold snarls. He walks away, his arm around Julia's shoulder.

'When he met her I was jubilant,' Hedy says, watching them walk up the gravel path. 'She's very much in love with him, despite his illness. I think that she is just so grateful that he didn't die, Detective Swan. It's not like she has kids to keep her here.'

I watch till they disappear into the house.

'The man who raped Moya Breslin – did he rape you too?' I'm hoping I might shock her, but she is unperturbed.

'You mean Inspector Whyte?'

'I do.'

'So what is it you want to know?'

She walks further along the jetty and I follow her. I see the mist descending from the mountains, but for now it is only interested in the woods on the far side of the lake.

'Whytie killed my father. Okay, my father shot himself through the head just over there, but it was Whytie who made him do it. I challenged him about it every time I met him, whether it was at some function or other or if I just met him on the street. Of course, he always denied my accusations. He said that Hugo lied and that he murdered that poor girl Biddy Foley. The inspector just couldn't get enough evidence to arrest my father, but then one day – it was about a year after my mother died – he called by and I foolishly I let him in. I was so young and innocent. I was barely sixteen and he was wearing his uniform. He said he had new information on Biddy Foley's disappearance, information that might clear my father's name. There was another guard with him, although he stayed in the patrol car for the duration. Yes, he raped me on the couch in the front room, right beside the blazing fire. I screamed and cried out but nobody came to my rescue. He kept slapping me and threatening me. All through it he was laughing. I can still smell his stinking alcoholic breath, Detective. I get sick at the memory of it all.'

I want to console her; tears are dripping down both her cheeks. Hedy had that little girl lost look that is so disturbing.

'I got pregnant,' she says.

'Oh my God!' is all I can think of to say. 'What happened the baby?'

'I sent him away. I paid for him to go away, but eventually he came back here and was adopted by a local family. I just paid for his upkeep.'

'Who is he?'

'Sergeant Boyle,' she says. 'Funny isn't it how he joined the police, just like his father.'

My cell phone beeps and I think it's Mike, but it's a message from a private number. 'Meet me at the old slaughterhouse if you want to know everything' it reads.

'Look, Hedy, I gotta go right now. I'll come back to visit you real soon. Come on, I'll walk you back to the house.'

* * *

Just like before, it is all too dark. The yard outside is sunken and the mountains of snow piled up by the digger have turned to hard ice. They look ridiculous against the backdrop of greenery. The ground is totally destroyed. Should I call someone? Who do I call? Can I trust anyone? Maybe Mike, but Mike and Terence are away in the forest right now. I have visions of them pitching their tent for the night. I am praying that Bruce hasn't fallen or bashed his head. Some thought when the humans doing the same thing don't concern me so much. But they can care for themselves; they are big and bold enough. Maybe I should call the sergeant and let him know what's going on. But I don't trust him either. Hedy has scared me away from him. I wonder how many children have been lost to this place and to one serial rapist. Were those that survived sent away only to return bitter and twisted? Was Terence Fleming bitter and twisted? If he was, then he didn't act so.

Perhaps, as Julia points out, the clues are in his writing.

'Hello,' I shout out, wondering if whoever opened the big steel doors was still about, lurking in the dark abattoir. I am afraid because, despite the passing years, it still smells of blood.

'Hello,' I shout again. 'It's Detective Swan.'

I am using the torch in my cell phone. I hear a sound behind me, but a rat scurries by.

'Where are you?'

I should have made that phone call.

A light switches on and the whole place changes. The rat turns and runs by me again, passing within a foot of me, so I step back. Once more I'm taken aback by the rows of chains and the old rusted machinery.

'The Witherspoons killed anything that moved in here.'

I can see him now, this tall, strong man. He walks towards me carrying a torch that's turned off. His face is friendly, so I am not afraid. I douse the torch in my cell phone.

'You startled me, Mr Tobin,'

'It's my funeral look. Over the years I've developed this bleak appearance. It goes with the trade, I'm afraid – dark clothes, grey hair and pale skin.'

'Yeah, I bet.'

'Thank you for coming, Detective Swan. I thought it best to meet here. Now stay with me. I want you to imagine something.'

'Fire away. Save for watching the rats, you have my full attention.'

'The rats are harmless. There's nothing in here for them to eat any more. I think they use this old place for shelter. If anything, we are disturbing them.'

'Hey, an undertaker who likes rodents!'

He smiles and goes to speak but then hesitates. 'I was six years old when the Witherspoons brought us here. There was seven of us down in the convent. We were the seven children that didn't exist.'

I want to tell him that I found his prayer book, but I don't.

'It was their idea of a joke. The father was like that, and Kevin … he wasn't much older than us. He might have been nine or ten. They loaded us into the old man's van and brought us out here. Just picture it – little boys and girls aged six frightened out of our wits. They were slaughtering pigs that day, and the pigs were screaming in a pen out in the yard. I remember Kevin whacking them on the back with a stick as they ran around in circles in their panic. Have you ever heard a pig cry? They know they are going to die. They are very clever creatures. Anyhow, the Witherspoons made us watch as they butchered each one by cruelly cutting their throats as they passed through here.'

Tobin points to a gangway that leads to a convoy of chains suspended from the ceiling.

'It must have been dreadful.'

'They saved as much blood as possible in large buckets, and when they had killed the last animal, Kevin emptied a bucket of blood over one boy's head. I'll always remember his laughing and his teasing.'

'So what is it you're telling me?'

'I'm telling you that seven kids that didn't exist got their revenge many years later.'

'Did you kill Kevin Witherspoon?'

'I did.'

'But why? So many years had passed. What he did was horrific, but he was still just a child. If anything his father was responsible.'

'No, you don't understand – he killed the love of my life.'

'Jane?'

'Yes, Jane told Kevin that she knew about the abattoir, about what happened here. Jane was giving a lecture on local history in the hotel and Kevin waited till it was over. He questioned her versions of many events around the village and denied that his father had brought any children to visit the abattoir. In the heat of an argument Jane told him that she knew about the unknown children from the convent who had been brought here, and how he and his father had traumatised them forever.'

'What did he do?'

'He kept pressing her, disputing that any children were traumatised. He said even if her claims were true that his father was only joking and teasing, as was his way. Kevin claimed that his father had been trying to help the children understand nature and the place of animals within nature. He said he had no problems with the children and he was glad they'd all escaped the chapel fire.'

'You slaughtered him, here in this dreadful place. Why didn't you just tell the sergeant?'

'I know the sergeant. I know the history and I know about Moya and her child. The sergeant isn't trustworthy.'

'So who killed Mary Ryan then? Come on, Eoin you seem to know it all.'

'I dunno. I only met her once, like I told you.'

'If you didn't do it, did Witherspoon?'

'No, I doubt it. He was only interested in Jane.'

'What about his wife?'

'Susan wouldn't hurt a fly.'

'I don't understand, Mr Tobin, why tell me now?'

'It's nothing to do with conscience – just to do with timing and you finding that girl of yours. Very soon I'll be following my adoptive father into Neverland. The case is closed, as they say. The medics have given me a month, max. It's a pity, but I can't bury myself. I'm the last in line, so the doors will shut. As I said, the love of my life is gone, but maybe I'll join her on the other side.'

I see the gun, but I'm not afraid as he doesn't point it at me.

'No, no!'

A single shot rings out and Tobin falls in a ball by my feet. A rat runs from underneath the machinery behind him, the biggest rat that I have ever seen – as big as a cat. Blood oozes from the side of Tobin's head and suddenly his skin bursts as if some worm-like creature is escaping. Then his blood freezes and turns dark. I am at a loss.

I try Mike but his phone rings out. So I call the hotel, but Moya is away and Marcia Mellon is on a day off. Then I ask if they have a number for Paula. I call Paula and she answers. She is at the station and is surprised anyone has rung her.

'Where's the sergeant?' I ask.

'He's gone up the mountain. It's his day off.'

'You need to get Dolan. Eoin Tobin has shot himself here at the abattoir. He claims that he murdered Kevin Witherspoon because Witherspoon killed Jane Watts. He shot himself right here in front of me, Paula.'

'Stay where you are. I'll be there in five minutes.'

The phone goes dead. I wonder should I have got Dolan's number so I can call him directly, as Paula and the sergeant are close, maybe too close. How on earth do I know I can trust her?

I move outside to grab some air, but then I worry about Tobin's body and the rats. I go back in but the rats are nowhere to be seen – just the sad bloody body.

I hear a car skid to a stop and the yard trembles.

'Jesus,' Paula says.

I no longer worry such is her look of petrification.

'Oh my God!'

'He did it right in front of me!'

I am tearful, and the normally reticent Paula hugs me.

'I rang Boyler, but he isn't answering. Sometimes the reception up in the woods comes and goes. I called Dolan too. He's on his way but it'll take a while. Why the hell did he do this?'

'He says he was told he'd only a month to live. He says he murdered Kevin so I guess he wanted to check out with an easy conscience.'

'That's one way of putting it.'

Paula is on her knees examining the body, but she is up just as quick as a rat runs right up to Tobin's head.

'Get out of here!' Paula screamed.

The rat runs away, disappearing under the old machinery.

'Jesus, I might need to get the gun out of the car. I might have to shoot a few of these buggers next.'

25

Steele was seeing all in the internal. It hurt to move his head, so he stopped trying. They placed the sack over his head to plug him in to himself, and they came in and out of the room, making loud noises like they were pulling chairs about across the floor. He knew Joe by now. How could he forget him and the bleach! And the detective still had a sore mouth. Earlier they gave him water with no ice. It was tepid and he spat it out. Joe hit him a punch in the cheek for his trouble. He was still dreaming of escape, but they had his hands tied behind his back. He was stuck fast to the chair. There was no way out except when they released him to use the toilet bucket in the corner. Maybe then. That was his only hope. But things were getting worse. He was slipping in and out of consciousness. At one point he thought Joe was interrogating him. He had jumped to alert and waited a good ten seconds before he was satisfied that it was a dream. Even if he made an escape where on earth would he run to, who did he know in this godforsaken place besides Moya, and he hardly knew her at all. If he asked her for help, she too would be in danger. if he could get to a phone and call Malone. Yes, that would do Whytie in. Malone wasn't afraid of Whytie. Yes, he must escape and get to a phone. Malone would send help.

The door opened. He heard it squeak. It made a long whining sound, then he heard footsteps. He thought it might be Joe again with more water, but it wasn't. He felt the big presence stand over him. He knew it was Whytie from the smell. There was a silence as if Whytie was inspecting his condition, then came that distinctive voice.

'You know, Detective, I was thinkin' about you. I was at this meeting earlier with all the usual suspects, those people you have on yer list – Dr Hammond and the bishop, those pesky politicians Wade and Meaney. We had lots of ideas to discuss. I'm sure you're not aware of this but our project at the convent was compromised. That puts us in a fix. It's a bit like you and the German. You can put him with Biddy Foley, but you can't prove he killed her. Frustratin'! So what do we do with seven unregistered kids? They don't know a thing about the outside world. Nobody owns them. They have no kin. What would you do, Detective, like if you were me?'

Whytie removed the sack, and even though the light was dim, Steele was blinded momentarily. Then Whytie turned to walk away as if he wanted to think about what he had to say next. The detective heard the door squeak again, a sign that Joe had entered the room.

'We're in a right state, Detective. We have seven children on our hands that nobody wants or gives a rat's shit about. What would you do? The quack wants to continue the project, the vain fool that he is, and the politicians are scared they'll be found out. As for the bishop, he's convinced he is saintly among all this. So it comes down to the shit-shovelers, the likes of you and me, Steele. While they all sleep soundly in their beds, you and me shovel the shit. I do the things I do for them. Don't you see that without me you'd all be in the shit? What thanks do I get, huh? None, I'm a cheap lump of crap. That's the way they look at me. They're all snobs, every one of them. So what do I do now?'

Steele didn't react. He wasn't sure what the hell Whytie was on. The smell of alcohol was palpable. Was he making a confession? Was he admitting that the German killed Biddy Foley? Did any of it matter now?

'I need you to help me, Steele. I need you to set the match – that's if you wanna live. I can't just let you go dancin' back to Malone with a cock-and-bull story about me. Nah, I need to keep you honest. You do this for me and you're compromised, but you get to live. Don't think that it won't be done just cause you refuse to do it either. It'll happen either way, Detective. The first option – you keep your hands clean but you die. The second, you help me out and you live. Either way those kids die. So what do you say?'

'You don't leave me much choice, Inspector. Malone would be proud of you.'

'Ah yes, Inspector Malone, the great man. Those mighty men of Opus Dei. You know, Steele, I'm beginnin' to get a fondness for you. You aren't like de rest of them. I think you could be my man. I think in that soft brain of yours you can see the logic in strikin' the match. I can, you know, but I hope you won't double-cross me, because that would be the end, wouldn't it.'

When Whytie left, that pungent smell of alcohol went with him. Joe remained for a few minutes, but even he got tired and bored and eventually upped and left, not bothering to replace the sack that had left the detective blind for so long. Steele thought about Whytie's request. It was the wish of a madman. He wanted Steele to light the match that would burn seven little children to death, just so he himself could live. He was in no doubt that Whytie would do him in regardless, but he was right to play along. For one thing it bought time. If he had refused, Whytie and Joe would have beaten him to death where he sat. No, at least this way there was still time.

An hour passed. Rather than sleep engulfing him he was suddenly wide awake. When the door creaked open again, he cried out, 'Joe, is that you? I need to use the bucket.'

The detective heard Joe curse under his breath and mumble and moan all the way to the chair. Steele felt him loosen the ropes around his hands; then he untied the detective's wrists.

'Ye are pleasin' the inspector. Yer learnin',' Joe said.

Steele could smell Joes stinking breath. He was on the same stuff as the inspector. Maybe Joe had had too much. Steele wondered if there was anyone else about. Was Whytie still lurking around? Joe helped him to his feet and set out to march Steele across the room to where the bucket was stuck in the darkest corner.

'Are you shittin' or pissin'?' Joe asked.

'I need to sit,' Steele said although he was indecisive.

'Fuck's sake,' Joe said. 'You'll stink the place out again. I wus jus' about to ate me food.'

Steele loosened his belt and his trousers hit the floor. Joe reluctantly turned his head away and Steele, seizing his opportunity, freed his belt with his right hand and wrapped it fast around Joes neck. It took Joe a second to realise what was happening. He bucked and tried hard to pull himself free, but he only succeeded in strangling himself further. After a frantic thirty seconds, Joe slumped to the ground.

The detective pulled up his pants, leaving the belt around Joe's neck. He opened the door slowly. The small kitchenette was empty. A small wooden table had a half-drunk cup of coffee and some sandwiches open in a paper bag. The radio was playing traditional Irish music, but it was very low. The blind was pulled so the room was dim. Steele ran down the small hallway and opened the front door in the fading light. He discovered he was in a small cottage, with a garden that would have sported blooming flowers in summer. He looked over his shoulder but there was no sign of Joe. The detective wondered had he inadvertently killed his minder. As Steele stepped out onto the narrow path, headlights appeared outside and a car stopped. Taking refuge behind a juvenile evergreen tree, he waited, trying to control his breath. The men walked slowly up the driveway, but on seeing the door ajar they broke into a trot, passing the detective's tree. He could make out Whytie's shape, and he could hear their curses as they found Joe in the room they had used for a cell. It was time to make a break for it, before they came looking for him. So he ran.

He made it out onto the road, passing their car. He wondered if they had been so stupid as to leave the keys in the ignition, but they hadn't, so he kept running. He heard screeching voices behind him, cursing and shouting, and then a bullet hit the ground somewhere beyond him. Another shot bounced off the road behind him. It made a spark and the detective jumped involuntarily. The third bullet hit him in the leg just below his left knee. Steele winced in pain, but he limped on, not knowing in which direction he was going. He knew his pursuers were running behind him, so he slipped into the woods and limped his way as far from the road as possible. Finally, when he could hear no sound he rested behind a tree.

His next task was to warn them at the convent, and he needed to find a telephone urgently. When he caught his breath he followed the curved line of the Eske River. He knew it emptied into the lower lake, so it would lead him back in the general direction of Lough Lyn. He took the well-worn path made by walkers and animals. For the most part it ran parallel to the water, but occasionally it veered inland for a few metres. Steele took the opportunity to rest, leaning against some solid tree trunks and when the path returned to the river, he dipped his shirt in the water to soothe his leg wound.

The world was so different here than it had been in the dark prison he had endured for the last few days. It allowed some rational thought to enter the fray. Surely the folk in the hotel were worried when he hadn't returned or slept in his bed. Then the negatives returned. They would report their concerns to the police and old Whytie would have a plausible explanation at the ready. No, there was little hope of assistance from that quarter.

His wound was open and raw. He really needed to remove the bullet. The skin was black and splintered around the gaping wound and it was still bleeding. The detective prayed that he would have enough reserves of strength to complete his task. The river narrowed as it reached the lake, ending up as a single channel which looked like a flooded ditch. Steele let it go on its way while he found the main road and limped his way towards the village, hiding behind trees and hopping into ditches if a car came by.

The woods around St Michael's were not so dense. There were large gaps between the trees and most of the trees were choked with ivy. Suddenly he was aware of persistent bird song.

The main door to the convent wasn't locked. Inside he was overawed by its grandeur and by its twisting granite staircase.

'Can I help you?' A novice looked him over cautiously, her eyes stopping at the wound on his leg.

'I need to see the Reverend Mother!' Steele said, surprised that his voice was so weak. He knew he looked a sight.

'Be off with you!' the novice said, going red in the face. 'The dispensary is open in the village. The doctor will examine your wound.'

She placed her hand on his shoulder to push him towards the door, but Steele put his arm around her neck and, dragging her a few feet, said, 'The Reverend Mother. Now!'

'Okay, all right.' The novice gasped for breath and pointed to a large oak door down the hallway.

When Steele released the novice, she fell to the ground. She looked a sight, battling for breath on the marble floor. Steele limped down the hallway, leaving tiny spots of blood in his wake. He didn't knock; he just burst through the heavy oak door. A startled Sister Agnes was sitting at her desk. She removed her glasses as the detective approached. She stood up as if she expected to fend off an attack.

'I need to use your phone,' Steele said. 'I need to call Dublin. You don't realise it, but the children you have here are in mortal danger. I need to use the phone.'

The Mother Superior went pale. It was like she didn't quite get what he was saying. She had lapsed into a dream.

'We don't have any children here!' she snapped.

Just then a door opened from a side room and Whytie was there with Joe and the fella with the agricultural accent.

'Detective Steele, you disappoint us. Of all the places you could've gone to hide! You've come runnin' home to mammy. Bad mistake, boy.'

Steele saw the Mother Superior fall back into her chair before Whytie's hoods escorted him out of the building. Whytie followed them to a car that was parked out the rear.

'Bring him down to Colla, and don't fuck up! Hog-tie him if you have to.'

Whytie turned and went back towards the convent while his cronies bundled Steele into the boot of the car.

When Steele felt the air again, he was lifted out of the boot and thrown on a damp stretch of grass that had been flattened by grazing sheep. He knew because he was face down in their droppings. Joe and his mate took Whytie at his word and hog-tied him. The detective cried out in excruciating pain when they stretched his wounded leg. Steele could smell the lake water and could hear it flap against the small jetty. A small boat was bobbing up and down; the noise he heard was it hitting against the stone.

'You're killing me.' Steele screamed as they put a blindfold on him.

They dragged him to the rowing boat. Once inside the motion of the water terrified him. He thought the boat was going to capsize, the men were moving about so much. They were tying his wounded leg to something heavy like a block of concrete or a large stone and arguing about the tautness of the rope. Finally Joe said, 'Fuck it, it'll do. It's not like he'll complain now, is it?' The man with the agricultural accent laughed, and then Steele heard the swish of oars as the small boat glided through the lake water.

After a few minutes the boat stopped

'Time to drop anchor,' Joe said.

The man with the agricultural accent laughed louder this time.

Steele tried to scream and beg, but the more he struggled the tighter the ropes became. Then he felt himself lifted.

'On the count of three – one, two, three,' Joe called out, and freezing water swallowed the detective.

The weight attached to his leg forced him down. He held his breath for as long as he could. He knew that once he opened his mouth, the icy water would destroy the back of his throat and invade his lungs until they expanded so much they'd burst, and he would die.

Steele never thought he would die like this, not in the line of duty. He had always imagined the old folks' home and the pretty nurses mopping his brow as he said his goodbyes to the world. But not this. What would Moya think if she saw him now, hog-tied and heading to his death by drowning. Would she even care if she knew about it. Maybe she'd swim to the bottom and save him? Finally, the detective opened his mouth and the iced water did its worst.

Within seconds his chest exploded and in his final moment, he thought he heard the oars swish through the water as the small boat rowed back to Colla pier, which looked so innocent from the shoreline. Steele lay on his side and life left him to sleep in the quiet depths.

26

1950

The first thoughts to run through my mind was that the fire wasn't ten minutes burning. I wasn't first on the scene. There were a few nuns staring helplessly at the blaze.

'It's no good!' one of them said.

I was made to step back by the heat of the inferno. I saw Moya as she ran along the circular path.

'Hugo, there are children in there.'

She looked exhausted. Her hair was all out of place and her skin was scorching in the heat. She had stopped at a rarely used side entrance.

'Save them, Hugo,' she screamed.

I pushed open the door and was greeted by a wave of thick, dark smoke. It was choking, even in the fresh air.

'For God's sake, do something?' Moya screamed again.

I went in blind. I never felt heat like it. I was sure I was about to melt. The inner door had collapsed. I couldn't see much, and timber was collapsing all round me. Then I heard the sound of a giant wooden beam drop. All before me was blazing and the infernal heat was melting my skin. I somehow managed to turn and run back out to the fresh air where, I am told, I collapsed on the grassy bank leading to the path at the foot of the nuns' cemetery.

'I couldn't find a soul,' I said to Moya as I roused.

'It's all right,' Moya said gently. 'You saved you – that's so important. Those poor kids are gone. Nothing we can do now.

'Did you call the police?'

'The police are here,' Moya said, 'but we both know I can't tell them what I really think happened here.'

She was staring down at me, and in all the confusion I got this desperate urge to kiss her.

* * *

That afternoon I went to sit by the jetty as Addie was giving Hedy a bath. It was a cool afternoon. I sensed that winter was coming to an end, and the lake was rejoicing as the daylight stretched for another twenty minutes. The birds chirped as the good news about the changing season spread. My injuries were superficial. Addie had placed wet towels on my face and arms. Then she carefully rubbed in some cold cream she had bought in the village chemist.

'You're so brave, Hugo. We're so lucky to have you back safe!'

I winced with the pain, but her wet towels were soothing, and that stinging pain and the emerging blisters were softened and made bearable. I couldn't very well seek medical advice at the scene. Yes, everything remains a secret in Lough Lyn, and sitting on the jetty I didn't feel brave. Maybe I had betrayed myself. It was Hadamar all over again. When things got dirty, I went missing. Now all those children were dead. Why hadn't I stood up to Whytie and his cronies? So what if they released the photo of me and the girl in the car? What could they do to me that was worth the deaths of those children? These people were ruthless; there was nothing they wouldn't do to protect themselves. I was trying to protect Addie and Hedy, but in essence

I was prepared to allow innocent children to die. I forgot about my pain. I don't care if my skin blisters and I appear hideous. It will reflect how I feel on the inside.

Addie arrived and tightened the buttons on Hedy's coat.

'I don't want her to catch a chill after her hot bath. How's your face?'

I turned around to show her.

'Still nasty, Hugo. I'll rub more cream into it when we go back to the house.'

I tried to smile. Hedy brushed by me. She walked fairy like to the end of the jetty.

'Be careful!' I shouted after her.

'I will,' she sang.

'The inspector telephoned earlier about this Detective Steele.'

'Steele?'

'Yeah, he was going about his investigation into this missing girl. He said Steele thinks you know something about it.'

'I only know they brought me to see her. I was supposed to analyse her. That is why they offered me the position here. For some unknown reason they wanted me to examine the dregs of society. Why, Addie, I'm not too sure.'

'I told the inspector that you had no knowledge about this girl.'

'Thank you, Addie,'

I was watching Hedy. She jumped each time a rogue wave came towards the jetty. She had created a new game for herself, but Hedy was small and vulnerable against the backdrop of the mighty lake. Beyond her, the power of the landscape stretched high to the mountains, yet she was but a dot.

'He's not a very nice man, Hugo.'

'No, Addie. I detest him!'

'He was trying to insinuate that you have some romantic thing for Moya.'

'That's ridiculous!'

'Yeah, I told him that.'

'Good.'

Addie went quiet and studied Hedy and her game for a moment. Then she broke her silence.

'Let's go home, Hugo.'

'I dunno, Addie. It might not be safe.'

'I'll take my chances. Berlin is much safer than here I'd bet.'

'I wouldn't count on that, my dear!'

* * *

Moya kissed me hard on the lips. It was so hard that I had to withdraw; my lips were still sore, even though the blisters had gone.

'Did I hurt you?'

'I'm still in pain.'

'Brave man,' she said, patting my head.

She turned to the bedside locker to get some water and I was taken by her perfect skin. She was tight and gleaming, and everything moved in unison within her powerful muscles. I got excited at her physical strength, so when she turned around again, I kissed her just as hard and she recoiled for a second.

'Do you want more?'

She placed her hand neatly on my penis, then held it gently in her palm. She started stroking it fully up and down. I gasped with excitement.

'My legs will always be open for you, Hugo.'

She was wet, and I felt the full length of my penis inside of her. Somehow it belonged in there. I withdrew and re-entered her more forcibly each time until she moaned and wrapped her legs around my back.

'I love you, Hugo!' she whispered softly.

I couldn't help myself – I spurted my seed inside of her. She smiled as she suddenly felt it within her.

I lay back on the propped pillows exhausted while Moya struggled to catch her breath too.

'I think I might be pregnant,' she said casually.

'Think?' I was now fully alert.

'I missed my period. Maybe I should go to the doctor.'

'Of course you should.'

'I will. Don't worry, Hugo, I won't tell a soul.'

'It's not that. I was just thinking of Addie.'

'Addie will be the last to know. When is she coming back?'

'Tomorrow. Her friend leaves Dublin tomorrow.'

'Do you think she knows about us, Hugo?'

'No. Save for the fucking inspector making trouble, she doesn't know. Addie thinks you're just keeping your mother's job safe while she convalesces.'

'Convalesces? My mother is dying, Hugo. She won't be coming back.'

I was surprised by the certainly in her tone.

'We can only hope.'

She didn't reply, but then she said, 'I better get dressed. I still have things to do around the kitchen. Funny, isn't it, about that detective. He just left us all of a sudden. The inspector said he was called back to Dublin urgently – so urgently that he left all his clothes behind in the hotel. He didn't settle his bill, but your nemesis said he would look after the bill, so the hotel won't be out of pocket. That must make you feel better, Hugo – no more detectives running after you?'

I watched her as she got up. Moya was tall for a woman and once more I was drawn to her perfect skin. She looked at me curiously, wondering if I was just feasting my eyes. Perhaps she thought me a pervert. When she finished dressing, she sat on the corner of the bed. She must have found me lazy and freakish. I was naked and I absentmindedly played with my manhood. Then Moya smiled and I let go of my penis.

'I'm worried the baby might be his.'

'Oh no!' That hadn't crossed my mind.

'How will I ever know, Hugo? I'll spend my life staring into his or her eyes for clues.'

'You're worrying yourself to death, my dear. Maybe the whole thing is a false alarm.'

I went to get dressed myself. My clothes lay innocently on a chair by the window. Out front, Jennings was digging over by the boundary fence and the cloudy sky was taking a dim view of the world.

'Go see what your doctor says. We can discuss it all then.'

Moya went rigid. 'I didn't mean that I'd go to a doctor around here. I can't do that. Do you want rid of it, Hugo, is that it? You don't want the shame, and Addie finding out and throwing you out on the street? Do you want me to go running to Whytie, see if he'll support me and our child? Is that what you want, Hugo?'

'No, no that's not what I want.'

She was back on the bed, crying uncontrollably like a child. I tried to pacify her but everything I said was wrong. Each time I said something, she began another tirade of tears. This went on till my patience was truly tested.

'Right, Moya, what I'm saying is that I will pay for you to go get rid of it.'

She stopped crying and looked up at me through a film of tears.

'You'll pay for me to get rid of it? My God, I was wrong about you, Hugo Bauer. You're not a brave man, not brave at all. You're just like the rest of them. You might as well have struck the match at the chapel. You're no different from them.'

She stormed out of the room and a minute later I heard the front door bang.

* * *

Whytie had drink taken. I knew because he referred to me as 'the Kraut' numerous times. The bishop was explaining something to Wade. I couldn't hear him, but I was able to pull my chair a little closer.

'It glows like heaven, I'm certain of it. I'm waiting for a reply from Rome.'

Wade nodded but then looked doubtfully at Meaney while Dr Hammond played with the place mat, standing it on its side, then tumbling it over before finally resting it on its opposite side.

'Gentlemen,' Whytie said, 'we've reached the end of our project. As you know, the chapel fire has ended our interest in St Michael's. I propose a drink to dat.' He lifted his glass of brandy.

They all joined in save for me. Whytie noticed and said, 'Our German friend doesn't join the toast?'

The bishop gave me a worried look, but the doctor, smiling, said, 'My dear Whytie, would *you* toast the end of *your* job? My good friend Hugo here is out of work. Hardly a thing to drink a toast to, now. Most likely he'll have to return to Berlin and face a firing squad or a hanging. I believe the British and the Americans are quite ruthless you know.'

'It makes no difference if he joins in a toast,' Wade said forcefully. 'Now our problems are over and the whole thing is signed, sealed, and delivered.'

'Thank God!' said Meaney, bowing his head.

'I wouldn't toast the murder of innocent children.' I shocked them with my anger.

Dr Hammond raised his eyes to heaven. 'Dear Hugo, you are such an innocent. Look it, your countrymen killed millions of innocent children during the war while people like you sat back and watched. Yet you come here with some sort of superior morality.'

Whytie banged the table with his fist. 'The detective wanted to interview you on the Biddy Foley case, but let's say he got called back to Dublin, Bauer, so you are in the clear, thanks to Whytie here. You can start planning your trip to see de firing squad or the hangman for all I care.'

'What on earth did he want to talk to me about?'

'Some photographs came to his attention, but he's gone now. I fixed it for you, even though I can't stand you.'

'You tried to frame me.' I tried to find some weakness in Whytie's eyes but, full of brandy, he didn't wince. 'I'll take you on, Inspector. How about I go to the authorities and squeal? You fuckers have murdered seven children. They will believe me as I have an ace up my sleeve. I was a witness at the chapel and I know what you did to Moya. I swear she will testify against you. I even went into the inferno to try and save those children. They will believe me, I can assure you. So call off your threats and your blackmail, Whytie, or I'll play my ace!'

Whytie laughed. 'Right now, I'm just short of tellin' yer missus about Moya. You think we don't know about Moya?'

'You think I won't play my ace?'

'Gentlemen!' the bishop intervened, 'let's keep it reasonable. There's no reason to be so foul. Mr Bauer, we did not murder those innocent children. That is not correct. There was an accidental fire. All the children you met in the convent are safe and well, living in America. We couldn't do it any other way. We have their names, their dates of birth, some proof of their identity. They have gone on their merry way. Do you have evidence of any dead children? If you have, I suggest that you present it here to the inspector. After all, he is the law around here. If you wish to return to Germany, Mr Bauer, feel free to do so. We'll give you a more than generous severance cheque.'

I latched on to the bishop's pious face. 'You have no idea of the evidence that I possess. I was inside that chapel when it was burning and I know it was arson. So I will be left alone, and no more clandestine phone calls to Addie, Inspector.'

'Just doin' me job.' Whytie smirked.

As I left Meaney and Wade wanted to shake hands. I refused, but Dr Hammond came around to my side of the table and he slapped me on the back.

'Don't do anything stupid, Bauer. The whole thing has collapsed. You should take the bishop's cheque and go. Bring your wife and kid and get out of here as fast as possible. That's my advice. Whytie will bury you, my friend. He's like a dog with a bone. Do you really think that detective just upped and left? Think about it, Hugo.'

* * *

'Why is this man doing this to us?' Addie had just seen Hedy off to bed. 'He's saying all these dreadful things, Hugo?'

'We can't go home, Addie. I know you want to go back to Berlin, but we can't go home. Hadamar is still big news and the investigations are continuing. Whytie has it in for me, and God knows what happened to Steele. Maybe he works for them now, or maybe something worse has befallen him.'

'Who are they?'

'These men that brought us here. They are evil – not trustworthy.'

She followed me into our bedroom. The evening was closing in and the long night was lying in wait.

'He says you are sleeping with Moya.'

I turned and looked at her. She nodded and went to the dresser.

'So I am stuck here in this godforsaken place with an eight-year-old daughter and a husband who is fucking the temporary maid. Let's see, that's after Whytie says he has compromising photographs of you with a girl who is missing, presumed dead. My God, what have you become? What if your mother could see us now?'

She sank on to the bed, bringing her hands up to her face. I wasn't sure if she was crying or not.

'There are things going on that I can't tell you about,' I said. 'All I can tell you is that I took no hand in hurting anyone. You know they killed that missing girl, not me.'

She removed her hands from her face.

'You're lying. You lied about Hadamar. You lie all the time, and you lie to me and your daughter. How do you expect me to believe you now, with that horrible man calling me? Do you know that he is offering me money for information about you? He even said that should anything happen you, Hedy and I would be taken care of! Such arrogance! What does he mean, *if something happens to you*?'

I went to the bedside table and slid the drawer open. There was the shining pistol and the required bullets. I would have to confront Whytie after all, and when I did, I would kill him.

'I don't trust you any more, Hugo. I'll arrange to go to my cousin in Bonn as soon as I can. You can spend your time with Moya then.' She turned her head into the bedspread and sobbed.

The gun fitted neatly into the inside pocket of my jacket, but I was tired. I hadn't been able to sleep the previous night and I was hungry too. So I made coffee and toast.

Moya didn't arrive so I presumed we were now maidless. Addie didn't come out of her room but as I left, Hedy said from the top of the stairs, 'Where are you going, Daddy?'

'I have some business to do, love.'

'Will you be long?'

'I don't know.'

'Can we go for a row later?'

'We'll see. It's a bit choppy.'

'What's wrong with Mother? She's crying.'

'She's tired love. I'll check in on her when I come back.'

'Okay. Love you, Daddy!'

I turned the key in the ignition. I was still wondering that if I killed Whytie, would I then kill them all one by one – the bishop, Wade, Meaney, the doctor, and whoever else? The secret that Moya and I carried – it was true that maybe the child's future depended on it remaining a secret. It was pointless and, just like at Hadamar, I was helpless. If I took them on, Addie and Hedy would be in danger, but if I didn't, they would destroy me and my family anyway. I believed they would take care of Addie and Hedy. They knew that it was best to keep them close – much easier to control and oversee; it would be too difficult to shut someone up who is in Germany or Belgium. Addie and Hedy would be better off without me, that was for sure. Then Addie wouldn't have to leave, and Hedy could grow up in this beautiful countryside by the lake.

I turned the engine off. I sensed it was hot but suddenly going cold.

* * *

I walked around the house. Jennings was planting a hedge down by the small stream that drained into the lake. I felt the gun press against my side. I stood on the jetty. The grey waves made the dirty water splash over the stone.

* * *

I held the gun to my temple.
  A voice screams
  'Daddy?'

The last paragraph was added by me, Arnold. Dec. 2017.

27

Dolan secures the crime scene. He does this with considerable ease, giving each of his team a specific job to do. Georgina gleefully informs Paula and I that our services are no longer required, so we are to retire to the station. Dolan will interview us when he is done.

'Go make yourself useful, Detective. Have another look over Jane Watt's files.'

That is his squeaky order but, hey, I am in no mood to argue. I just saw a man blow his brains out. The idea of sitting down, drinking coffee and chatting to Paula about everything really appeals to me. Paula goes to make coffee and she points to Jane's file sitting on the corner of the desk. The last peruser left it open on a page about Kevin Witherspoon. I am suddenly sad this poor man is dead. Paula's coffee is good. She serves it strong and hot; she has the sense to lace it with sugar. Suddenly the life returns to my tired brain. I read all about the Witherspoons and wonder at the blatant gap where a photo has been removed. I move on, turning the pages impatiently till I get to the convent and its history and a piece about Sister Agnes, the Reverend Mother. I read down and I am getting bored until I read a handwritten footnote. I presume the scribble is by Jane Watts. I read on:

> Sister Agnes attended the inquiry. Her testimony was stark but to the point. She stressed several times that she was no longer a nun and had retired from her vocation days after a fire engulfed the convent chapel. She said that she didn't want revenge on anyone. As far as she was concerned the fire was an accident, but she stated categorically that no children were present in the convent on the day of the fire and that all the children who were under the care of the sisters were documented and placed in loving families within the wider community.

Paula is standing over me with her mug of coffee. She is very warm towards me and I truly appreciate it on this horrible day.

'How are you, Avril. The colour is returning to your cheeks.'

'It's your coffee, Paula.'

'I keep thinking of Boyler up the mountain. He's missing all this. Typical for the guns to start firing when he has a day off. He'll be ragin'. Day after day goes by and nought happens. He takes a day off, and the lid blows off the world. He's very sensitive, you know.' She looks at me like I should know, and I do – kinda.

'What do you think of this?' I show her Jane Watts' scribbles.

'I dunno. I never heard of any inquiry. Boyler or Dolan never said anythin' about an inquiry.'

'Can you check it up? Can you find out on that computer of yours?'

'Sure.'

Paula hands the file back to me, rather than just turn it around, and a photograph slips out onto the desk. I pick it up and stare at the black-and-white image.

'So what will I search under?' Paula asks. She is used to being subservient and to receiving instruction.

'I dunno. Try "inquiry Lough Lyn" – something like that.' I continue to stare at the photo, and then I turn back a page in the file. Before Paula leaves I ask, 'Is this the same person? Is this the Reverend Mother?'

Paula does an about-turn and comes round my side of the desk to look.

'Who does that remind you of?' I ask.

Paula studies the photo carefully before she beats her right fist against her chest. 'That's the spit of Susan Witherspoon – when she was younger ... before she let herself go.'

'I'm thinking the same.' I make a dash for the door.

'Where are you going, Avril?' Paula asks.

'I'm going to see Susan. It's about time I got the truth about the goings-on around here.'

'What about my search?' Paula says as if she is dreading being alone.

'Go ahead and search. I hope to back in an hour. If I'm not, you better come lookin'.'

* * *

Susan has a sad look. It's as if the world has plucked the life out of her and left her naked against its constant harassment.

'Hello, Mrs Witherspoon, I hope you're getting back to normal. The police have a suspect in Kevin's murder. You'll be shocked to hear that Eoin Tobin has admitted to killing your husband. I'm afraid he took his own life, right in front of me.'

'I haven't come to terms with Kevin's death. No, I haven't now and I doubt I ever will. As for Eoin Tobin – he hated Kevin. They never got along, but he probably had his sadistic reasons. I dunno.'

She ushers me through the paper curtain and to the same seat by the window where I sat on my first visit. The yard has lost its greyness; the sun shines on the surrounding walls and the cats play hide and seek, teasing each other.

'Folk around here didn't take to Kevin, but they didn't know him like I did. Yes, he was a hard man to please, and a tyrant behind closed doors, but he was a good man really. It was his father that ruined him in childhood. His father was brutal man – too fond of his fists. Kevin – the type of fellow he was, he forgave his father for giving him such a hard time as a kid.'

'Yes, our childhood shapes us.' I am thinking of Ma and Granma and all the arguments after drinking whiskey. 'I brought this photo for you to see. I'm sorry I never showed it to you before but I only came across it earlier.'

Susan Witherspoon takes the photograph and I notice her expression change.

'Do you know this person, Susan?'

'Yes, I do. Are you tellin me that Tobin is dead?'

'Yes.'

'Good riddance! That's my mother in the photograph. She was the Reverend Mother in the convent when I lived there. She was sweet to me, but she couldn't show me favour over the others.'

'So when were you in the convent Susan?'

'You don't know, Detective?' She looks at me incredulously. 'I was there at the same time as Tobin and the others. The fact that I'm a nun's daughter was a secret. I did everythin' the others did, but it all changed after old Witherspoon forced Kevin to bring us to the abattoir. Kevin was only young. He teased us and stuff, but we survived. But the nuns got wind of some plot to burn down the chapel at Sunday prayers, so my mother made plans to get us out of there. She lobbied good families around the district, and one by one we were sent away. Then one day after we all left, the chapel burned down and my mother had a nervous episode. She never recovered, not fully.'

'How could the Reverend Mother be your birth mother, Susan?'

'Because they raped her. She was raped, along with all the other women. Whytie left it to the soldiers to make sure we were conceived, but my mother put it up to him that this was all wrong. So she too was raped for standing up to him. She paid the price for taking him on.'

'Gees, and your mother told you all of this?'

'Yeah, over the years – before she died.'

'When did she die?'

'My mother died in the Mullingar asylum in December 1962.'

'I see. So do you know where the other children ended up?'

Susan goes quiet like she is thinking hard. Maybe she is ordering her brain to *stop* thinking. She glances out the window as the cats scale the high walls.

'I had to tell Grainger to feed them, scrawny cats.'

Now I am ashamed of my first appraisal of Susan. Yes, in her current condition she is plain ugly, but when she turns her head to face me again I can see that once she was a plain but sweet-looking young woman. The damage was inflicted by time and neglect of self.

'So where did the other kids end up, do you know?'

'Besides Tobin, there was me and another girl. We called her Three, but on the outside, she was known as Jean. I was number one. Two and Five died of childhood diseases a few years after we left the convent. I don't know where Six went or what happened to him. Me and Tobin never got on. I think he thought I got special treatment because of who my mother was. He hated the Witherspoons for the abattoir, and then I go and marry Kevin. He wanted to bury the past and everything to do with my mother and the convent, and any mention of his father.'

'So your mother saved them all? She was a heroine?'

'She did her best, Detective. She always said she hated Whytie. She was terrified of the inspector and his cronies.'

'I can't say I blame her. Listen, I best be going, Susan. I'm sorry for giving you the news about Tobin. He said before he died that Kevin killed Jane Watts because he was afraid of some revelation about those times. Do you know did Kevin kill Jane?'

Susan once again looks at the cats who by this time are sitting peacefully by the shed, enjoying the long-lost sun.

'Kevin wasn't afraid of any revelation, not for himself. He didn't do anything bad. The abattoir was his father's doin'. Kevin was just as terrified as the rest of us, but he did his father's bidding. He was sorry about it but didn't feel guilty about it, if you get the difference. Kevin was protecting me. He didn't want folk in the village knowing about my mother and me and how it all came about. My mother went to great pains at the inquiry to keep our secret safe. He didn't want Jane Watts and Tobin to undo all her good work now.'

'Are you telling me that Kevin did kill Jane?'

'He had no choice. We started to get calls from both Tobin and Jane. They said they knew everythin', everythin' we had done to cover up our past. They threatened to out us so as everyone in the district would know. Kevin went to see Jane to hammer it out with her, maybe come to some compromise, but she refused point blank. So in a fit of temper he killed her and then tried to make it look like the work of an intruder or a madman. I guess Tobin knew what he did and waited quietly for his revenge.'

'Where was the inquiry held? What exactly were they inquiring into?

'It would have been 1956. I was still young. The inquiry was into the missing detective from Dublin. I can't remember his name. They never found him – he disappeared. They sent a team from Dublin but they found nothing. There were rumours that he was investigating the murder of a teenager and that he had visited the convent to inform my mother that the children under her care were in danger, but the inquiry proved nothing. All the eminent people involved gave evidence, but there was no real conclusion. They never found the detective's body.'

'His name was Dan Steele.'

'Yes, that's right!'

I can see that Susan is tired. Her hand trembles and tears are launching from deep within her eyes.

'I'm sorry, Susan, I have to ask you this. Did Kevin have anything to do with the disappearance of Mary Ryan?'

'No, no, Kevin wasn't afraid of what Mary knew. She didn't know much, to be honest – not the day she called by here.'

My cell rings and it's Paula.

'Got a call from Hedy Bauer,' she tells me. 'Arnold's gone off up the mountain and he's mad. He thinks Boyler and your buddy Terence are hunting deer illegally. She said he isn't acting like himself. She's terrified he's going to do something mad. Jaysus, if anythin' happens to Boyler I'll die. Can you go up, Avril? I can't because Dolan wants to interview me and he's not taking Arnold's threats seriously.'

28

The road up the mountain goes on forever. What's worse is it just stops suddenly with no warning. I am on a forestry access road. The grass is high down its centre, and the conifers on each side are dark. Below them, the red pine needles cover the damp earth. It is no wonder the deer live up here. This is as far away from civilisation as they can get.

I left Paula to update Dolan on blood and rats. I wonder has he relented and is he on his way. He is a squeaky rat too. Maybe Tobin has managed to solve Dolan's case for him. His only mystery now surrounds the body of a girl who lay in this moist earth for nearly seventy years. Of course, Mary Ryan is still listed as missing or disappeared, but I don't think anyone cares any more, not the police or anyone else.

All I want is to find Mike and Terence and tell them my news, but as the forestry track twists and turns I am sorry that I'm alone. Suddenly I come to a dead end. My only choice now is to stop or drive on into the trees. I must be mad for I have no idea where they are. They could be anywhere within a twenty-mile radius. I am sure I am wasting my time. Best to turn back and catch up later. So I switch off the ignition for a minute and enjoy the stillness.

I listen to the fresh breeze combing the trees, and the birdsong. It is deep and dark, matching the interior of the wood. If Tobin killed Witherspoon and Witherspoon killed Jane, who killed Mary or caused her to disappear. Tobin said he didn't know what happened to Mary and I suppose I believe him. Mike is right–she could just have upped and left. Nah, it isn't her. I take a deep breath. She might be anywhere. There are a million places out here to hide a body, but who could have killed Mary and why?

Julia Bauer says that Terence Fleming kills all the women in his books, but he is a writer and he is entitled to. I step out of the jeep and stretch my upper body. I walk a few feet along the track. Lough Lyn teaches me, and its natural beauty and stillness enchant me, but for years those people in positions of power controlled everything. The abuse of power is remarkable right across the spectrum – the politicians, the clergy, the medical profession, the police, all protecting things and hiding secrets. But for what gain? I conclude they did it because they *could* do it. Was it about the protection of wealth, of religion. Maybe it was just their way of abusing the poor.

I hear a shot! It's no more than twenty yards away. Perhaps Terence has shot a deer. I slip carefully down a slope into the woods and follow a track made by animals. But soon my track deteriorates and I am squeezing through between the trees. My jacket is catching on stray branches, the corners of twigs cutting into to my skin. I am glad that some are blunt. Once again, I regret my actions and wonder if I have gone insane.

I hear another shot. This time I judge it to be about twenty feet away. I get closer and I see the sergeant line up his rifle. He is protected by the thick trunk of a tree. I see him but he doesn't see me. I crouch down behind the remains of a fallen tree. He peers around the trunk and lines up his rifle to fire once again. I want to scream at him to stop. Here he is, the son of Hedy Bauer, deep in the woods, firing his rifle at God knows what. I have a terrible thought – it is Boyle all along using his police uniform as cover. Mary finds out his birth secret so he gets rid of her. Arnold says he is a crack shot, the best hunter in the district. Yes, Boyle hunts Mary down and kills her. I want to scream at him, but he stands still, the tree trunk covering his entire body. But a shot hits the tree and dry wood splinters everywhere. The sergeant is on his knees as two more shots disturb the earth beside him. I think I will crawl; he won't see me. Once I get back to the narrow gaps between the conifers, I will make my escape. But another shot rings out and something makes me look back. The sergeant has dropped to a sitting position, and I see blood spurting from a wound on his right shoulder. Boyle grimaces and lays his rifle down beside him. He uses his right hand to try and stop the flow. Another a shot rings out, and it hits him on the left leg. More spurting blood. Now I realise that someone is trying to kill the sergeant.

It's kinda funny, but he isn't surprised to see me.

'Stay down, Avril.' He keeps his voice low and he struggles to move towards me.

More shots hit the ground where he had been previously.

'I dropped my phone. It's over by that tree.' He points to the base of a tree six feet away.

'Who is it? Who is trying to kill you?'

'I will hunt you down like the dog you are.' shouts a voice, getting nearer.

'You win the prize. Hey, brother, there's no counting on your friends now. They're dead, and I shot the dog too. Do you know that my wife prefers you to me, so she does, she does, she does!'

I hear a shot hit the trunk of the tree higher up than before.

'You can still get out of this, Arnold?' the sergeant shouts.

'Now!' Boyle says to me. I race to the tree and collapse to the ground. I pick up his phone.

'Stay there, Avril. Just toss it over to me.'

'Why does my wife like you better?' Arnold shouts.

'She doesn't, Arnold. I just helped her sort out the problems with her car.'

'I should have done to Julia what I did to that nosey bitch, Mary. She took my grandfather's diaries, all his private letters and notes, and she lied about it – said she didn't have them.' The voice is only ten feet away.

'Okay, Arnold, you tell me where Mary is and I promise I'll get them back for you,' Boyle shouts back.

He makes a big effort to throw the rifle to me and it lands at my feet. He tries vainly to use his cell phone but I see that he is losing so much blood he hasn't the strength left to use it.

'Aren't you dead yet, Sergeant? How many times have I got to shoot you? Hedy tells me you were nearly a man before I was born – nearly a man. Are you nearly a man?'

The sergeant is ready to pass out, his face is white and the earth around him is turning red.

'Where did you put her?' Boyle asks, gathering strength from somewhere.

'In the freezer in the boathouse, you nuts! Some policework. I kept her there for so long, but when I took her out she started to stink the place out, so I put her in the lake. I was thinking she might want to reunite with her car at the bottom of the lake. Before I strangled her she told me she loved her car. Now they're all dead, my half-brother. They were breaking the law, you know – hunting illegally, committing a crime, bro.'

Arnold steps out into the clearing.

He studies Sergeant Boyle and, seeing he is dying, he drops his rifle by his side. I see the barrel of his gun is pointing to the damp earth.

'This is the end, brother. Time to put you down.'

Boyle crouches low as he awaits the bullet. It is his final act of submission.

I have never fired a rifle before, but I know that I have no time. Arnold raises his gun and points it at Boyle's head. My bullet goes straight through Arnold's nose. In slow motion it removes half of his face, and he slumps to the ground face down. I am in shock.

Eventually, the sergeant is air-lifted to hospital. They are taking him directly to Dublin for emergency surgery. Paula comforts me, and I follow her and Dolan down a steep bank to small clearing. Terence Fleming lies dead, a bullet through his temple, but Mike is just wounded and will be fine. The bullet missed his head and lodged in his shoulder; the paramedics are minding him now. I go to him and sit by his side. Then I see Bruce lying still behind his master. I keep waiting for some phantom animator to bring him back to life, but no such luck. Dolan's whole persona changes. He and his team cover Terence with a sheet that the paramedics brought.

'We thought he was a deer at first,' Mike says for the third time. 'But when we got closer, we recognised him. He shot Bruce first. Just one bullet took him down. Terence lost it and charged at him. He just blew Terence away. Jesus!'

'Sssh now, Mike!' I am trying to be brave.

'It's a shit world, Avril,' he says, and I see the tears cascade down his cheeks.

* * *

Moya Breslin offers strong coffee and gives everyone free whiskey. Mike and Paula join me, but Moya is too stunned to even bother. She wants to talk about her son, but we all know that she didn't know very much about him to say anything substantial. Marcia Mellon takes to giving out the drinks.

'At least Boyler will make it,' Paula says, trying to say something positive.

'What got into Arnold? He used be such a nice fella,' Marcia says to Moya who just looks at her.

She finally accepts a glass of whiskey and goes to sit alone at small table by the door. I wanna follow her to keep her company, but heck, I am an emotional wreck myself. I have seen loads of dead bodies in my time, but the sight of Terence lying there with blood seeping from his forehead will haunt me forever.

'What will you do now, Avril?' Mike asks, trying hard to be strong. I know he is bluffing; he is shaking.

Dolan arrives with Georgina. He is very serious looking. Gone are all traces of arrogance that taint his personality.

'I have some more sad news,' he says. The squeak in his voice has lessened, like he has graduated in stature.

Paula tenses up. I can see the blood drain from her face. Is it sad news about the sergeant?

'We found Mary's car in the lower lake, and a few minutes ago the divers recovered what's left of her body.'

Marcia gives Dolan and Georgina a glass of whiskey for which they are both very grateful.

'So it's over,' Mike says.

'I need to go home.'

Mike gives me a sad look like he is telling me that he will miss me.

I stay in Lough Lyn for another three days. It's funny how the human mind adapts to catastrophic realities. I am no different to other folk. My mind tricks itself into believing that life can somehow be normal again and that in time I will be cured. The loss of Terence and Mary will be buried someplace deep in my heart.

Paula brings me good news about Sergeant Boyle. He will get better and be home soon. She tells me that in 1956, the inquiry lasted just ten days. It brought about the resignation of Whytie They couldn't prove that he murdered Detective Dan Steele as there was no definite proof that Steele was dead. Whytie went on to spend ten years in the NYPD and died in his sleep in 1970. Wade didn't get re-elected after his involvement in the scandal, but paradoxically Meaney went on to become a minister in the Irish government. However, Meaney was killed in 1960 in motor accident on the Naas dual carriageway. He was on his way to an emergency vote in the Dáil Eireann. Bishop Cassidy was called to Rome and died there in 1964 of a heart attack. The information on Dr Hammond wasn't too clear. It is thought that he went to London after the inquiry and then on to the Congo. He died there in 1965 from liver disease.

I leave Lough Lyn with a heavy heart and a profound sense of failure. In truth there wasn't much more I could do to help or save anyone. In the end the world is what it is, and even though I despair of it, I know that in the midst of all that darkness, I found the source of goodness too.

***

She waited for him. When he came in, she was silent at first.

'So you must leave?' he said, coming close to her.

'Yes I must. I'll speak out.'

'Speaking out will make no difference,' he said.

She brushed him away with the palm of her hand. 'If I don't speak out then who will?'

'The world is a sycophant. Its ways are corruption, disease and suffering. You will never change that.'

'No, but I'll speak out about this until I am killed by it.'

'Then you might step alone through the dark forest.'

He came close to her again, pressing against her outstretched hand.

'I will walk proudly, no matter what ferocious creatures lurk, and I will speak out against their ferociousness.'

'Good,' he said kindly. 'But remember, never go beyond the point of no return. It is the darkest place in the wood. You will die there, never to come home ...'

From the novel The Darkness of Trees by T. Fleming.